Praise for *The Rogue You Know*

"The pace is lively, the sexual tension palpable, and the love story perfectly delightful. Fun and touching, this magical read is a keeper."

—*RT Book Reviews*, 4.5 Stars, Top Pick!

"A page-turning adventure, a love story that assails all the senses and keeps the heart rate high. Good Reading!"

—*Long and Short Reviews*

"Ms. Galen writes with a sure, deft touch...plenty of humor as well as a real emotional depth."

—*All About Romance*

"Highly entertaining, humorous, action-packed, and so much fun!"

—*Night Owl Reviews*, 4 Stars

"Captivating...I loved how the romance progressed, how genuine it felt...a lot of action, plot twists galore, and more surprises than you can imagine. Another superb addition to the Covent Garden Cubs series!"

—*Fresh Fiction*

"Romantic and tremendously fun. Galen is known for her adventurous love stories, and this romp is filled with charming characters (including a dog) and a grin-inducing happily-ever-after conclusion."

—*The Washington Post*

Also by Shana Galen

I Kissed A Rogue

SHANA GALEN

sourcebooks
casablanca

Published by Sourcebooks Casablanca, an imprint of Sourcebooks, Inc.
P.O. Box 4410, Naperville, Illinois 60567-4410
(630) 961-3900
Fax: (630) 961-2168
www.sourcebooks.com

Printed and bound in Canada.
MBP 10 9 8 7 6 5 4 3 2 1

*For Gayle Cochrane, who helps me
more than she can know.*

One

SHE HAD TO ESCAPE. SHE COULDN'T DIE DOWN HERE, IN the rank dark, alone. She might deserve such a death, but she'd fight it with every last ounce of strength. She'd almost freed her hands by twisting and working the rope against her chafed wrists until it slackened. Her captors hadn't tied it very tightly, but that was the only mistake they'd made.

Lila had no idea how long she'd been in the dank, cold cellar, but she knew the moment her life went completely astray. The carriage had raced along the dark streets of London, the familiar clip-clop of the horses' hooves almost like music in her ears. She'd pulled her thick pelisse more tightly around her bare shoulders and rested her dancing slippers on the warm brick at her feet.

All she'd wanted was her cozy bed and a cup of tea. She hadn't even cared that by leaving her cousin Rose's betrothal ball early, she'd risked her father's wrath in the morning. She'd attended the betrothal tea, the betrothal dinner, and now the betrothal ball. Would that Rose marry and be done with it. It was during that uncharitable line of thinking that she had heard John Coachman call out and the carriage slowed.

Lila had parted the curtains in an effort to see what was the matter, but all she'd seen was the swirl of London fog and the amorphous shapes of the outriders moving to stand protectively in front of the carriage door. She'd sighed with impatient annoyance.

"Now wh—?" She'd clamped her mouth shut at the sound of a thump and an unfamiliar man's voice. The carriage rocked as the horses danced with fear. She waited for John Coachman's reassuring words and heard only a muffled shout and the pop of what sounded like her father's rifle.

Her heart pounding in fear, she'd slid one lock into place and had been reaching for the other when a tall, lanky man yanked the door open.

He'd smiled, his thin lips and cheeks stretching over his facial bones. "Hello, Lady Lillian-Anne."

From there, everything was a blur. She'd been dragged from the carriage, hooded, and pushed against the conveyance, her hands roughly bound. Lila had been so shocked at her mistreatment, she hadn't even screamed, and then she'd been lifted and tossed over a man's shoulders. She hadn't been carried far before she'd heard the squeak and squeal of a door being pried open and the echo of boots on slatted wood floors. Another door, then another, and her captor had carried her down a flight of stairs and dropped her on her bottom.

She'd screamed then and scurried backward, only to run up against a pair of hard boots. A voice, much like the one who'd greeted her, hissed in her ear. "Shut yer potato hole. Keep quiet or I stuff my drawers down yer throat. You hear me, Duchess?"

She'd nodded and closed her mouth. She'd pulled her legs in and hunched her shoulders, making herself small, waiting for what seemed an eternity for what was to happen next. Would they rob her? Rape her?

She was not a duchess, only the daughter of one. She had the wild thought that perhaps the men wanted her stepmother, the Duchess of Lennox. But no. They'd called her Lady Lillian-Anne. They knew who she was. They'd planned the abduction and whatever was to come next.

Lila had shivered, her body shaking uncontrollably with fear and cold. Finally, the man had moved away. At his word, the others had followed, and she'd heard their boots on the stairs and then the thud as the door closed.

She sat on the hard floor, the small pebbles and rocks digging into her skin through her silk ball gown and the pelisse. She jumped at the creaks and pops of the building settling, fearing each minute sound was the men returning for her. Gradually, she grew accustomed to the sounds but not the smell, never the smell. Something had died down here—*many* somethings— and with the hood over her face, she could only imagine. Lila envisioned rat corpses responsible for the sharp, sickly fragrance that burned her nostrils. When she began to imagine human bodies, she bit her lip hard to stop the rising panic.

Strange that in the middle of London, all was silent but for her teeth chattering.

They'd stopped chattering now—after too many

hours to count. Lila was too numb to feel the cold any longer. The rope around her wrists was all she cared about. She twisted and pulled until finally she managed to squeeze one hand free. She bit her raw lip against the pain of the rough rope sliding against her hand. The gloves she'd painstakingly inched off might have protected her bare skin, but they were one more layer between her and freedom.

With a wince, her wrists slid apart, and she exhaled softly, hugging her arms around her chest. Her shoulders throbbed, and the simple act of rotating them in the opposite direction was sheer bliss. She felt for the opening of the hood she wore and quickly tore it off. Charcoal gray replaced the blackness. If the cellar had openings of any kind, she couldn't spot them in the dark of night. She prayed it was still night and that morning would show her some sort of escape.

And not a stack of rotting bodies.

She had to find a way out. By now her father must have realized she'd been abducted. He would be frantic with worry. Had her captors sent a ransom note? Was that what this was about? Colin would make the duke pay it. Colin and Lila had grown closer since their mother's death. He wouldn't allow their father to ignore a ransom note.

If there was a ransom note.

What if the Duchess of Lennox was behind this? Lila's stepmother hated her, but even she would not stoop to hiring mercenaries to abduct her stepdaughter.

Lady Selina would. She and Lila had hated each other since their first Seasons, when Lord Hugh had asked Lila to dance before Selina. From then on, it had been war.

Selina was married now and certainly too busy to plan attacks on Lila. But Madeleine Stratham, her cousin Rose's friend, was not too busy, and she had intentionally stepped on Lila's gown at the ball tonight, hissing, "Watch out!"

Had that been a warning?

Lila's head spun. If she tried to count all of her enemies, it would take hours. And who knew what her abductors would do to her when they returned. She pressed her hands against the cold, dirt floor beneath her, moving her fingers until she found her gloves. She pulled them on again, for warmth as much as protection, and moved cautiously forward, hands outstretched. Her knees trembled and wobbled.

"Please no bodies. Please no bodies," she chanted under her breath.

The cellar was blissfully empty. She discovered a wall and followed it around to the base of the stairwell. Her hands traveled over that rough wood until she found the opening. The stairwell had no railing, so she carefully lifted her skirts and moved slowly and silently upward. Her fingertips touched the wood of the door at the top, and she stood listening.

She heard nothing but silence and the strains of music farther away. Perhaps a tavern or gin house was nearby. She couldn't be certain a guard wasn't on the other side of the door, but she tried the handle anyway. The handle moved, but the door did not budge when she pushed on it.

Some sort of lock kept it closed and secure.

Lila waited, again listening for movement or an indication her efforts to escape had been noted. When she heard nothing, she rattled the door. The wood was flimsy and old. One serious push against it, and she could compromise the lock.

She took a jagged breath and said a quick prayer. She'd never prayed so much—no, she'd been her own god for too many years. Lila stepped back, careful not to go too far and tumble down the stairs, then rammed the door with her shoulder.

Pain exploded at the point of impact, the sharp heat of it radiating through her neck and back. And then she was falling forward as the door gave way and she stumbled, unchecked. She groped for something to break her fall, but there was nothing. Her feet tangled in her skirts, sending her plummeting to her knees. More pain sliced through her, eliciting a small sob.

On hands and knees, she raised her head and peered about in the darkness. She did not know where she was—an abandoned building or house? There were no windows where she crouched, and she could not judge the time. There were also no voices except for the sounds from the street outside. Wherever she was, it was not near a busy street. The voices sounded far away and muffled. Please let that mean she was alone.

Lila rose and crept forward, tripping over objects in her path—a ragged piece of wood, broken pottery, a tangle of clothing or blankets. Finally, she rounded a corner and spotted the gray haze of early morning through a filmy window. It had been after midnight when she'd left the ball, and now she judged the time close to five in the morning.

Crouching down, she sidled forward, wanting to see what lay beyond her prison. The closer she got to the window, the clearer the voices she had heard earlier became. Finally, she stood to one side of the window and chanced peeking around. The glass, if there ever had been glass, had long been broken or removed, and the window was open to the cold of the early morning. Outside the window was not a street at all, as she had thought, but a small courtyard or square—though that description was far too grand for the small, rubbish-strewn area she glimpsed.

She could not hear the music on this side of the building, but now she knew the origin of the voices. Four men stood in the courtyard, speaking in low tones. One man, the one who faced her, wore a long greatcoat and a beaver hat. He was quite portly, much heavier than any of the other men. That was not saying much as the others were small and scrawny and not dressed for the chilly night.

Except for one.

He was the one who'd taken her, and that realization sent Lila cowering in the shadows.

When the men's conversation went on as before, she looked out again. The man who'd taken her wore a ragged, thigh-length coat and gestured with purpose. He was the leader of these rogues, and watching him, Lila realized he argued with the wealthy gentleman.

The pounding of her heart and the blood in her ears quieted enough that she could hear snatches of the conversation.

"—didn't do yer part."

"Now wait just a minute. Who do you think you

are?" That from the gentleman. She could hear the cultured accent in his voice.

At a signal she wouldn't have seen had she not been watching from a distance, the rogues moved closer to the gentleman, stepping into position until they surrounded him. The leader still stood in front of the blubbering gentleman, who did not seem to realize he was in any danger.

"Want to know who I am?" The leader cut the gentleman off. "I'll show ye."

Lila gasped at the flash of metal in the dim light and almost screamed when two of the rogues caught the gentleman and held him fast. All was over and done so quickly that Lila hadn't had time to look away. The knife flashed and a gash of red opened on the gentleman's neck. Then he'd crumpled to the ground, a dark pool growing around him.

Dead, dead, dead. Lila's brain would not stop repeating the word.

"Take care of him," the leader said to the others, gesturing carelessly to the dead man.

Dead, dead, dead.

Would she be next? Would he put that knife to her throat and open her up like a fish to be gutted? She crumpled her fist against her mouth and stared at the leader in horror.

It was then she realized he was staring back at her.

Their gazes met, and the leader shook his head and started for her.

"Ye'll wish ye hadn't seen that."

Lila stumbled away from the window in terror, but it was too late.

⚜

"Sir."

Someone shook his shoulder, and Brook opened his eyes. He was instantly awake and alert, his body tensed and ready for action.

"Sir."

"What is it?" He sat, scrubbed his face once, and stared at Hunt. Part valet, part secretary, part inspector, Hunt was a veritable jack-of-all-trades. Brook found him indispensable.

"A footman has come from Derring House. You have a caller."

Brook absorbed the information even as the woman in bed beside him groaned and rolled over, pulling a pillow over her head. Hunt's eyes never strayed from Brook's face. The yellow light from the candle the servant held flickered over his cleanly shaven jaw, dark eyes, and chiseled features. Brook didn't know how the man managed to look so bloody awake at—

"What time is it?" Brook asked.

"Half four, sir."

Brook paused in the act of setting his bare feet on the floor. "In the morning?"

"Yes, sir."

"Who the hell wants me at four in the morning? Tell him to come to my office at a decent hour."

"I would have given those instructions, sir."

Brook waited. Hunt was no fool. He would not have pulled Brook from Arabella's warm arms if he didn't have a reason.

"But?" Brook asked with a longing look at Arabella's slim form, naked under the bedclothes.

"The footman says the man calling for you is the Duke of Lennox."

Brook heard the word *duke* and rose, but at the rest of the title, he paused.

"Lennox?"

Hunt nodded, his expression one of chagrin.

"What the devil does he want?"

"The footman didn't say, sir." Hunt held out Brook's dressing gown, which he donned before making use of the chamber pot behind a screen.

While Hunt silently dressed him, a thousand possibilities raced through Brook's mind: the duke had been robbed; his new wife had been accosted; his prize thoroughbred had been poisoned.

He wouldn't allow himself to think of *her*. He wouldn't allow himself to acknowledge the clench of his belly when the image of Lady Lila arose in his mind.

He hadn't thought of her for years, and that was not by accident.

"Let's go," he said, waving away his rumpled cravat. He used this flat on occasion when he wanted privacy from his mother and the rest of the family at Derring House. He kept only the bare essentials here. Hunt could probably find him a clean, starched cravat, but Brook didn't want to bother with it. Some contrary part of him wanted to greet the duke without it.

At the bedroom door, Brook looked back at Hunt impatiently. Hunt cleared his throat and nodded to the bed. He'd forgotten Arabella.

She'd been onstage at the theater until late last night; then he'd taken her to dine before bringing her back here. She wouldn't wake for hours. Brook looked about for pen and paper. Finding neither, he started for the parlor and the desk there, but Hunt produced a sheet of foolscap and a pen and inkwell.

Brook gave the items a long look. "What else do you have hidden in your coat?"

"Oh, this and that, sir."

"Huh." Brook penned a quick note to Arabella, set it on the pillow where he'd been sleeping less than a quarter of an hour before, and followed Hunt out of the flat.

Twenty minutes later he stood in his mother's drawing room. Crawford, his mother's butler, offered him tea as though it were a reasonable hour instead of half five in the bloody morning.

"Where is my mother?" Brook asked Crawford, declining the tea and noting the way Lennox sat with his back rigid against the chair he occupied. He balanced a full, untouched cup of tea on his knee.

"She has gone back to bed, sir," Crawford said. "I am to inform Edwards if you require her ladyship's attention."

"Very good, Crawford. Leave us."

When the butler had closed the door and Lennox and Brook were alone, Brook crossed to the mantel and leaned one arm negligently against it. The action caused his shirt, open at the throat, to gape slightly. He hadn't taken a comb or brush to his hair and, though it was short, he hoped it looked rumpled.

"This is a surprise," Brook said. "How kind of you to grace our lowly home."

The duke said nothing, simply stared at his tea. He was obviously distraught, and Brook almost felt sorry for him.

Almost.

Finally, the duke looked up. His eyes were bloodshot, and his face looked haggard. The dark hair streaked with gray that he always wore combed back from his high forehead fell in unkempt waves over his brow.

"I didn't know where else to turn. I know you must hate me—"

"Hate is far too strong a word. It implies an emotion, and you inspire no emotions in me, Duke. I care not whether you live or die."

The teacup rattled and liquid sloshed over the rim as Lennox set it roughly on a table. "This isn't about me." He stood, rising to his full height, which was very nearly equal to Brook's. "I came because I thought you might be able to put aside the past, and because I hear you are the best."

"The best?"

"You found the missing Flynn boy and the daughter of the Marquess of Lyndon. If you won't do it for me, do it for Lila."

"What has she to do with any of this?"

"She was abducted earlier this evening, just after midnight. My coachman and one outrider are dead. Another is hanging on to life by a thread."

Everything in Brook went very still then—the crackle of the fire behind him, the clip-clop of the horses pulling carts to market, the chime of the tall case clock in the corridor faded into the distance.

Lila had been taken. She might be injured, raped, dead. He hadn't seen her for seven years, and still the knowledge that something might have happened to her ripped through him. Brook tamped down the fear fiercely and clenched one hand behind his back. He must be calm, rational, precise.

"Tell me the details."

For the first time that night, the duke's shoulders squared. "Then you will help?"

"I'll find her. Where is this outrider?"

"At my house. I'll take you to him."

"On the way, you can tell me the events of the night as you know them." Brook started for the door, but the duke's hand on his shoulder stopped him.

"I cannot say how much I appreciate this, Derring. I'll pay you whatever you ask."

Brook blew out a disgusted breath. "You have *nothing* I want."

By an hour after daybreak, Brook stood in the place the coach and four had been waylaid. The spot was just a few streets from Seven Dials and the thieves and criminals there had wasted no time stripping the conveyance of every adornment. Even the door with the ducal crest had been pried away. The horses were gone. The injured outrider had taken one to make his way back to Lennox House, but the other three had either run off or been stolen.

The coroner had come to examine the bodies and several constables milled around, watching Brook circle the wreck of what had once been a fine coach and four. The attack had been planned, and planned well. The fact that it had happened here certainly pointed to one of the gangs inhabiting Seven Dials as the likely culprit. The rooks might have been brave, but they weren't known for abducting grown women in protected conveyances.

If it was a woman they wanted, the rookeries teemed with them. Blunt had to be the motive. So why hadn't a ransom note been sent?

"It's cold enough to freeze my balls off," a man said, approaching the carriage. His hands were shoved in his greatcoat and a hat rode low over his temple, concealing a scar.

"Dorrington," Brook said with a nod. "You going soft?"

"Say that again and you'll see just how soft my fist feels when it connects with your teeth."

Brook smiled. The other inspector had been working with him for almost two years now, and he hadn't changed a bit. He was still foulmouthed, cunning, and sharp as a blade. But he knew this area better than anyone else Brook could think of, probably because he had once lived here under another name.

"Hunt gave you the particulars?"

Dorrington nodded, then crouched down to study the blood-spattered ground. "Duke's daughter on the way home from a ball with a coachman and two outriders. Coach is waylaid. She's taken and two of the men were shot dead. One was stabbed multiple times. Probably won't make it." He looked up at Brook. "Did you talk to the survivor?"

"He wasn't much help. Said there were four men, couldn't describe any of them. Two of them had pistols, and the others, knives that they used on him. The lady was dragged from the carriage and taken that way." Brook pointed toward Seven Dials, where a sickly yellow fog had rolled in. "He thinks. He was on this side of the coach, bleeding all over, and he says she wasn't carried off past him."

"So this is his blood?"

Without waiting for an answer, Dorrington crossed to the other side of the vehicle. When he didn't return right away, Brook joined him. Dorrington stared in the direction of Seven Dials, now shadowed in mist. "Not much hope of finding her if they took her in there. No one will snitch, and there are a thousand places to hide her or dispose of the body. We can't narrow it down, unless…"

"We know who took her." Brook stuffed his icy hands in his pockets. His face was frozen, but he ignored the burn of his chafed skin. "If they are in Seven Dials, your old cronies are the most likely suspects. They run Covent Garden, and Beezle's just ambitious enough to try something like this."

Dorrington lowered his head, shielding his face in what was probably an entirely unconscious attempt to hide his features. "He's done it before."

"We don't have proof of that."

"The cove he took described him right down to the freckle on his arse. That's all the proof I need."

Brook didn't argue. He'd thought of the case last year as well. The son of a viscount had been slumming in the rookeries one evening when his friends lost track of him. His parents hadn't been too concerned. The father figured his boy was holed up enjoying himself in a brothel. But when the ransom note had come, they'd called for Brook.

Unfortunately, they'd already paid the ransom, and the boy was delivered home—unhurt but for a few scrapes and bruises—before Brook could do much of anything. He and Dorrington had interviewed the lad, but he'd been hooded and tied, and hadn't seen anything except for the face of the man who'd taken him.

His description of a tall, skinny man with dark hair and a hawk-like nose was a far cry from the detailed description Dorrington made it seem.

"But if Beezle did it, where's the ransom note?" Dorrington asked.

"That's my question."

"Suppose we sit back and wait until it turns up."

Brook shook his head. "No, we go in and start searching."

"If Beezle's involved, I'm out. He recognizes me as"—Dorrington lowered his voice—"Gideon Harrow, and it's more than my arse hanging in the wind. There's Susanna to think of."

"We've risked it before. You've never been recognized." Sometimes Brook didn't even recognize the man for the thief he'd once been—not with his hair neatly trimmed, his clothes pressed, and a few more pounds on his lanky frame.

Dorrington stared at him. "Why the risk? Who is this Lennox mort? She mean something to you?"

"She did. Once."

"And now?"

Brook pulled the collar of his coat up to shield his neck from the cold. "And now I need someone to show me all of Beezle's hidey-holes. You're the man for the job." And he started for Seven Dials, trusting Dorrington to follow.

"You'll get us both killed," Dorrington called after him.

"You have something better to do today?"

Dorrington grumbled, but a moment later he caught up and, with a curse, pulled Brook down a dark alley and into hell.

Two

LILA COULD HEAR THE MEN TALKING. THEY WOULD kill her. They were probably plotting how to do it right now. She didn't understand why they hadn't killed her yet. When the man who'd slit the gentleman's throat had caught her, she had thought that was the end.

But instead of slitting her throat, he'd dragged her back down to the dark cellar and left her. He hadn't bothered to tie her hands this time, but she'd heard something that sounded heavy scrape across the floor above. She imagined an enormous obstacle blocked the door. She'd never escape.

Perhaps that was the idea all along.

She was so thirsty. Perhaps they'd leave her down here to die of starvation.

She'd never thought she'd die this way. She hadn't wanted to die like her mother, delirious with pain and coughing blood. But at least her mother had died in bed with her family around her.

Lila would die alone.

She didn't know how much time had passed. In the

darkness, she could judge only by the violence of her hunger, but that came and went. Her thirst was a constant. She didn't sleep, but she had nodded off a time or two, waking when she began to slide to the ground. She did not want to lie on the ground. Not yet.

She rested her head on her knees and then lifted it again. Where were the voices? Had the men left her? Cautiously, she stood and strained to hear again. All was silence.

No, wait. That wasn't quite true. She heard the creak of a board, the thump of a footfall. Someone was still up there and moving about.

She began to sink back down when a man grunted and something heavy slid across the floorboards.

They were coming for her.

Lila slunk away, into the deepest shadows of the cellar, and then clenched her fingers and moved back before the staircase. Was she so much a coward that she'd cower in a corner? It would buy her no more time.

The door rattled, and she bit her already bloody and parched lips. She would not scream or cry or beg for mercy.

The door opened and a weak shaft of light penetrated the gloom. In that light, she saw the form of a man. She knew instantly it wasn't one of her captors. This man was solid, not bone thin.

"Lady Lillian-Anne?" he whispered.

Lila's parched throat would not allow her to answer. She made a croak, and he stepped onto the first step. He held no lamp, not even a candle. She didn't know whether to trust him—not that she had many other options.

"Yes," she finally managed. "I'm here."

"Come on, then."

She hesitated, uncertain whether to trust this man. His accent was not much better than that of the men who'd taken her. How did she know he didn't have something worse planned for her?

"Are you tied up?" he asked. "Can you walk?"

"Yes, but—"

He sighed with impatience. "Always introductions with you gentry morts," he muttered. "I'm with Sir Brook Derring. We're here to save you."

"Brook Derring?" That was a name she had not thought about for a long, long time.

"He's entertaining Beezle and the cubs with a Banbury story at the moment, but they'll be back and nab us both if you don't hurry."

If her muscles hadn't been so cramped from hours of disuse, she would have run up the steps. As it was, she moved quickly and the man at the top took her elbow. He pulled her into the kitchen, then paused to shove the battered wardrobe in front of the door.

He winked at her when he was done. "That might give us some time."

He took her elbow again and led her confidently through the building and out a door that led into a narrow alley. So narrow was it that she had to turn sideways to fit. The ground sloped inward and the smell was that of human and animal waste. Lila tried not to breathe as she followed the man along the wall. They'd gone perhaps twenty yards when he yanked on one of the doors that opened into the alley and disappeared inside. A moment later, he poked his head back out.

"Coming?"

She followed him through a twisting maze of back alleys, dark buildings, and even over rooftops. A thick fog shrouded everything, and she wasn't certain if it was day or night. She was glad for the fog. It kept them hidden. Still, she jumped every time she heard voices, afraid they'd been found. Finally, her leader stopped in the middle of an alley that led onto a busier street. She could see men and women walking by where the alley opened, and the movement had dispersed some of the fog.

"Stay here," the man said to her. She couldn't see his face. He wore his hat too low on his brow.

"No!" Like a child, she grabbed hold of his arm. "Don't leave me."

"I'll be back, and I'll bring Derring."

"Can't we send someone else to fetch him? One of those women?" She gestured to three prostitutes leaning against the walls of the alley and watching them curiously.

"Raise yer skirts and do the deed already!" one of them called. All three cackled.

"I'll be back in a moment. Stay here, and don't talk to anyone." He moved away, then came back. "Don't even look at anyone."

Lila hugged herself and pressed her back against the wall.

He'll be right back.

And if he wasn't, she was free now. She could walk right out of here, hail a hackney, and go home. She might have no idea where she was, but she was still in London. She couldn't be too far from home.

The prostitutes at the end of the alley called out to the man as he walked past them. He answered back, jesting with them in the strange cant the lower classes used. She didn't understand them, and she didn't want to.

Brook Derring. *Sir* Brook Derring. That honor had been bestowed after she'd known him. The king had given it to him for his service to the Crown. Lila wasn't certain what the service had been, but she knew Brook was known now for finding people who had been abducted. She didn't go out as much as she had when she'd known him, but she'd heard him spoken of at dinner parties now and then. He was nothing short of a national hero. He'd found the son of a baron or viscount. Poor man had been languishing in an opium den in Brighton, or had it been Bath? And Derring had found a woman too.

That was why he was here. She was the one who had been abducted this time. Her father must have gone to him and asked for help. Lennox must have bruised his pride, going to Derring, especially after the way the duke had treated him.

After the abominable way they'd both treated Sir Brook.

She knew only moments had passed, but it seemed hours. Perhaps Sir Brook would leave her here. Was that his revenge? But if he'd wanted revenge, he could have left her in the cellar.

And why would the other man lead her in circles if only to abandon her here?

He'll be right back.

Now that she wasn't moving, she was cold again. And thirsty, so thirsty. She tried to swallow, but her mouth was too dry.

"You just going to stand there all night?" one of the prostitutes called.

The three of them had grown bored of calling out to passing men and turned their attentions on her.

Lila didn't answer. Derring's man had told her not to speak. She wouldn't speak.

"Wot's wrong?" one of them, dressed in a low-cut reddish blouse, asked. "Cat got yer tongue?"

"She don't know wot to do wit' 'er tongue." That was from the youngest of the three. Lila thought she looked little more than a child.

The first, short and with thinning hair, approached her. "This 'ere is our place. Get out."

Lila looked up at her and immediately back down again. The woman had skin like leather, and the stench of her rotting teeth made Lila want to gag. The prostitute leaned down, her dark, greasy hair brushing against Lila's sleeve.

"I said, get out."

Lila shook her head. Oh, where was Derring's man?

"She wants to stay, Rosie." That from the buxom girl in red. "If ye stay, dearie, ye have to earn yer keep."

Lila stared at her slippers, black with God knew what.

"That's right," the young one chimed in. "Ye pay us a fee. I'll take that fancy coat."

Lila tightened her arms, but it was no use when two of the women grabbed her and forced her pelisse from her back. She fought back, but it was three against one. She received a slap and a punch in the stomach for her pains.

The girl in red snatched at the combs in her hair, and the short prostitute snapped the necklace from her neck. Lila blinked back the tears from the sting of the hair that had been ripped out, then pushed the women away.

"Take them and leave me alone."

"Oh, now, listen to 'er," said the short one, who Lila was beginning to think was the leader. "Don't she sound all 'igh and mighty."

"*Take 'em and leave me alone*," the youngest one mocked her, nose in the air, chest out. She strutted about, fluffing her new pelisse.

"I know wot will bring 'er down a peg or two. A good rogering will show 'er wot's wot."

The prostitutes grabbed her by the arms, and though Lila dug her heels in and tried to shake them off, she was dragged inexorably forward. She kicked and writhed until she was knocked in her already-sore lip. The sharp pain made her forget about the rest until the women had dragged her onto the street.

"Boys, lookee 'ere. Fancy a tumble? You pay ol' Rosie 'ere a 'alf crown, you can 'ave 'er the 'ole night."

"No!" Lila struggled, only to be knocked in the teeth with an elbow.

"Want a poke? Try 'er out for a sixpence."

"Let go!" Lila finally pulled free, only to stumble on her skirts and fall to her knees. She looked up and into the gleam of a pair of shiny, black boots.

The man held his hand down, offering it to her. The small gesture of kindness took her off guard and, before she could think the better of it, she took it. He pulled her to her feet, and when she looked into his face, she caught her breath.

Brook.

After all these years, she still knew him. As though her touch burned him, he pulled his hand out of hers and pushed her aside. The man who'd led her from the cellar was there, and he took her arm and started walking.

"'Ey, now! Ye can't just take 'er. She's ours. Ye 'ave to pay."

The man beside her never stopped moving, but she heard Brook Derring's voice clearly. "You want me to pay? How about I do you a favor? How about I don't throw you in Newgate or have you transported for kidnapping?"

"Aw, come on, guv. We was just 'aving a bit o' sport."

"Take your sport back to the hole you crawled out of."

A moment later, he was beside her. His arm came around her back. "I have her now."

The other man released her, as though transferring ownership.

"Thank you," Lila said, looking up at him.

He gave her a puzzled look and pushed her forward. "Don't stop until I say."

"If Beezle isn't down, he will be soon," the other man said.

"All the more reason for you to disappear now. I have her. Get out of here before Beezle sees you."

"You don't need to tell me twice." And the other man slipped into the fog and was gone.

"Where are you taking me?" she asked as he continued to push her along.

"Stop talking."

"I remember you being nicer," she said as they moved around a group of men throwing a die. Several of them eyed her curiously. Without her pelisse, she wore only her lilac silk ball gown, and though it was wrinkled and stained, it was still finer than most of them had seen.

"I'm surprised you remember me at all."

"If you despise me so, why did you rescue me?"

He glanced at her, and she knew before he even spoke the words would be cutting. His dark brown eyes glinted like hard agate.

"I like charity cases."

Lila looked away. She knew what his words implied. She wasn't well liked among the *ton*. No one would have minded too much if she were to disappear. No one would have troubled too much to come after her.

"What, no rejoinder?" Sir Brook asked, raising his arm to catch the attention of a jarvey sitting on the box of a hackney. "Where's that silver tongue, Lady Lila?"

In the grave with my mother, she thought.

Before handing her into the hackney, he draped his greatcoat over her. It wasn't until the warm wool, infused with the scents of bergamot and brandy, enveloped her that she realized how cold she'd been. The first gusts of a wintry wind swept the fog away and cut through her right down to the bone. The coat, still warm from Derring's body, was like an embrace.

She shivered and lowered her nose into the collar.

After giving the jarvey the address, he handed her into the hackney—that and the coat told her he could still be chivalrous—and seated himself across from her, taking the less desirable position. Lila could only stare down at her ruined gown and shoes and wonder just how awful the rest of her looked.

Not that she cared what Sir Brook thought. Not that she cared what anyone thought.

She was away. She was free. Lila considered, for the first time in hours, that she might not die today. She should have felt elated, but all she felt was the pounding in her head and the burning in her eyes from lack of food and sleep.

"Once we reach your father's home, you'll undoubtedly be whisked away, so let me ask my questions now."

Lila raised her eyes. She'd thought they would sit in silence.

"What time is it?" she asked, her tongue thick in her mouth, making her words come slowly.

"Half three," he said. "In the afternoon. You've been gone for a night and a day."

Sir Brook had removed his hat and, though the last vestiges of fog still covered the world in nebulous gray, she could make out his features now. He'd always been handsome. Not handsome in the way his brother, the earl, was. The earl was smooth and polished and had the charming good looks to match his charming personality.

Brook was more edges and ridges, his face sharper and rougher. His nose was straight as a knife, his cheeks cut high, his brows a slash of honey brown over eyes the color of mahogany. When she'd known him years ago—six years? No, closer to seven—he'd still been a youth, barely a man. His cheeks had been soft, his lips full, his eyes warm. Now his chin was covered with light brown and blond stubble, and his lips were pressed firmly together. His hair had been longer then too. He'd worn it tousled and curled like the dandies. She'd thought he looked a bit feminine with those curls, but there was nothing feminine about him now. His cropped hair was light brown with some blond mixed in. It was not styled fashionably. The severity only made him appear that much harder.

She'd liked the boy better. The man seemed impenetrable.

He met her gaze directly, not looking down or away. His eyes revealed nothing of his thoughts. She wondered if he still thought her beautiful.

Silly chit, she chided herself. What did she care? With her hair in knots and streaks of dirt and grime all over, she probably looked no better than the loose women who'd tried to sell her. She closed her eyes, so dry they stung, and tried not to feel the humiliation of it all over again.

"Dorrington said Beezle had you in the cellar of one of his flash kens."

Flash ken. That was an interesting term for the thieves' den. She opened her eyes, running her tongue over her dry, swollen lips. She'd never known thirst could be so agonizing.

"Do you know why Beezle took you?"

She shook her head.

"Could it have been a random attack?"

"No, it wasn't random. Do you have any water? Something to drink?" She touched her throat, trying to clear it of what felt like sand wedged there.

Brook pounded on the roof of the hackney. The jarvey opened the hatch and peered inside.

"Stop at the next tavern and fetch the lady bread and watered wine. I'll pay you double for your pains."

"Yes, sir!" The jarvey dropped the hatch and the conveyance drove on.

"Thank you," she said quietly. "My father will pay you back—"

"I don't want his money."

Lila wondered if that was a reference to her father's accusation, all those years ago, that he only wanted Lila for her dowry. The hackney slowed, and she heard the jarvey dismount. Wine. She would have wine in a few moments.

"You must allow us to repay you in some manner," she said.

His mouth curved up in a sneer. "So polite and gracious. What an actress."

She didn't want to argue. She was too tired to do so. And yet, she couldn't resist murmuring a response. "I am grateful."

"I wager that's the first time you've ever said those words."

The door opened, bringing the sharp edge of cold with it, and the jarvey handed Derring a cup of wine and a hunk of bread. "I 'ave to bring the cup back."

Derring cut his gaze to the door. "Give us a moment." He passed her the cup. "Drink slowly, my lady."

Her hands shook when she wrapped them around

the wooden cup and brought it to her parched lips. Her head told her to heed his advice, but her body was overeager. She gulped the wine, choked, and had to hand Derring the cup while she coughed and coughed.

The next thing she knew, he was beside her, his body larger than she remembered and so solid and warm. He waved a handkerchief under her nose, and she took it, grateful, again, for his kindness. She, who had never valued kindness, could not seem to have enough of it this day.

When the coughing passed, Derring held the cup to her lips, allowed her to sip, and withdrew it before she could drink too deeply. Her body screamed for more, but she managed to drink it all slowly and without another coughing fit.

She was still thirsty, but the need was not so great.

Derring handed her the bread, instructed her to nibble it slowly, then moved back to his seat. He opened the door, and Lila shivered again at the burst of cold air. The poor jarvey and his horse must have been freezing. The man took the cup and a few moments later, they were once again underway.

"As I was saying," Derring said, snagging her attention.

She'd closed her eyes again, and this time she felt as though she were floating. The wine had been watered, but the lack of food had still caused it to go to her head. The world seemed to spin.

"I don't want anything from you, save answers. You said the attack was not random. How do you know this?"

Lila pressed a finger to her temple. "Because…

because he said my name." She met Derring's mahogany eyes. "He called me Lady Lillian-Anne when he pulled me from the coach."

"Who pulled you from the coach?"

"I don't know his name."

"Describe him."

The questions came fast and sure, and she tried to focus. "It was a man. He had brown hair."

"My color?"

She looked at Derring's hair. It was light brown with lovely blond highlights in it. Had it been a little longer, she might have thought about running her hands through it.

"No, it wasn't as pretty as yours."

"What?"

He sounded shocked, and Lila realized she'd spoken aloud. She closed her eyes, tried to gather her thoughts.

"It was darker, I think. He…was tall."

"My height or taller?"

Now she looked at Derring's body. He didn't seem quite so tall, sitting across from her. But she remembered the feel of him beside her.

"I don't know. He seemed impossibly tall to me, but I don't suppose he was."

Derring sighed, and she knew she was not giving him useful information. But the events of the night blurred in her mind. Her surroundings had been dark, and she'd been terrified.

"Is there anything else you remember? Anything that might distinguish him?"

"No, but I thought you said you knew who took me. Beetle, was it?"

"Beezle, and yes, I suspect him, but I need proof."

"I'm sorry. Perhaps I might remember something later." She lowered her nose into the collar of the coat again, sniffed his scent, and closed her eyes.

"I have one more question."

She looked up.

"Pardon me for asking about such a delicate matter, but did Beezle—or whoever took you—did any of the men violate you?"

She felt her cheeks burst into flame. Of course, she'd known she might be raped. She'd feared it constantly, but to speak of such a thing...

She shook her head, looked down.

"Lady Lila, I need the truth. Whether you wish to tell your father or anyone else is your decision. I will keep silent, but I need to know."

She looked up at him, startled by the vehemence in his voice. She couldn't see what difference it made. The man who'd taken her would hang for kidnapping alone.

But she could see Derring would press until he had his answer.

"He did not touch me...in that way," she said. "I was afraid he might when he caught me at the window. He was angry then, and he dragged me back to the cellar, but he left me there without hurting me."

"There was a window in the cellar?" Derring asked.

Lila pressed her fingers to her eyes. She might have cried had she the water for tears. "No. I escaped into the building—or I suppose it might have been a house."

"You escaped?" Derring stared at her, his expression disbelieving.

She straightened. "Yes. Did you think I would sit there, waiting for a knight to rescue me? When all was quiet, I stalked up the stairs and tried to get away. I found a window and saw the men who'd taken me, at least I think that's who they were, in a sort of court-yard with another man. A gentleman."

"How do you know it was a gentleman?"

Lila explained about his clothing and his speech, but when she came to the part where the leader had taken a knife to his throat, she couldn't manage to speak it.

Derring moved beside her again, but this time his presence did not comfort her. She pushed herself into a corner and put her hands over her face.

"Say it fast, Lila. If you say it fast, it's easier."

She did not want to remember it. She did not.

"He had a knife, and he grabbed the gentleman by the throat. I don't know how he did it. It happened so quickly, but he made a motion and then the man's throat was open and blood…"

Derring took her hand in his and pressed it tightly. "That's enough. I don't need you to say more."

"I just want to go home," she whispered from behind her hand. She'd not said those words in several years, not since her father had married again. "I just want to be safe."

"You are home."

She realized that at some point when she'd been speaking, the carriage had stopped. A glance out the window showed the white stone facade of Lennox House.

She moved toward the door, but Derring didn't release her hand.

"But you aren't safe."

Three

LENNOX HOUSE HAD NOT CHANGED, BROOK THOUGHT after he'd stepped inside. As predicted, Lady Lila had been whisked away by a horde of maids. Always one for a production, she had made a show of stumbling when she walked, and one of the footmen had carried her up the staircase.

Brook had rolled his eyes.

He'd been shown into a small, masculine sitting room paneled in dark wood and opening onto a terrace. The trees in the garden shook and shivered with the cold, and the wail of the winter wind rattled at the windows. The butler had offered him refreshment—everything from tea to brandy—but Brook had declined. He could have sorely used a drink and wouldn't have minded something to eat, but he'd meant what he'd said in the hackney.

He didn't want anything from Lennox.

And so he sat in a dark blue armchair, tapping his fingers on the rich upholstery. He'd been waiting almost an hour, and he supposed he might wait longer still. The duke would want to see his daughter. The king would want to see his princess.

She was still a princess, for all her *thank yous*. Perhaps she'd learned gratitude over the past seven years, but little else had changed. She'd sat perfectly straight, even in a rumpled dress that he imagined her lady's maid would burn. Her voice was still haughty, her nose still stuck in the air, her composure barely wavering.

It had wavered, which meant she was human after all. He'd sometimes doubted it.

He rolled his head around, stretching the tense muscles of his neck, then let his head fall back on the chair's cushioned top rail.

She was still beautiful. He didn't expect her to change, but why did he still have to find her attractive? Even knowing what she was, he wanted her. He couldn't see how any man could look at her and not want her.

All that long, dark hair and those wide-set golden-brown eyes. She appeared so innocent when she looked at him with those eyes. She looked ripe to be kissed on her perfect, pink lips, just the right color of pink against her pale, perfect, and porcelain complexion. How he wished he might fault her figure, but she was neither too thin nor too round. Her breasts swelled beautifully at the bodice of her modestly cut gown. And the thought of one of those plump globes in his hand made his body throb with need.

"Why?" he moaned. "Why her?"

"Who you talking to?"

Brook snapped up at the small voice and peered around. He saw nothing and no one, but somewhere, a child was hiding.

"Who said that?" he asked, keeping his voice light and playful. He had nephews and a niece. He knew how to speak to children.

Someone giggled and the curtains near the doors to the terrace rustled. Brook couldn't stop a smile. Children always thought if they couldn't see you, you couldn't see them.

"Hmm," he said, making a show of looking everywhere in the room but behind the curtain. A small head full of blond curls poked out and then back in. More giggles.

"I wonder where she could be hiding." Brook rose. "Under the desk?" He pretended to look under the desk. "No."

More giggles.

"I know. Under the chair." He lifted the chair. "No, not there. Wait, I have it! Under the rug!"

Now the little girl laughed so hard she could not contain it. She tumbled out from the curtains. "You can't hide under the rug. That's silly!"

"You can't?"

She shook her head, her blond curls bouncing.

"I would never have looked behind the curtain. You're very good at this game."

"I know. Nanny can't find me!"

Brook glanced toward the door, which was closed. He hoped Nanny wasn't frantic with worry. "Perhaps you should tell Nanny you've won."

"I will." The girl scampered toward the door, then looked back at him. "Who are you?"

Brook pretended to be taken aback. "I'm terribly sorry. I've been unforgivably rude."

The child laughed again, her cheeks growing pink with merriment now.

He bowed. "I am Sir Brook Derring. And who might you be, young lady?"

"Ginny. That's short for Genevieve." She gave an awkward curtsy, just catching herself before she lost her balance.

"And how old are you, Ginny, or should I say Lady Ginny?"

"That's right."

He nodded. He'd thought so. The child couldn't have been older than four, and if memory served, the duke had remarried four or five years before. This must be Lila's sister.

"I'm four!" She held up four fingers. "How old are you?"

"Oh, I'm very old. I'm practically ancient."

"How old?" she asked, eyes wide.

"One and thirty."

"That's not very old. Papa is much older than that!"

"How old is he?"

"I forgot."

In the distance, they heard footsteps. "Ginny! Ginny, come out this instant!"

Brook raised his brows at the girl. "Is that Nanny?"

"That's Mama. I'd better go."

"Good-bye then."

She didn't take the time to say good-bye, just yanked open the door and dashed away, her shoes clicking on the wooden floors.

Brook shook his head and shoved his hands into his pockets. Lila certainly had competition in that little one. She wasn't the only princess in the house any longer.

A moment later, the door opened and the Earl of Granbury entered. Brook hadn't known the duke's son and heir was home, but he supposed the duke had sent for his son when Lila had gone missing.

"Sir Brook," Granbury said, coming forward and bowing. "How can we thank you?"

Brook bowed in return. Granbury was younger than Lila and had the look of sincerity. His brown eyes, shaped like Lila's but a darker color, were almost too big for his youthful face.

"I don't need thanks, your lordship. I wanted only to speak with your father."

"He is on his way." Granbury poured a measure of brandy, handed it to Brook, and then poured one for himself. Though Brook had been determined not to take anything from Lennox, he didn't feel the same compunction with Granbury. He sipped and wondered if the earl knew anything of his history with Lila.

"I only saw her for a moment," Granbury said, "but she seemed fine. How did you find her?"

"Luck," Brook said, not wishing to bring Dorrington into the conversation. It was better if no one asked too many questions about his associate.

"Remind me never to gamble with you," Danbury said.

The two sipped their brandy in silence for a few moments, in which Brook fervently wished the duke would make his appearance. What did one say to a brother after having rescued his sister from Seven Dials?

Finally, Danbury cleared his throat. "Hell of a thing about the MP from Lincolnshire."

Brook didn't follow politics. That was his brother's domain. But he liked to think he kept abreast of Parliament's activities when they were in session. He'd even been called to address Parliament a time or two on the question of crime in the city.

At present, Parliament was not in session. Most of the members were at their country estates or in their home counties.

"What happened?" Brook asked, glancing toward the bracket clock on a table. How much longer would the duke make him wait? He wanted a hot bath, a hot meal, and his bed. In that order.

"The man was found dead this morning near the Covent Garden Theater."

Brook set down his glass. He'd been near Covent Garden himself that morning, investigating Lila's disappearance. "Natural causes?" he asked.

"Murder. His throat was cut from one end to the other."

Brook's entire body went cold, and his focus sharpened like a knife.

"Do they have the assassin?"

Danbury settled himself in a large armchair. "No. Right now the Bow Street Runners are asking for witnesses."

Oh, he had a witness, but he wasn't trusting her to the Runners. Most of them were good men, but there were a few who would sell their souls for a few extra coins.

"Have to ask yourself what kind of world we live

in when our own government officials are murdered on the street."

"Yes."

Brook knew exactly the kind of world they lived in, probably better than the earl would ever know. His question was what sort of relationship the dead MP had with Beezle—if that was who'd taken Lila and who she'd seen murder the member from Lincolnshire.

His next question was how to protect Lila. If she'd seen Beezle murder an MP, she wasn't safe. Kidnapping was one thing, murder quite another. She was a target now, and she had to be protected.

The door opened, and Granbury stood as his father entered. Lennox waved his son back down and crossed directly to the ormolu table holding the brandy, sherry, and port decanters. He poured himself a measure of sherry, downed it, then poured another. Crystal-cut glass in hand, he turned to face Brook.

"Well, you've done it again. My daughter is home, safe and sound."

"She is home," Brook acknowledged.

"She seems none the worse for her ordeal, a little tired and hungry, but that can be remedied. It's her reputation that concerns me now."

Of course that's what mattered to the duke. Lila had to make a good match. That, after all, was the purpose of a duke's daughter. How Lennox must have chafed at his wife's illness and death. The period of mourning only prolonged Lila's maidenhood.

The duke himself, however, had certainly not waited to marry again.

"Did Lady Lillian-Anne tell you *all* that happened to her?" Brook asked.

The duke waved a hand. "She told me enough." He gestured to his son to rise from the chair Granbury occupied and then took it himself. Granbury retreated to the window, seeming content to stay in his father's shadow.

"She is still intact, still able to marry. That is, if you agree," the duke said.

"If I agree?" Brook had been standing still, but he went stiller yet.

"To keep this little incident to yourself. I'll pay you to keep silent, of course."

Brook raised a hand. "As I've said before, I don't want your money, and you insult me by supposing I would ever tarnish a lady's reputation. If the abduction is discovered, the news of it won't have come from me."

"I have your word on that?" the duke asked.

As far as Brook was concerned, he'd already given his word. "I believe we have a more pressing concern than your daughter's reputation. She witnessed a murder last night, and based on the information Granbury just gave me, I believe the man murdered was the MP from Lincolnshire."

"What?" Granbury pushed away from the window. "I never said anything about Lila and the MP."

"No, but I put the facts together and made a deduction."

"I don't follow," the duke said. "What is this about Lila and a murder?"

"Did she tell you she saw her captor slit a man's throat last night in Seven Dials?"

"No."

"She doesn't want to think about it," Brook said. "I had to pry the information from her."

"If she doesn't want to think about it, why not let it lie?" Granbury asked.

"Because if it's the MP she saw murdered, she's a target. Bee—the men who took her won't want witnesses. They know who she is, where she lives. They'll come for her and kill her."

"This is preposterous!" The duke rose. He was not a tall man, but he had broad shoulders and the face of a Roman general—tall forehead, aquiline nose, sharp blue eyes. "How can you be certain the man she saw murdered was the MP—what's his name?"

"Fitzsimmons," Granbury supplied.

"How can you know it was the same man? Surely a handful of men are murdered every night in Seven Dials. And Fitzsimmons was found near the theater."

"Which is on the outskirts of Seven Dials," Brook added. Though the rookeries bordered the respectable neighborhoods throughout the city, he found that the gentry liked to believe they were far, far away from the rabble in their own homes and favorite shops or clubs.

"It would be a relatively simple matter to dump the body there."

"Relatively simple?" the duke sputtered. "And you know this from experience?"

Brook let the snub slide. "I will check with my contacts at Bow Street and inquire as to the possibility of there being another corpse killed by the severing of the jugular. Until I return, I still think it prudent to take additional security measures. I don't know who took Lady Lillian-Anne—"

"Some investigator," the duke snorted.

"—but I will find out. If it's the man I think, your daughter, your whole family, is in danger."

"We will take precautious," Granbury said. "In fact, it might be a wise idea to remove to the country."

"And how do we explain our absence at my niece's wedding then?" the duke asked.

"Rose will understand that this is an emergency," Granbury said.

"How?" the duke demanded. "We will have to tell her that Lila was taken, and though I love the girl, her mouth runs more than my prize thoroughbred."

"I understand your dilemma," Brook said, "but surely your family's safety trumps etiquette."

The look the duke gave him reminded him of one his mother often bestowed when he gave her similar advice. To men like the duke and women like the dowager countess, *nothing* trumped proper etiquette.

"I'll go to Bow Street and return with more information," Brook said. "In the meantime, Lady Lillian-Anne needs rest. There's time yet to discuss removing to the country."

"If you think that's even a consideration, you don't know the duchess," the duke said with a wry smile.

He didn't know the Duchess of Lennox, Brook thought as he followed the butler to the front door. But he had met her young daughter. The girl had obviously been petted and spoiled. One word to the duchess that her daughter might be in jeopardy, and she would leave soon enough.

But would that be enough to save Lila?

❧

Lila woke in the middle of the night. She'd been dreaming of the cellar, of fighting and clawing her way out, of the darkness closing in and burying her underneath it. And then the dirt had turned to blood. Blood gushed over her like it had from the gentleman's throat.

She sat with a quick intake of breath and put a hand over her pounding heart.

In the seat beside the bed, her lady's maid, Lizzy, snored quietly. She was probably supposed to be keeping vigil, but Lila was glad she slept. She did not want reports of nightmares reaching her father. He frowned upon any sign of weakness, any sign of imperfection. Already she was such a disappointment to him. At five and twenty, she should have been married and a mother. Yet, here she was, still unclaimed.

She was a duke's daughter and therefore not subject to the same rules as other women. But even a duke's daughter received raised eyebrows when she was unmarried past five and twenty. Her father had made it clear the upcoming Season was the one. She must marry and marry well.

Prospective grooms—most of them old and titled— had been listed, plans made, new gowns for every occasion ordered. Only the most fashionable and most expensive fabrics for the eldest daughter of the Duke of Lennox. Thousands of pounds had been spent and thousands more would be spent still.

She could not let her family down.

The abduction had put a wrinkle in the plans. People had seen her where she oughtn't have been, unchaperoned, and with a man who was not her blood relative. Lila did not worry that Brook might wag his tongue. If nothing else, Brook was a gentleman. He'd proved that years ago when he'd stayed silent, despite her abominable behavior toward him.

But what about the man who'd taken her out of the cellar? What about the jarvey? Those prostitutes? Did they know who she was? Would they sell their stories to the press?

Oh, wouldn't the *ton* love a bit of malicious gossip about Lady Lila? She'd made her enemies among the upper ten thousand, right from her come out. She'd angered the women by stealing their beaux and demanding fealty from those gentlemen who courted her. They were to dance with no one else, call on no other young lady. Some of the older gentlemen scoffed at her little games, but she publicly snubbed them when they came to call. When she could stir up rumors, she always did, relishing in the power to damage a reputation with a mere hint of scandal. She had not been loved, but she'd been universally feared.

Now she was the one who feared scandal.

Lila took a deep breath and rose from her warm bed. The clock on the mantel told her it was still before midnight. She felt as though she'd slept a day and a night. Her body ached with weariness. She should have slept more, but she did not want the nightmare returning.

Perhaps a quick walk to the kitchens for a cake or a piece of toast and tea might clear her head. She'd eaten soup and bread for dinner, but she was hungry again.

Lila donned her wrap and pushed her feet into slippers, then, taking a candle and its holder, quietly opened her door. Lizzy didn't wake, and Lila padded along the carpeted hallway until she reached the stairs. The house was quiet. Her father and mother had not gone out. They'd probably retired early, which meant the servants could do so as well.

Colin might have gone to his club, and his valet would have no reason to expect him for several more hours.

Lila lit the candle from a wall sconce and started down the stairs, holding her candle high and lifting the hem of her nightgown so she did not trip. It was not until she'd reached the last few steps that she felt the eyes on her.

She looked up and almost stumbled.

Brook Derring stood in the vestibule, watching her.

At first, she could only blink at him and wonder if she was not dreaming or merely imagining him. Seeing him again this afternoon, even under the circumstances, had made her desire to see him again. He was all the things she shouldn't like in a man—young, virile, dangerous.

He had neither extraordinary wealth nor title. He was the son of an earl, but he was the second son. Added to that unfortunate fact, he worked as an inspector. He hadn't even done the respectable thing and become a vicar or taken a commission in the navy.

And yet for all that, she couldn't take her eyes off him.

His gaze never left her, and almost immediately, she realized she was not dressed. She was covered, of course, but her hair hung loose and tangled and she wore no gloves or other adornments.

Finally, Brook bowed. "Lady Lila."

"What are you doing here?"

It wasn't what she'd wanted to say. Indeed, she did not know what she wanted to say. *Not that.* It sounded so insolent when she owed everything to this man. But she'd been so desperate to hide how much she did want him to be there that she'd overcompensated.

"How good to know your warm welcome has not changed."

Lila descended the last two steps. "I only meant I was surprised to see you."

"As I am you." His gaze swept over her, causing heat to rise to her cheeks. It wasn't a lascivious gaze, but she felt a tingle on her skin nonetheless. She wished he would look at her again, even if it were only to scoff at her unkempt appearance.

"I have business with your father."

"But I thought—" She did not know how to finish. She wasn't so vulgar as to speak of money and payment, but he had said he wanted no part of her father's money. Had he changed his mind?

And, if so, why should that disappoint her? It wasn't as though he had come for her because he cared about her.

"You might as well know," he said. "This concerns you."

"Did you catch the man who took me?"

"No. But I discovered something that distresses me."

She waited, wanting to know and fearing what he would say next.

"The man you saw murdered last night was almost certainly a member of Parliament."

She took a step back, the implications of the statement like a load of bricks falling on top of her. "No."

"It's true. I—"

"What is this?" the butler said, returning. "My lady, surely you should return to bed."

"Thank you, Franklin, but I would speak with my father and Sir Brook."

"Your father has not asked for you, my lady."

Lila notched her chin up. "Will you show me to him, or must I find my own way?"

The furrowed lines on Franklin's face deepened yet further. "He is in the library. Follow me."

Lila did so, with only a quick glance at Sir Brook, whose legs were longer and brought him effortlessly to her side. "And don't you tell me to go to bed."

"I wouldn't dream of it. As I said, this concerns you."

She nodded, dread pooling in her stomach like too much sherry.

"But, Lady Lila," Brook added, "I don't think you'll like what you are about to hear."

Four

SHE LOOKED PALE, TIRED, AND IMPOSSIBLY LOVELY. Something about her hair falling down around her shoulders in an ebony cascade made her appear more vulnerable than the stiff-necked, perfectly coiffed chit he was used to seeing. Make no mistake, she still had the stiff neck and the rigid spine, but her loose hair softened the stick-up-her-arse look about her considerably.

Franklin, who had looked as though he had two sticks up his arse, led them to the duke's library. Brook knew it was the library without having to be told. He'd been here once before. He preferred not to think back to that humiliating day, the worst of his life until then. He wasn't there to ask for Lila's hand in marriage tonight.

The duke rose when Franklin announced Lila, his mouth turning down into a frown. "Go back to bed, Lillian-Anne. I'll discuss what Sir Brook and I decide in the morning."

From behind her, Brook saw her shoulders straighten and square. She didn't like that suggestion in the least. Brook could hardly blame her. He wouldn't like having his future decided for him either.

"If it's all the same, Father, I'd like to stay and listen." She held up a hand to forestall her father's argument. "I can't sleep anyway, and Sir Brook has informed me this matter concerns me."

The duke's eyes cut to Brook, and Brook read disapproval before Lennox looked back at his daughter. "Lila—"

She took the chair closest to the fire and settled herself, seeming to dare her father, or anyone else, to try and ban her.

Brook knew Lila rarely, if ever, defied her father. He knew this from experience. The duke's bewildered expression seemed to prove that he was as surprised at her stubbornness as anyone.

"Very well, then." The duke nodded to the butler. "That will be all for now, Franklin. Sir Brook." He gestured to the chair in front of his antique maple desk.

Brook took the chair, angling his body so he could see Lila. She sat with her hands in her lap, her slippered feet primly on the floor, the fire crackling behind her and lending a soft, burnished color to her hair and skin.

"Sir Brook, I trust you had ample time to make the inquiries we discussed earlier."

"I did." He kept his response brief, following the duke's example. It didn't escape Brook's notice that no refreshment had been offered, not that he would have taken it, but he did not appreciate being treated as though he were in the duke's employ. He had completed the task he and the duke had agreed upon.

As far as Brook was concerned, this call was purely a courtesy.

"Unfortunately, it appears the worries Lord Granbury expressed this afternoon are warranted."

"And what worries are those?" Lady Lila asked, unwilling to be left out of the conversation.

"Lord Granbury mentioned one of the MPs had been found this morning near Covent Garden. His throat had been cut," Brook answered before the duke could give her some nonsense. She deserved to know she was in danger.

Her hand rose to cover her mouth.

"Bow Street thinks it more than likely that Mr. Fitzsimmons is the man you saw murdered last night. They would like to send a man to ask you a few questions." Now Brook glanced at the duke. "That is, if you approve, Duke." Brook was not strictly one of Lennox's familiars. Lennox would have probably preferred Brook called him *Your Grace*. All the more reason Brook would call the man whatever the hell he pleased.

"I do not. No Runner will come to my house and question my daughter."

"Helpful as always," Brook muttered.

"Furthermore, what sort of training do these Runners receive? It's purely ridiculous to think that a man of Mr. Fitzsimmon's rank and standing would be milling about in Seven Dials and associating with…ruffians."

Lila's eyes skipped from her father to Brook and back again. She'd uncovered her mouth, but now her knuckles pressed white against her lips.

"That was my initial question as well. However, upon speaking with Mr. Easterday, the head of the Bow Street Runners, who is a very good friend of mine, I discovered the Runners have been troubled by Mr. Fitzsimmons's activities for several weeks now."

"But this is preposterous!" the duke said, rising. "Are honest citizens now to be investigated by the Bow Street Runners? It is revolutionary France all over again!"

"What reason do the Runners have for making inquiries about Mr. Fitzsimmons?" Lila asked, smoothing over her father's outburst.

"The Runners were hired by a man whose identity they did not wish to reveal to look into a spate of burglaries in the homes and offices of the enemies of Mr. Fitzsimmons. It seems in the last six months or so, anyone politically opposed to Fitzsimmons has become a target for burglary. Key papers and private correspondence are taken along with valuables. I must admit, I find it strange that a common rook would want papers and correspondence. Most of them cannot read."

"Surely you do not think a member of the House of Parliament has been breaking into homes and pilfering them." The duke leaned on his palms.

"Of course not. He wouldn't have the skills or knowledge."

"But the men who abducted me would," Lila said quietly.

"Yes. The Runners are investigating possible connections between Mr. Fitzsimmons and several gangs in the Covent Garden area, including the gang I think responsible for Lady Lila's abduction."

"Good. The Runners should earn their pay for once," the duke announced. "If that is all, then—"

"Forgive me, sir, but that is not all. In all likelihood, Lady Lila witnessed the murder of a prominent member of Parliament. Let us assume for a moment, Mr. Fitzsimmons paid Beezle, the leader of the Covent Garden Cubs, to crack the houses and offices of his enemies. Last night, their agreement went terribly wrong, and Beezle or another member of the gang murdered Fitzsimmons. That's a capital crime. The gang members involved will surely hang."

"I imagine they might hang for any number of their offenses," Lila added.

"Yes, but they haven't been hanged because they haven't been caught. You, Lady Lila, witnessed the murder. That puts you in danger because Beezle—if it was Beezle—knows you saw him. He'll want no witnesses because, mark my word, Beezle does not intend to hang."

"Then we send Lila to the country after Rose's wedding."

"And what makes you think Lady Lila will be safe in the country? Moreover, what's to stop Beezle from attempting to kill her while she is in London?"

"No thief would be so bold," the duke declared as though he had any knowledge whatsoever concerning the matter.

"These men are bold and growing bolder still." Much of that could be attributed to the reluctance of men like the Duke of Lennox to sanction a metropolitan police force in London. There weren't enough Charlies and Runners to catch the criminals, much less prevent or deter crime. Assaults, rapes, thefts, and now abductions were on the rise and had reached new heights.

"But that is not my only concern," Brook said.

"You are certainly full of them tonight."

"Yes, Duke. My other concern is that perhaps Mr. Fitzsimmons was not working alone. Yes, he has standing and power as a member of the Commons, but there are many other men with much more clout than he."

"Bosh!" the duke said. "This is pure conjecture."

"Even so, I'd like to hear what Sir Brook has to say," Lila added, her voice quiet.

Brook inclined his head toward her. "My question is why would Beezle—or whoever was behind the murder and abduction—kill Fitzsimmons? After all, with Fitzsimmons dead, the source of revenue dries up."

"And you think someone else, someone with more power than Fitzsimmons, ordered him killed?" This came from Lila, who sat forward as she spoke.

"I think it highly likely Fitzsimmons either discovered something he was not supposed to or outlived his usefulness, and Beezle was paid to dispatch him. Only the promise of more blunt than the gang made cracking houses would entice Beezle to cut off his revenue source. Whoever paid Beezle to do it must have been wealthy."

"Which means I am still in danger," Lila said, twisting her hands together.

"You saw the murder, and that means Beezle was sloppy. He'll want to eradicate any proof of his mistake before the man paying him realizes he might be vulnerable. It's true what they say." Brook looked from Lila to her father. "There's no honor among thieves. Beezle will snitch on the man who hired him—not because it will save him, but because he'll want that man to go down too."

The fire crackled in the hearth, and the duke's chair creaked as he sat down. "Then I need you to protect my daughter."

Brook shook his head. "That's not what I do."

"I'll pay you whatever you ask."

Brook stood. "It's not about compensation. I'm not a guard dog. There are men who—"

"I don't want some hulking brute of a man in my home or near my daughter. Not only that, but I have no intention of announcing to Society we've hired a protector for my daughter. The Season will be upon us soon, and God knows her prospects are slim as it is."

Lila made a small sound of offense.

"Have you thought of the ramifications of having me as her constant companion?" Brook asked. "You think tongues won't wag?"

The duke clearly had not thought of that. He sat back and seemed to consider. Brook imagined he was weighing the benefits and disadvantages of such gossip.

Brook suddenly felt as though he were on the auction block. "As you made quite clear years ago, I am not a suitable match for your daughter. I seem to recall something being said about my *lowly status*."

"Oh, now, I don't think I ever said that."

Brook paced in front of the desk. He remembered every single word of the brief interview, and the duke had said far worse. "In any case, I understand your desire to have a gentleman in charge of your daughter's protection. I am not that gentleman, however. I fear circumstances could occur whereby our association might be misconstrued. At which time, I would be forced to marry Lady Lila, and I have no intention of ever marrying Lady Lila." Brook glanced at her, sitting tight-lipped. "No offense, my lady."

"I see." The duke stood now.

"I do beg your pardon for bringing you such deplorable news." Brook gathered his hat. "I must insist, however, that this be the end of our association."

"You insist?" the duke said, his tone one Brook had not heard before. The hair on the back of his neck stood up in warning.

"No need to call the butler. I will see myself out."

Without waiting for the duke's leave, he opened the door and stepped out, heading straight for the vestibule. The house was quiet and dark. Brook supposed the brooding Franklin was about somewhere, waiting to be summoned, but Brook imagined the man could wait just as well in his quarters as in the vestibule.

He reached the door when he heard the slippered steps on the marble. He resisted the instinct to turn and closed his eyes instead. "Go back to bed, Lady Lila. You and I have nothing to discuss."

"I just need a moment, Sir Brook."

A moment he did not want to grant. He did not want to look at her again, with all that lovely black hair flowing down her back, and those large, honey-brown eyes pleading for him to save her.

She was not his to save.

Because he did not turn, she stopped behind him and placed her hand on his coat. He could not feel the heat of her skin, but the pressure of her touch burned him just the same. He turned abruptly, making her hand fall away.

"Am I really in danger?" she asked.

"In my opinion."

Her head tilted up slightly so she might look him in the eye, and he could imagine cupping the back of her neck, feeling the slip of her hair against his bare hands, and lowering his lips to hers.

"What shall I do?"

"If I were you, I'd disappear."

"For how long?"

"Until this is resolved and you are safe again. If you'd like, I can send word to your father when it's safe for you to return. The fewer people who know where you are, the better."

But she was shaking her head. "My father won't send me away. I'll miss the Season."

"Forgive me, but you'll also miss the Season if you are dead."

She gave no indication of being shocked at his words except a small intake of breath. "I understand," she said. "I couldn't care less if I miss the Season."

"That's not true." He stepped forward, inadvertently inhaling her sweet scent. He remembered that she'd smelled of lily of the valley all those years ago. At one time, the fragrance had all but obsessed him. Little had he known then that the woman was much like the flower—poisonous.

"No, it's not. I'm five and twenty. This might be

my last chance to make a good match, and you know as well as I that I am nothing but a burden if I don't marry." Her eyes implored him, but his heart was immune. "Couldn't you—" she began.

"No."

"You haven't even heard what I have to say."

"You want me to guard you in the guise of courting you."

Her eyes widened. "Yes. You can attend all the events of the Season without anyone questioning your presence."

"And I can act the lovesick puppy and follow you about. I've done that once before. I won't be your lapdog again."

She waved a hand. "Sir Brook, that's not what I'm asking."

He grasped her wrist before she could wave a finger in front of his face again. "Isn't it? You think only of yourself—how you can attend the Season. But you don't consider how it will look for me to shadow you. Not to mention, I have no desire to attend the events of the Season."

She opened her mouth.

"And if, by God, you mention that your father will pay me"—he pushed her back against the door—"I will make you very, very sorry."

She looked up at him, her breath coming quickly, and her breasts rising and falling in the *V* of the robe that had parted slightly. "I do not think anyone would mistake you for a lapdog." Her voice trembled.

"Good."

"But I do need your help."

The words cut him. He'd thought he'd won, and his guard had slipped. Leave it to Lila to expose the chink in his armor. He steeled himself, released her arm, and pushed her away from the door.

"Sorry. I'm all out of favors."

∾

Back in her room, Lila stood by the fire to warm herself.

She hated him. Amazing how one might exist for years and never think of a person, and then less than a day after becoming reacquainted, she absolutely despised him. She would not have thought Brook Derring interesting enough to warrant hatred. He'd certainly not made an impression on her seven years before. She'd practically forgotten about him.

He had not forgotten about her. She'd wronged him in the past. She knew that now. She knew it then, but the difference was she cared now. Her mother's death had changed her, made her appreciate the value of kindness and generosity. Before she'd been a spoiled, selfish child. The more beaux the better, in her opinion. Brook had been a casualty of her vanity.

But she wasn't trying to be selfish now. She honestly needed his help. She had to find a husband, and the best way to do that was to attend the Season. She would not even be very picky. She would take the first man her parents approved.

If she didn't find a husband...

She looked up the stairs and thought of her step-mother. Her father's new wife was but a few years older than Lila and as spoiled and selfish as Lila had been at eighteen. She'd never liked Lila, but she was friendly enough when the duke had courted her. After she'd become his wife, she'd done everything she could to distance Lila from her father and from her home. Valencia would think of reasons Lila must stay in the country when the duke and duchess were in Town. Or she would send Lila to stay with one relative after another when the duke and duchess retired to Blakesford for the winter. Lila had not spent a Christmas at her home in four years.

The only reason she was in London with the duchess was because of her cousin's wedding. Lila's absence would have been noted and remarked upon, and the duchess had not been able to convince Lennox to leave Lila at Blakesford. And so Lila had come, suffering the cold looks of her stepmother in the coach and being told to stay away from Ginny.

Lila could not see how she was any sort of threat to the little girl. She was four and the only sister Lila had ever had. When the baby had been born, she'd been excited at the prospect of holding her, rocking her, singing to her. She'd been lonely without her mother, and Colin was never at home either. But Valencia had screeched the first time Lila had taken the baby in her arms, and Lila had been kept away after that.

She couldn't go on like this. She couldn't spend the rest of her life being passed from one distant relative to another. She didn't want to be the object of pity. She didn't want to become a spinster. She wanted a child of her own, a home of her own, and, if not love, affection. The recent events meant she would be sent away again, ostensibly to keep her safe but also to keep her away from Valencia.

Lila didn't doubt her father loved her, in his way, but he loved peace and harmony more. If sending Lila away meant his wife was happy, Lila would be gone within the hour.

She'd better have her maid pack her valise in the morning. She would not be there much longer.

Her father and Colin rose when she entered the dining room the next morning. Valencia, as a married woman, could breakfast in bed and never missed the opportunity. Lila took her seat and accepted a cup of tea. She glanced at her father, expecting to see exile written in his eyes, but she could not read his expression.

Colin winked at her before going back to shoveling food in his mouth. She was not hungry, though she'd barely eaten anything the last few days.

"Your mother and I have been talking," the duke said after Lila had a sip of her tea.

She made herself swallow, though a lump had risen in her throat. "She is not my mother."

"You know what I mean," the duke said, waving a hand.

"No, I don't." She was being obstinate, but it stalled her dismissal for a few extra moments. "Valencia was still in the nursery when I was born. It's impossible for her to be my mother. She was younger than Ginny when Colin was born."

Her brother glared at her from across the table. Valencia and Colin had an amicable relationship, and, like his father, Colin preferred peace and had no wish to be drawn into Lila's disagreements. Lila wondered if the cordial relationship between stepmother and stepson might change if Valencia ever produced a son. After all, then Colin would stand in the way of her son becoming a duke.

But Colin hadn't thought of that, had he?

"Very well. Valencia and I have been talking."

Lila set her teacup down with deliberate care. "I have already asked Lizzy to pack my things."

The duke raised his brows. "I did not say you were leaving—not yet anyway."

"What do you mean?"

"I agree with Valencia that you should go. If Derring is correct and there is some danger, your presence here threatens all of us."

"Most of all me," Lila pointed out, though she knew Ginny was the one Valencia cared about.

"Exactly, which is why we cannot simply send you to Aunt Millicent's or your cousins in Wales. I think it unlikely, but you could be followed. We would put our family in danger, and you could be killed. You need protection."

"Sir Brook said he is not a guard dog."

"Sir Brook does not know who he is dealing with."

Now Lila felt the tea in her belly churn and boil. She could only imagine what her father planned.

"What will you do?" Colin asked the question she was too afraid to voice.

"I have an audience with His Majesty."

The king? Lila failed to see what the king had to do with any of this.

"He's in Town?" Colin asked.

"For the wedding," Lila murmured. Rose's parents were extremely wealthy, and King George IV had a tendency to overspend. He cultivated the good graces of wealthy families, receiving loans in return for using his influence in other ways.

"I believe the king and I will deal with the issue of Brook Derring." The duke glanced at his pocket watch and rose. "I must be on my way. I wouldn't want to keep His Majesty waiting."

More likely he would be gone most of the day, kept waiting himself for hours on end. Lila watched him go, dread making her head pound with every footstep he took.

She looked at Colin. "What does he have planned?"

"I don't know. I can't think you'll like it."

"I can't think Sir Brook will like it either."

"He doesn't like anything. Straight as they come and a dead bore."

"What do you mean?" Lila leaned forward, interested despite herself. The impression she'd had of Brook Derring from the women of her acquaintance was that of a hero who could do no wrong. It surprised her that her brother should see him differently. "I thought he was a hero."

"Yawn." He brought his hand to his mouth and pretended to yawn. "He doesn't gamble, rarely drinks more than a sip or two of brandy, and spends all his time in the rookeries—not for diversion either."

Having recently escaped the rookeries and having seen firsthand the squalor and filth, Lila couldn't think what diversions the slums held for any man, her brother included.

"And that's not all," Colin added. "The female population is falling all over him and his so-called heroic deeds."

"Having been on the receiving end of his deeds, I'm inclined to think they are more fact than supposition."

"Be that as it may, the man has his choice of women."

The subject made Lila vaguely uncomfortable, reminding her that Colin, though younger than she, by virtue of being a man, knew much more of the world than she did. But it was more than the novelty of discussing such a mysterious and prohibited topic. Lila found that while she did not particularly care who her brother bedded, she did not want to know Sir Brook's bed partners.

"Colin, I don't think—"

But he ignored her interruption. "And he could care less. Doesn't even look twice at the most choice courtesans. I've been trying to snag Mrs. Arbuckle for a month, and she all but tosses her skirts up every time Derring enters the room."

"I don't want to hear this."

Colin had warmed to his topic, and he either didn't care or didn't hear. "I half think if the Duchess of Dalliance hadn't married and gone off to produce a passel of brats, he'd look right past her. And she was the most beautiful courtesan in the last hundred years."

Lila rolled her eyes. "All that says is Brook doesn't care for courtesans. Perhaps he finds it distasteful to pay for a woman. You speak of women like they are horses to be bought and sold."

Colin gave her a look of pity. "I don't expect you to understand."

"I don't wish to understand. You've only reinforced my belief that Sir Brook is a good man, who saved me from certain death."

"Not yet he hasn't," Colin pointed out. "Not very gentlemanlike to leave you when you are still in danger."

"I haven't heard you volunteer to protect me either."

"Me?" Colin's face went white. "I can't put myself in that sort of danger. I'm the heir."

"For the moment. I imagine father and Valencia are working to produce a spare."

Colin's lip curled. "Now I've lost my appetite."

"So have I! Funny how being the target of a murderer has that effect."

Colin nodded and took another bite of scone. He'd apparently forgotten he couldn't bear to eat. "Demmed inconvenient of you to witness that murder."

"Especially for me."

"The duke will fix it," Colin said with a faith in their father Lila did not share. "He'll make sure Derring protects you."

"I don't want Derring forced to protect me. He already hates me."

"Why?"

Lila looked away. She wouldn't reveal that sordid bit of history to her brother. "He just…does."

"He doesn't hate you. He doesn't hate anyone. Doesn't love them either. He's not a man of passions. Trust me, you'll be perfectly safe with Derring."

But Lila was not so sure.

Five

BROOK WOULD MURDER LADY LILA HIMSELF. How dare she trap him in this fashion?

The king had gone on and on about annulments and contracts and special licenses. Brook hadn't heard a word. He'd fastened his gaze on the Duke of Lennox, who stood at the king's right arm. Lennox, that bastard. It was as though he'd made it his life's work to humiliate Brook.

Brook hadn't tried to argue with George. There was no point. Once the king made up his mind, he would not change it. Not if money was involved at any rate, and Brook was willing to believe quite a bit of blunt had been deposited in the king's coffers to seal Brook's fate.

He might have asked his mother to come to his aid. The Dowager Countess of Dane still had some influence, but his mother would likely side with the king. She wanted Brook to marry.

His brother, the earl, might come to London to intervene, but he might also laugh his arse off.

Brook had other friends—Viscount Chesham and

the Marquess of Lyndon—but the time it took to rally them would give Beezle the time he needed to dispose of Lila. Brook might not want to marry the chit, but he didn't want her dead.

If she managed to survive the time it took for Brook and his friends to argue with the king, the result would still be the same. Lennox would make another donation to King George's treasury, and Brook would be ordered to obey his sovereign.

And so he sat in the coach outside Derring House and stared at the special license in his hands. He'd put off telling his mother as long as he could. He'd put off having Hunt polish his shoes and starch his cravat. If there was one thing Brook knew, it was when to admit defeat. That did not mean he gave up.

It simply meant he needed a new strategy.

❧

The church was all but empty. Brook's mother and her husband sat with his sister and Dorrington on one side, while the Duke of Lennox and the Earl of Granbury sat on the other. Behind them, one of the king's attendants took a seat. Brook supposed he was there to ensure the king's wishes were followed precisely.

There hadn't been time for Dane and his wife to come in from the country. If his older brother had been present, Brook would have asked him to stand beside him. As it was, Lila had no attendants, so perhaps it was for the best Brook stood before the bishop alone as well.

The bishop, a jowly man with white hair and a ruddy face, cleared his throat and began. For the first time since her father had brought her in, Lila looked up at him. Her warm brown eyes appeared too big against her pale skin, which was as white as the silk gown she wore. The gown had a leaf design in silver netting, and she wore a small, silver leaf to ornament her hair. Pearls circled her throat and danced at her ears, and with her hair piled high in a coil of ebony, she looked every inch the duke's daughter.

The bishop had droned on—something about God's will and not entering into marriage unadvisedly; clearly the bishop did not know about the king's will and advice—but now the officiate paused and cleared his throat again.

"Into this holy union Sir Brook Erasmus Derring and Lady Lillian-Anne Pevensy now come to be joined. If any of you can show just cause why they may not lawfully be married, speak now." The bishop paused at this, looking first at Lila then Brook. "Or else forever hold your peace."

Brook ground his teeth together and glared at Lila. She lowered her gaze again.

"I require and charge you both—" the bishop began.

"May I have one moment with my—er, betrothed?" Lila said.

She had spoken to the bishop, but her gaze was on Brook. He raised a brow.

"You can speak to him after the ceremony," the duke said from the pew.

"Just for one moment, Father," she said.

"My Lord," the duke said to the bishop. "Please continue."

"I am sorry, Your Grace, but I cannot. Lady

Lillian-Anne must come to this union of her own free will." He glanced at Lila. "If you need a moment, my lady, you may use the sacristy."

She nodded and gave Brook an imploring look. With a shrug directed at his mother, whose face was the picture of disapproval, he followed Lila to the side chamber. The room was full of books and vestments, all in order, and in the middle were a small altar and a sacrarium, where the bishop washed his hands.

Lila stood before the altar, like a sacrificial lamb. Brook stood just inside the door, keeping it open for propriety.

"Delaying the inevitable?" he asked.

"I had to make certain you knew this was not my doing," she said, her voice breathless. "I never told my father to go to the king. I did not want to force you into marriage."

Brook leaned a shoulder against the doorjamb. "I must admit, your previous refusal was quite definitive and robust. This sudden change of heart surprised me."

"Oh, stop speaking so formally! I am trying to tell you I have no more choice in this than you."

"The bishop will ask for your consent in a few moments. All you need say is *I won't*."

"And then my father will disown me, and Vile Valencia will make certain I am shipped off to Cheapside to live with my mother's great-aunt, who is so poor she can ill afford to feed herself much less me."

"Beezle will find you inside a week there."

She closed her eyes, seeming to summon patience. He couldn't blame her. He was being an arse. "You must be the one to say you won't have me," she said.

"Oh, no." He pushed away from the jamb. "And have the king throw me in the Tower? Not bloody likely."

"He won't throw you in the Tower." She folded her arms under the square neck of the gown, pushing her breasts up until they swelled at the bodice.

"I'm not taking that chance."

"Then we have no choice but to marry."

"I assumed that was the reason we were both in the church at half eight in the morning—you in your bridal silk and me in this stiff-necked cravat Hunt tied far too tightly."

"But you don't want to marry me!"

"I want to be thrown into the Tower even less."

"Nice to know I rank above imprisonment."

"Barely," he said, pointing a finger at her. "Besides, the king mentioned annulment. I'm to keep you safe and capture the man who killed Fitzsimmons and abducted you, and the king will see the union annulled."

"On what grounds?"

"How the devil do I know? On whatever grounds His Majesty fabricates."

"But what if you don't capture this Beezle, or whoever it was?"

"I will."

"And what's to happen to me after the marriage is annulled?"

"I don't know, and I don't care." He glanced behind him and into the sanctuary. Lennox had risen and was looking pointedly in his direction. The king's attendant was scribbling something on a sheet of vellum. "Let's finish this."

He turned to exit the sacristy, but her hand on his upper arm made him pause. He looked down at the gloved fingers, so white against his dark blue coat, and then at her pale face.

"Brook, I don't—I just don't want you to hate me for this."

"It's far too late for that."

She didn't look at him again during the ceremony. She spoke her vows, her voice quiet but steady. If he thought he saw tears sparkling on her black eyelashes a time or two, she didn't allow them to fall. That was to her advantage. He'd never liked women who manipulated men with their tears and feminine wiles.

Finally, the deed was done, and the party retired to Lennox House for the wedding breakfast. At least everyone but Brook did. He met Hunt at his office on Bow Street and reviewed the reports on Fitzsimmons the Runners he knew had compiled.

"I don't know if the man was in league with one of the Covent Garden gangs, but he had something on the side. These purchases he made in the last year or so require income far above his."

"Perhaps he came into some money," Hunt suggested.

"I'll have Dorrington look into that and into his habits at the gaming table. I'll find out who he had ties with in Parliament. Has anyone interviewed his widow?"

"I know Sawyer wanted to, but he was told it would be unseemly to bother her at this time of grief."

"I don't mind being unseemly."

The door, which had been only half-closed, swung open. "I'm glad to hear it because you missed your own wedding breakfast," Dorrington said, strolling into the office. "If that isn't what you nobs call *unseemly*, I don't know what is." He slouched into one of the chairs across from Brook's and propped his boots on the desk. Brook glared at the boots, but Dorrington didn't remove them.

"I don't have time for wedding breakfasts. I have a killer to catch and an annulment to request."

"Your mother is furious," Dorrington said with a smile.

"I'll bring her flowers."

"Your wife is humiliated."

Good. She'd humiliated him. Let her see what it tasted like. Brook sat and crossed his arms. "Your point?"

"I do have to give the gentry mort credit. She held her head high."

"Then all that training finally proved useful."

"Dane and Marlowe sent their best wishes to the breakfast and said they would come to Town soon," Dorrington said.

They would undoubtedly stay at Derring House, and he would have to make a point of speaking with Marlowe when she arrived. Like Gideon, now called Dorrington, across from him, she'd once been part of Beezle's gang. She might have insights he'd overlooked.

"Marlowe must be breeding again," Dorrington said.

Brook supposed it was possible. His nephew was almost a year old now. "Why do you say that?"

"When I saw her at Christmas, she ate half a kidney pie."

"I've seen her eat more than that."

"I haven't. Not since she started having regular meals. She's bellyful. Mark my words."

Brook sat forward. "We can discuss my brother's growing family another time. Today I need you to look into Fitzsimmons's gambling habits. Make the rounds of the hells catering to gentlemen and ask about him. If you don't find anything at those—"

"Try the rookeries. I know what to do, but hadn't you better go claim your bride?"

"Why?"

"It's almost six. Or did you intend to leave her alone on your wedding night?"

Brook glanced at the clock on his desk and cursed. The day had slipped through his fingers. He hadn't thought what he would do with Lila on their wedding night. It wasn't as though she'd welcome him into her bed. Not that it should matter. He was her husband, and she was his for the taking. Whether or not he bedded her made no difference for the annulment. The king would have to find some technicality on which to declare the marriage unlawful. Even if he didn't take Lila to bed, everyone would assume he had.

And why should he deny himself? He ought to have some pleasure from this arrangement.

Except, of course, there was no pleasure in bedding a woman who didn't want him.

Brook looked at Hunt, hoping his man had considered the domestic arrangements. "You can't take her to Derring House, sir."

"No." And that was too bad because Derring House was large and full of servants and family. He could stay well away from her at Derring House. But he wouldn't endanger his family and home by having her there. Beezle would have no qualms about slitting the throats of every man, woman, and child in residence if it accomplished his goal.

"I don't suppose we can leave her at Lennox House. Her father doesn't take the threat seriously enough," Hunt added. "The duke hasn't even hired additional footmen to stand guard."

"He took it seriously enough to marry her to Brook," Dorrington said.

"That's because he's lazy and has a termagant wife to contend with," Brook said. "He'd rather foist his eldest on another man than exert himself to protect her." Brook felt a twinge of sympathy for Lila, but he pushed it down. Her situation was little different than many unmarried women's.

Except now she was married. To him.

"I suppose we have to take her to the flat," Hunt said.

Brook groaned. Even as he wanted to argue, he knew Hunt was correct. Only a handful of people knew of his flat. Lila would be safe there for the time being.

But it meant taking her to the one place that was truly his. It was the place where he did not have to play the part of earl's son or knight errant, where he could just be Brook.

And now the woman he hated most in the world would be living there as well.

❧

Lila hadn't known what to think when the handsome man who purported to be Brook's valet had come to claim her at quarter past seven on the night of her wedding. After Brook had not made an appearance at the wedding breakfast, she'd assumed he was done with her. Perhaps he hoped she would be murdered. Then he wouldn't have to go through the trouble of securing an annulment.

She'd finally changed from her wedding dress, which she had loved, despite the fact that she had to marry Brook Derring in it. The short puff sleeves with a leaf on each sleeve, matching those in silver netting on the bodice and hem, were just lovely. She hated to take it off.

But she'd finally dressed for dinner in a white gown with flowers embroidered in red and gold and had sat down to have her hair styled. Lizzy had only just taken her hair out of its elaborate wedding style when Lila was summoned downstairs. She might have asked Lizzy to pin it hastily, but her head ached from the weight of the hair and the tight style in which she'd worn it all day, and she was glad for the respite.

Now she stood with her hair in a tail down her back, watching her father quiz her husband's valet. The valet, who was clean shaven, tall, and possessed a strong jaw and lovely blue eyes, did not cower or grovel in the presence of the duke, like most of his fellows would have.

"How do I know you are employed by Sir Brook?" the duke demanded.

Hunt—that was the man's name—cocked his head toward the front of the house. "He sent his carriage for her. Go ask the coachman and the outriders if you don't believe me."

The duke would do no such thing, but he seemed

satisfied enough. So Brook had sent his coach for her. He'd sent for her. He did want her after all.

"Where are you taking her? Derring House?"

"Begging your pardon, Your Grace, but I can't reveal that. It's for the lady's own safety."

"So you are taking my daughter away and you will not tell me where. This is unacceptable!"

Valencia, who until this point had been sitting near the fire, a smug smile on her pointed face, now rose. "Lennox, surely Lila will be allowed to write to you. She can assure you all is well."

Lila glanced at Hunt, who nodded. "I'll bring a letter tomorrow if you want."

"There. You see?"

Lila saw clearly enough. Vile Valencia had just rid herself of the daughter she'd never wanted. Lila doubted her stepmother cared whether she was off to a dungeon or the palace, as long as she was far, far away.

"Then I suppose I should say good-bye," Lila said, filling the silence. She looked at her father. "I will write this evening when I arrive."

He nodded. Lila wondered, briefly, if she should embrace him but decided against it. Such displays of affection were unseemly. She curtsied instead. "Good-bye, Father. Valencia."

Colin was not at home, but she would write him separately. Ginny was in the nursery with her nanny.

"May I say good-bye to Ginny?" she asked.

"I don't think that's wise," Valencia said. "She will be in bed by now, and I don't want her upset."

Lila knew for a fact Ginny was a stubborn child who did not go to bed easily and often not until after eight or nine. But she didn't argue with her step-mother. She supposed she might never see her little sister again. And if she did, Ginny would probably not remember or know her.

Her eyes stung as she left the room, following Hunt down the steps to the vestibule. She saw the carriage through the door Franklin held open. Two footmen were loading her valise inside.

Lila didn't see Lizzy. "Is my lady's maid already inside?" she asked.

Hunt gave her a pitying sort of look, which made her cheeks flush with embarrassment. "Your father said you weren't to bring any servants."

She could translate that without the valet's help. Her father had most likely said if she would have servants, Brook could damn well provide them.

"It's better this way," Hunt said, attempting to soften the blow. "The fewer people who know where you are the better. And these quarters aren't large. You'd be cramped with a lady's maid."

"I see. Well, I had best be off then." She lifted her skirts and took the hand of the footman. Inside the coach, she fussed with her skirts until John Coachman called to the horses and they were underway.

She only parted the curtains once to look back at her home.

No one had waited to see her off.

The journey to Brook's quarters was faster than she had anticipated. Hunt had instructed her to keep the curtains closed, so she wasn't sure where in London she had landed. It was dark by the time she was ushered out of the coach and up a flight of stairs into a dark, cold flat. For some reason, she had expected Brook to be waiting for her.

But except for Hunt, she was quite alone.

The valet lit a fire in the hearth of the common room and directed a footman to bring her valise to a room at the back, presumably her private chambers. Finally, he'd informed her there were victuals in the cupboard and fresh water in the pitchers, and she should take care to keep the shutters closed and make as little noise as possible.

And then he'd left, and Lila's heart had thundered when she'd realized he'd locked the door behind him. She was locked inside, a prisoner in this unfamiliar place.

For a full moment, terror coursed through her as well as fears of being forgotten or abandoned, and then she squared her shoulders. "Lila, you are a grown woman. It's time you acted like one."

Apparently, that included talking to herself. As no one was present to hear her, that seemed a trifle.

"The first thing you should do is investigate," she told herself in a matter-of-fact tone. She set about doing just that, finding bread and jam in a cupboard and water in the pitchers, as Hunt had promised.

"That's not much of a dinner," she said with a frown, but at least she would not go hungry. "Too bad Hunt didn't wait to collect me until after dinner at Lennox House." Her father always ordered six- or seven-course meals. It was wasteful and extravagant, but Lila had grown used to it, and bread and water did not appeal.

Besides a sturdy table, that was the kitchen, and

Lila returned to the common room. The fire crackled and popped in the hearth now, warming the room considerably. In the dim light, she could see the room boasted a large green rug, a desk with a chair, and a couch. It was a small room, so this was quite enough to fill it, but Lila felt the lack of embellishments.

"Not a single vase or even an ornamental table," she said, walking the circumference. She could not argue that the room fit her impressions of Brook. "Basic and utilitarian," she concluded. "And perfectly tedious." She sighed.

The desk held neat stacks of folders and papers, but she doubted they would be of any interest and headed for the back room instead.

Lila stopped short. "Oh no."

What she had thought a dressing room that would lead into two bedchambers was a bedroom.

The bedroom.

The flat had one bedroom. One bed.

Did Brook think she would share it with him? Not likely! He'd made it more than clear he didn't want to marry her. He'd begun planning the annulment before he'd even said his wedding vows. After the ceremony, he hadn't been able to get away fast enough.

Strangely enough, her shame at being abandoned at the wedding breakfast was not what hurt the most. He hadn't even looked at her when he'd pledged to love, honor, comfort, and keep Lila. His hard, coffee-colored eyes had stared at a point somewhere over her head.

Lila would be the first to admit she was a fanciful girl. She'd grown up the daughter of a duke, in grand country houses and town houses with ornate ballrooms and soaring staircases. She'd been dressed in velvets and silks before she could walk. It had been no stretch of the imagination to pretend she was a princess. She had been a princess.

Of course she'd imagined her wedding day. She'd dreamed of the gown she would wear, the handsome duke she would marry, the way he would stare into her eyes as though she were the only woman on earth.

None of that had come to pass. Even her wedding gown was one she'd worn before and which held no special significance for her except that it was a favorite.

Brook was most certainly not a duke, but she could have overlooked that. She wasn't a child anymore. She knew better than to judge a man based on titles or riches. Brook was a good man, but she did not even exist in his world.

He couldn't even bear to look at her during their wedding.

She had hardly been able to look away. He'd been so handsome in his dark blue coat and buff breeches. He had broad shoulders and slim hips and someone— probably that valet of his—had actually styled his hair. Combed back from his forehead, the strong lines of his face had been on display. He had a square jaw, defined cheekbones, soft lips.

She'd wanted to kiss those lips, had imagined them pressing gently to hers.

Perhaps she was a foolish girl after all because Brook had walked away from her without even a by-your-leave.

No doubt he didn't even intend to sleep in this bed with her tonight or ever. Perhaps he'd keep her locked here until he could obtain the annulment he so desperately desired.

Lila forced herself to move into the room and examine its meager contents. The bed was large and took up most of the space. It looked comfortable enough, though there was nothing stylish about the blue coverlet and two pillows.

Interesting that there should be two pillows. Was one for her or had Brook entertained other women here?

She pulled the coverlet back and noted the freshly pressed sheets. Someone—she would lay her wager on Hunt again—had made certain the linens were clean.

Pushed against a wall, a rosewood wardrobe stood with the door partly open. She peered inside, saw shirts and coats stored neatly. Nothing of interest there. Finally, she rounded the bed and stared down at the small bedside table. That had to be Brook's side, as a book lay open on top of several papers.

She lifted the book, read the title, and set it down again. *A History of the Peloponnesian War*. She didn't even know what that was, much less care to read about it. Under the book was a draft of a letter to a Mr. Simmons of Chancery Hall. Lila shouldn't have read it. It was obviously private correspondence and she had no right to pry into it.

On the other hand, what else did she have to do, and if Brook hadn't wanted her to read it, he shouldn't have locked her in there and left it out.

The letter inquired after a young boy by the name of Geoffrey, asking how he had settled in and thanking

Mr. Simmons again for undertaking his training. Apparently this Mr. Simmons was a butler of a country house, and this Geoffrey had been taken in as one of the servants.

But why should Sir Brook care about this Geoffrey? Could he be Sir Brook's bastard?

She lifted another sheet of paper. This letter was not a draft. It had been folded but lacked the wax seal. There were several others below it that were also folded. Perhaps Brook had not mailed these yet because he needed more wax to seal them.

With a furtive look at the door, she opened that letter. This one was addressed to a Mrs. Parson of Timberside Lane in Hampshire. It inquired as to the progress of Miss Mary Smith in the kitchens as the kitchen maid.

Another bastard? Did Brook send all his by-blows to other parts of the country to be reared as servants?

She read another letter and another, all in the same vein.

Exactly how many bastards had Brook Derring sired?

She looked at the bed again, at the plain blue coverlet. Dozens of children had been begotten in that bed, under that quite serviceable blue coverlet. Did Brook Derring actually expect her to sleep in it?

Then Lila remembered she was to write to her father and assure him she was well. That was not all she would write in her letter. With newfound purpose, she returned to the common room, sat at the desk, and withdrew a sheet of foolscap. Dipping the quill in the ink pot, she began to write.

Six

"Sir, I really do think you should go home."

Brook glanced away from the flash ken he'd been watching and peered through the sheets of rain at his man. Rain had been pouring for hours, and the water sluiced down Hunt's hat and onto his shoulders in fat rivulets. Brook's own hat kept the water out of his eyes but little more. He was soaked through to the bone, his hands and feet gone numb two hours ago.

Beezle and two of his cubs—Brook thought they were called Racer and Stub—had gone inside. He'd been tailing them all day, but now it looked as though they intended to stay inside. He could hardly blame them. The foul weather kept all but the most stalwart indoors. But Beezle would emerge sooner or later, and when he did, Brook would be waiting to follow him.

"A little rain never hurt anyone," Brook said, returning his gaze to the flash ken the Covent Garden Cubs gang called home. It was little more than a dilapidated building a strong wind would have blown over. Brook was surprised the heavy rains hadn't flattened it yet. "But perhaps you'd like to return to

Derring House and sip tea by the fire with my mother and the other ladies."

Hunt said something under his breath. Brook hadn't been able to make it out, but he assumed it was a curse.

"That's not what I mean, sir. I meant, you should return to the flat. You should see your wife."

Brook didn't like the sound of the word *wife*. He'd managed to forget he was married the past three days, and he rather liked that state of consciousness.

"Why? Have the men we posted outside the building seen something suspicious?"

"No, she's quite safe. Guarded all day and all night. No one but me and the guards are allowed inside or out."

"She's fine then," Brook said.

Hunt shook his head, splattering rain on Brook's cheek. "No, sir. You don't understand. She's been writing letters."

Brook cut his gaze toward Hunt. "What sort of letters?"

"That's what I want you to see, sir. If this keeps up, we'll need to hire another guard to fetch and carry."

Brook turned to face Hunt. "Another? I have four men watching the flat!"

Hunt dipped his head and water ran off his hat and into the puddle at their booted feet. "The men can't be expected to guard her and carry out all her orders."

"Her *orders*?" Brook stared at Hunt. "What sort of orders?"

"Pillows, sir. That's the latest thing. She's ordered pillows in velvet."

"Why?" What the hell did she want with velvet pillows? "What else has she ordered?"

"I think you'd better see for yourself, sir."

Brook glanced back at the flash ken. Beezle wouldn't be emerging anytime soon, and Brook could send Dorrington or another man to watch the gang. So far neither he nor Dorrington had been able to find any connection between Fitzsimmons and the Covent Garden Cubs, but Brook was persistent. And Beezle couldn't hide forever.

Brook pulled his collar up and motioned for Hunt to follow him. Once they were away from Seven Dials, they'd hire a hackney to take them to the flat. "Why didn't you mention Lady"—he glanced around and began again—"my wife's *orders* sooner?"

"I didn't want to trouble you with it, sir."

"And now?"

Hunt seemed to consider his words before he spoke. "I think it's best if you see for yourself."

Brook put his head down and plowed through the rain, stepping around those residents of the rookery unlucky enough to have nowhere but the street to weather the storm. There were plenty of them, and once or twice, Brook felt eyes on his back. He looked around, tried to spot who watched him. The old hag hunched against a broken cart? The prostitute shivering under the eave of a gin house? The little boy crouched in the doorway?

It might have been any of them or all of them, but Brook couldn't afford to take chances. "Hunt, make sure the hackney takes the long way around."

"You think we'll be followed in this weather and by a man on foot?"

Brook didn't speak, allowing his silence to speak for him.

Hunt sighed, a long-suffering sigh. "Yes, sir. The long way it is."

～～

Damp, blue with cold, and ravenous, Brook arrived at his flat in St. James's Street an hour later. He greeted the men he'd hired to watch the flat, who were inside the building and out of the rain. Even so, they looked tired and worn out.

"Thank God you're here, sir," one of the men who called himself Finnegan said. "I don't think we can take much more."

Brook slicked his damp hair off his forehead. "Yes, I can see it's been a difficult day for you—inside, warm, and out of the rain."

"It's only because of the rain that we've had any time to rest," said the other man, a tall blond called Turner. "The rain slowed her down some, sir."

Brook looked at Hunt, but his man was absorbed in shaking water off his coat.

"Wait here," Brook said and started for the steps. At the door to his flat, he shed his heavy greatcoat and patted his waistcoat until he found the key. Using it, he stepped inside.

And immediately stepped back out again to check the number. Where the hell was he? This wasn't his flat.

But the number was correct, and when he stepped

inside again, he recognized the layout if not any of the flat's contents.

"Is that the dining table, Finnegan?" a feminine voice called.

Brook shut the door behind him, pocketed the key, and moved gingerly inside. His rug, couch, and desk were gone. In their place was a large gold Turkey carpet, a white-and-gold velvet upholstered chaise longue, and a small escritoire with a dainty chair he would probably break if he ever sat in it. The hearth blazed with a crackling fire, which he did appreciate, but when he moved closer, he saw the mantel had been decorated with porcelain vases and Sevres bowls.

What the devil had Lila done to his rug? His desk? His couch? His bloody flat?

He turned when he heard footsteps and their eyes met when she entered the room from the bedroom. He had a moment of dread when he considered what she might have done in there, but then she was blinking at him, her burnished eyes so big and dark, and he forgot his horror for the moment.

One look from those eyes, and heat shot through him. The rain and cold seeped out of him, and a slow burn began in his belly and shot lower. She had lion eyes; her honey-colored irises seemed to look right through him. Into him.

He lowered his gaze, looking away from those eyes, and that was a mistake. Her lips were full and red, her cheeks pink with color from the exertions of—he remembered the velvet longue and the Sevres plates—refurbishing. Her dark hair had escaped the confines of what looked to have been a simple bun and now hung in long, curled ribbons down her back and over her shoulders. She wore a peach-colored gown ornamented with orange and pink flowers and green leaves. Something sparkly— spangles or metallic thread—had been sewn into the flowers lining the bodice and the leaves, and the gown seemed to sparkle and shimmer when it caught the light of the fire.

"It's you," she said, finally breaking the silence. "I thought—" She broke off and gestured vaguely.

"You thought I was the dining table." He glanced around the room again. "What is all this? Where is my desk, my couch?"

"I had them put in storage."

She'd removed his furniture and had it put in storage? "How did you manage that?"

She lifted one pale shoulder. "I asked Hunt to find a suitable warehouse. He's really quite useful, you know. I was astonished you didn't have accounts at some of my favorite shops on Bond Street. He took care of that."

Brook took a step back. "*I* paid for all this?"

One eyebrow arched. "It's not as though I came into this union with nothing. I know my father made arrangements."

The agreement had been five thousand a year until he caught the murderer and then if he chose to stay married to Lila, the rest of her dowry. At the time, Brook had thought five thousand a year ridiculously generous.

Not anymore.

"You spent my money"—she made a sound, and

he held up his hands—"*our* money on all of this? You didn't even consult me."

"Consult you? You're a man! Not to mention I thought I'd be living here alone. I haven't seen you since the morning of our wedding."

That was true enough, and since he didn't want to argue, he moved toward her. With a small cry, she jumped aside, and he stomped into the bedroom.

"Bloody hell!"

He didn't even recognize the room that had once been his sanctuary. A dressing table sat just inside the door, and its surface was covered with brushes, combs, and glass bottles. His bed was gone, replaced by a four poster swathed in some sort of filmy white fabric. On the bed was more velvet—a deep, rich brown velvet blanket and gold and white pillows. A Chinese screen stood in another corner, along with a tulipwood armoire that matched the dressing table.

"Where are my clothes? Where's my bed?"

"Your clothes are in storage until the new wardrobe arrives. I suppose I should have kept a few things here. You're dripping on the Aubusson carpet."

Brook looked down. Indeed a new rug in brown, gold, and burgundy had been laid beneath his feet.

He shrugged off his greatcoat, but before he could drop it on the floor in a soggy heap, she snatched it and hung it on a hook by the fire.

"As for your bed," she said in a prissy tone, "I couldn't possibly sleep under that blue coverlet or in the same bed where you sired all those children. Speaking of which, I have wax now, so you might seal and send your missives."

Brook's head spun.

It might have been the rumble of hunger in his belly. It might have been the damp seeping into his brain. It might have been that he'd walked into a stranger's home. It might be that his wife was absolutely daft.

He turned at look at her, or rather, above her, as when he looked at her, he tended to forget he was angry.

"Might we go back over that last exchange? You procured wax. Very good. The blue coverlet was not to your taste. Very well. But what children are you speaking of?"

Her cheeks colored, and she lowered her head. "The children you wrote about in the letters. I shouldn't have read them, but they weren't sealed. That's why I bought the wax."

"You read my letters?" *What letters?*

"Yes, the letters about your by-blows."

"By-blows? Bastards? I don't have any bastards."

She huffed. "Of course not. And if Mary and Geoffrey and Thomas aren't your children, then whose are they?"

"Mary and Geoffrey…" Quite suddenly it all made sense. Could he have been spared the refurbishing if she'd known none of those children were his, that he'd only sought to help them out of their wretched lives in the rookeries?

"I see you recall your offspring now." Her tone was frosty.

"They're not—" He paused, tried to clear his mind, and realized he was too hungry and cold to think clearly. "I'll call for food and warm water." He started for the door, then paused. "Unless you've hired a cook."

She gave him a look that said she thought he was the daft one. He would not throttle her. He *would not* throttle her.

"I've had Hunt or Finnegan bring me meals, but I didn't know how to acquire hot water other than heating it over the hearth," she admitted.

"The landlord's wife will bring it if you ask. She'll cook a simple meal or two if you tell her you want it in advance."

"I see. Then you intend to stay here and eat dinner?"

"Yes. Just as soon as I shed these wet clothes."

He walked through the door, but not before he heard her small squeak of alarm.

Lila peered out the door after him. Their flat opened onto a narrow landing and a set of steps. This flat was at the top of the building, and she had not heard anyone moving around below her. Was the rest of the building unoccupied?

Footsteps sounded on the stairs again, and she moved back inside. As much as she wanted to go outside again soon, she felt safe in the flat. And now that she'd refurbished it exactly as she liked, she was happy to stay there for some time to come.

Perhaps when the rain stopped and the weather warmed, she would be able to open the window and look out and let the fresh air in.

Brook entered, then pushed the door closed with his booted foot. He secured the locks and yanked at his drooping cravat.

"Did you speak with Hunt?"

"Yes. Since you threw out all my clothing—"

"I put it in storage."

"—I'm forced to send him back into the rain to fetch me dry garments. Dinner is on its way." He dropped the length of neckcloth on the ground with a wet splat.

Since the water leaked onto the wood floor and not her new rug, she did not object…until he began pulling at the sleeves of his coat. She stepped back, bumped into the chaise longue, and sat down hard to avoid falling. From that vantage point, she had an unobstructed view of Brook disrobing.

The coat, which was not as fitted as was the fashion, joined the cravat on the floor in a wet heap. Then came his boots and stockings. It seemed strangely intimate to see him in shirtsleeves and bare feet. The linen shirt molded nicely to his chest. She had a lovely view of his muscled back when he moved nearer the fire to warm himself. She looked down at his feet and was surprised to see they were long and well shaped. She honestly couldn't recall ever having seen a man's feet before…or his bare calves. Without the boots and stockings, his firm calves were on display.

A muscle in one flexed as he moved closer to the hearth—*closer to her*—and Lila looked away, heat rising in her face.

She should not be looking at his body. This was not a marriage in truth. He did not want her as his wife or in his bed. He certainly didn't want to be ogled by her.

And then he reached to his waist, grabbed hold of the shirt, and lifted it over his head. Lila couldn't help but stare, especially when he tossed the wet shirt onto the pile by the door.

She must have made some small sound of dismay because he glanced at her over his shoulder. "Are you choking?"

She shook her head, closing her eyes to shut out the image of his broad back, mostly in shadow, but the room boasted light enough that she could see the tendons of his shoulders and the way his sides tapered into a slim waist.

His back was smooth and muscled, and she could almost imagine he was a sculpture in a museum.

A warm sculpture she desperately wanted to touch.

She closed her eyes again, attempting to rein in her thoughts and focus them on what was right and proper.

This was his home. He had every right to undress in it. And she was his wife. There was nothing wrong in the eyes of God or man with him prancing around nude in front of her.

That thought produced quite an image, and she gulped in a breath.

His clothes would be arriving soon. If she just kept her eyes closed until he was dressed again…

She could feel him, feel the heat of him beside her.

Lila opened her eyes and looked at the fall of his breeches. Horrified, she quickly directed her gaze upward, over a taut abdomen, a firm chest, and bare arms with rounded muscles at the biceps. And all of this perfect flesh was burnished by the fire in the hearth. She squeaked and closed her eyes again.

His clothes would be there any moment.

"Are you well?" he asked.

She nodded, eyes still closed. "Quite well. Why do you ask?"

"You're making a sort of wheezing sound when you breathe. Come to think of it, your breathing is rather rapid. Are you certain you are well?" She felt him bend down, and she jumped up, brushing her arm against some bare part of him and flinching as though burned.

"I'm quite well. No need to touch me. Where is Hunt with your clothes?" She scooted away, trying to train her gaze anywhere but on him.

He put his hands on his slim hips, not seeming in the least embarrassed by his partial nudity. With his hands on his hips, she noticed his breeches were a bit too big at the waist and hung rather low on those hips, giving her a tantalizing peek at the forbidden area just below his navel.

She closed her eyes again.

"I imagine Hunt will be an hour or more," he said. "Do I make you uncomfortable?"

"No. Why should you say that?"

"You're wringing your hands together and squeezing your eyes shut. Haven't you ever seen a man's chest before?"

She opened her eyes and immediately wanted to close them again. Out of sheer force of will, she gazed at him and notched her head up. Of course, she could feel the color rise in her cheeks as well, but she could not control that. "Of course I've seen a man's chest. I've been to the museum."

"Ah, the museum." He stepped closer. He was still

across the room, and she wanted him to stay there. "I meant a real man. Not one made of marble."

"And where would I have seen that?"

"So I do make you uncomfortable."

She pressed a hand to her forehead and felt a sheen of perspiration on her brow. "No. Yes. I don't know. I suppose I do wish you were clothed."

"I can't stay in those wet garments. I'll catch my death of cold. And I can't don dry garments because you threw them out."

She glared at him. "No, I did not. I had them put in storage. It's entirely different. And I think you could show some consideration for me. You won't catch your death if you stay in wet clothes for a few minutes. You were obviously out in the rain for some time."

He took another step toward her, and she backed up a step. Her slipper squashed into the wet clothing, and she jumped aside.

"You think I don't show you any consideration?"

His eyes had taken on a dark, challenging look. Lila could spot a trap when she saw one and didn't answer.

"I left my breeches on. Perhaps I should show you exactly how *in*considerate I can be." He reached for the waistband.

"No!" she cried. "You have been most considerate."

A knock sounded on the door behind her, and she let out a small scream. And then she thanked God for the intrusion. Anything to stop Brook from shedding any more clothing. She reached for the locks, but Brook was beside her in an instant, batting her hands away.

His bare chest brushed against her ungloved arms, and she shivered at the frisson that leaped between them at the contact. Had he felt that as well or was it just her imagination?

"Do not ever open the door without asking who it is," he murmured in her ear.

She nodded, eager to do anything if he would move away and stop whispering in her ear. "W-who is it?"

"Mrs. O'Dwyer with your dinner, love." She had the lilt of Ireland in her speech. "Open the door now afore I drop it."

She glanced at Brook for approval, and he nodded. She fumbled with the top locks, and he inserted a key into the bottom. She pulled the door open, and a young woman with bright red hair and freckles on her cheeks and nose bustled in.

"Where shall I put it, miss?" she said, holding up the tray.

Lila considered, then pointed to the escritoire. The dining table hadn't arrived yet, so the desk would have to do.

"Sure and that's a right enough place for it," Mrs. O'Dwyer said moving toward the desk. "You look cozy enough in here," she said with a nod at the fire. "It's like the devil's weather outside tonight. A good night to stay by the fire. And then where's Sir Brook?"

"I…ah…" That was an excellent question. Where had he disappeared to? "He was here a moment ago."

"And those must be his clothes on the floor. They'll dry much faster by the fire then, darlin'."

"Yes, he went to ah…put on warm clothes."

"Ah, now, sure he did. Give him my regards, and I hope you enjoy the broth."

And with a quick curtsy she was out the door again. Lila's stomach grumbled at the fragrant smells coming from the other side of the room, and she crossed to the tray and lifted the cover of the soup tureen.

She frowned, for though the soup smelled delicious, it was a very simple broth and not at all the sort of fare she was used to. Beside it was a hunk of brown bread and cheese that looked several days old. She lifted a spoon to dip into the broth and taste it.

"What the devil are you doing?"

The spoon flew across the room, and Lila inhaled sharply. Brook had returned without making a sound, and he gestured at her angrily.

"Our dinner arrived."

"And you didn't lock the door?" He crossed to the door, turned every lock and key, and then stomped over to her.

"I would have."

"You could have been dead by now. Beezle only needs a moment."

"Finnegan and the other"—what was his name?—"are below."

"And what if their throats have been slit? Do you want to be next?"

"No! And stop trying to scare me."

"I shouldn't have to try and scare you," he said, towering over her. "You should be scared enough on your own. Do you think this marriage and hiding here are for fun?"

"No."

"Did you think this was just an opportunity to shop?" He gestured to the new furnishings.

"No! But I can hardly sit here for hours and days on end twiddling my thumbs, *waiting* to be murdered. It's not as though you are here to converse with." She did not care if he towered over her or shouted at her. She could shout too.

"Oh, I'm sorry I'm not here to entertain you with idle conversation. While you lounged warm and dry on your velvet pillows, I stood in the shit of the gutters of Seven Dials, the rain pounding down on me, and waited for Beezle to make an appearance. I'm trying to save your life, Lila."

"How dare you speak to me like that!"

"We're married." He moved closer again until she was flush against the wall. "I am permitted to call you Lila in private."

"That's not what I meant. You said…about the gutters…"

He stared at her for a long moment. Then he scrubbed his hands over his cropped hair. "Bloody hell."

His arm came around her, and he hauled her up against him. "Forgive me in advance, Mrs. Derring. I just can't resist."

His lips came down on hers, and though she tried to protest, no sound escaped. His warm mouth covered hers, and she couldn't think of anything but making certain he never stopped.

Seven

HE HADN'T WANTED TO KISS HER. GOD KNEW HE'D teased her enough. But what the devil was he supposed to do when she stood, all prim and proper, in her princess-in-a-tower room and stared at him with that shocked expression.

That *adorably* shocked expression. He didn't want to find her adorable. He didn't want to enjoy shocking her, but he couldn't seem to help it. It reminded him of when he'd been a boy and unable to resist needling his older brother.

Except Lila was nothing like his older brother.

And he hadn't meant to kiss her. He'd been angry because she had no concept of the danger she was in and because she'd taken over the only place that had ever been his alone and—very well—because he'd had to marry her and she was beautiful and he couldn't stop wanting to kiss her.

Only half of that was her fault.

But when she'd yelled back at him, her spine perfectly straight, her head held high, her hands folded primly before her, he hadn't been able to resist. He wanted to ruffle her composure, hear her make a sound other than a squeak of disapproval.

And so he'd yanked her against him and kissed her. A quick kiss to show her she didn't control him. But once his lips brushed over hers, he hadn't been in such a hurry to pull back. Once he felt the softness of her mouth, he wanted to feel more.

He danced his lips lightly over hers once, twice, three times. On the third time, she opened her lips with a light gasp or sigh—he was not certain which— and he slid his hand up her back and into her hair. He slanted his mouth over hers, angling her head to give him better access.

Her body was rigid in his arms, but she didn't protest. And as he moved his mouth over hers, she began to melt into him, slowly at first, until her arms came around his neck, and she clung to him as though he were the last lifeline of a sinking ship.

Her soft body pressed against him, her heat making him forget the cold rain and the chill of the hours he'd spent outside. Her scent, which seemed to be a mixture of lily of the valley and laundered linen, teased his senses, making him want more and more. She did not kiss him back, but when he ran his tongue lightly along the seam of her lips, she gave a soft moan.

He rather doubted she'd been kissed much since he'd last kissed her and not by any man who knew what he was about.

Hell, Brook hadn't known how to kiss a woman properly himself seven years ago.

But he knew now.

He might have deepened the kiss then. He certainly

wanted to. His body wanted more than a kiss, but he held back. This path was a slippery slope. Kissing her was only making him want her, and no good could come from that. This sham of a marriage would be over in a few days' time. Easier for both of them if they made a clean break.

Brook broke away from her, stepping back and releasing her. She clung to him for another moment before realizing she was free and forcing her legs to hold her weight.

Her eyes were so dark they were almost amber. Her cheeks were flushed, her lips red as a ripe rose and just as plump. Brook clenched his hands in order to resist taking her in his arms again.

"I don't forgive you," she said, her voice breaking on the last word. "In the future, I'd appreciate it if you didn't accost me."

He raised a brow. "Accost you? Is that what it's called?"

"I don't wish to have you paw at me whenever the mood strikes you."

Brook's hands clenched again but not from desire. "I neither accosted you nor pawed you, madam." He stepped closer to her, but she didn't back up. Even if she'd wanted to, her back was to the wall. "I kissed you, and you bloody well liked it."

"No, I didn't."

"I beg your pardon, but your moans and the way your hands clung to my person confused me momentarily."

Her color rose higher and so did her chin. "Do not kiss me again."

"I'll kiss you whenever I want. Someone ought to. You don't know the first thing about it."

Her jaw dropped, which had the added effect of bringing her chin down a notch. "Are you implying I don't kiss well?"

"If you think that was only implied, you haven't understood a word I said."

She let out a cry of outrage and rushed at him. Brook wasn't certain what she would have done had he allowed her to touch him. He had agile reflexes, honed by years in the rookeries, and he moved quickly aside. She stumbled past him with a startled cry.

"Get out!" she yelled.

"This is my flat. You get out."

She turned toward the door, as though to do just that, and then seemed to reconsider. For all her fury, she wasn't too angry to think straight.

Slowly, she turned back to face him. "I can't leave. I have nowhere to go."

"And a price on your head."

"A fat lot you care." She swiped her hand out. "You only want my father's money."

"I don't give a damn about your father's money. He could give me a hundred thousand pounds, and it wouldn't be enough to put up with the likes of you. You're a stubborn, spoiled brat, and you always have been."

"You're an immoral, ill-mannered arse!"

He would concede the ill-mannered arse. He could be both at times, but he was rather proud of his morals. "Immoral? What the devil do you know of my morals?"

"I know you have half a dozen by-blows spread throughout the countryside!" She'd positioned her hands on her waist, and her tone was that of one who thinks she has won the argument.

Brook leaned a hip against the dainty escritoire. "This is the second mention you have made of bastards. As I said, I have no bastards. The children you read of in my *private* correspondence are youths I pulled out of the rookeries. These children were orphans who only wanted a better life and asked for my help. I gave it to them by finding them positions as servants in large, well-to-do homes. They're safe, fed, and well away from the gangs and thugs who would have preyed on them in the city."

She stared at him, her mouth slightly parted with what he imagined was her next riposte. Then she closed her mouth and swallowed. Color rose in her cheeks again, but he imagined this time it was from shame.

"You helped those children?"

"I'm trying to. Not all of them are children either. Geoffrey is almost seventeen. I would have had to sire him at fourteen or fifteen. I promise you, I had any number of items on my mind at that age and none of them were tossing up a girl's skirts."

"I see." She wrung her hands together. "I suppose I should apologize."

"Go ahead." *Now* he was being an ill-mannered arse.

"Very well, I am sorry for assuming the worst about you."

He would have nodded. The apology was enough for him. He'd actually been surprised she'd made one at all.

"And I also apologize for reading your private letters. I should not have done that, and I really have no excuse."

"All is—"

"And I probably should not have had your flat refurbished without asking for your permission. That was quite selfish of me and probably a rather underhanded method of punishing you for stashing me away here." She lowered her lashes and swiped at her cheek.

Did she brush tears away or was it merely an itch?

"It's unjust of me to blame you," Lila said. "You are only trying to help me, the same way you helped those children. I do appreciate it, and I beg you to understand that the events of the past few days have been quite a shock. I hope you will forgive me."

She raised her gaze to his, and Brook tried to remember what he had been angry about. "Who the devil are you?" he asked. "What have you done with Lady Lila?"

"Very funny."

"I'm not attempting to amuse you. Is this apology some sort of jest?"

She exhaled, her expression a mixture of hurt and shock. "I suppose that will teach me to apologize. You don't even believe me."

"No, I don't. I know you, Lila."

"That's where you are wrong. I'm not the girl you knew."

With that, she turned her back on him and flounced away—acting very much like the girl he'd known. With a dramatic flourish, she slammed the door to the bedroom, leaving him alone in the common room.

Alone except for the dinner.

Brook couldn't argue with those circumstances.

If he was truly the ill-mannered arse she made him

out to be, he would have eaten all of the meal Mrs. O'Dwyer had brought. Instead, he left some for Lila to eat if and when she emerged from exile.

His belly full, he lay down in front of the hearth and closed his eyes, opening them again as soon as he heard Hunt's foot on the steps. Hunt knocked softly, identified himself, and Brook opened the door and took the valise.

He stripped off his wet breeches and pulled on dry ones.

He reached for a clean, pressed shirt, but Hunt produced the shaving kit.

Brook gave him a warning look.

"The landlady is on her way with warm water. What else did you want it for?"

Brook sighed. He might have taken a bath, except that he didn't have a tub at the flat. Instead, when Mrs. O'Dwyer knocked a few minutes later, Hunt took the warm water, poured some into a bowl to use for shaving, and gave the rest to Brook, who used it and a clean towel to wash the dirt and grime from the last few days off.

Then he sat to be shaved, leaning his head back, and closing his eyes. He could catch ten minutes' sleep in this fashion and not need to rest for another three or four hours.

"Where's the missus?" Hunt asked, placing a warm wet towel on Brook's face.

Brook opened his eyes.

Hunt used the strop to sharpen the razor, continuing his task as though he didn't see the way Brook glared at him.

"Finnegan and Turner said she's kept herself, and them, quite busy."

Brook gestured to the room. "As you see."

Hunt nodded and proceeded to employ the brush to spread the shaving soap on Brook's cheeks and jaw. "Much improved."

Brook pushed forward and glanced around again. "What was wrong with it before?"

"Not a thing." Hunt waited for him to sit back again and then began sliding the razor in neat strips along Brook's cheek. "But now it has a woman's touch."

"If by that you mean it has an abundance of velvet and satin, I concur. And I have no doubt she's in the bedroom right this minute planning her next purchase, but I won't have her using Turner and Finnegan as her lackeys."

"That won't go over well with her."

"She already called me an immoral, ill-mannered arse. It can't get worse."

"Oh, yes it can. And you're not immoral."

Brook pointed at him. "Thank you."

For a few moments, there was only the sound of the razor on stubble. "You might give her another chance," Hunt said, shaving Brook's neck, which meant Brook dare not reply or even breathe. "After all, she's attempting to take an interest."

Brook lowered his brows in question.

Hunt nodded at the nearby chaise longue. "The book on the Peloponnesian War. The one you've been reading for three years. She's reading it now."

As soon as Hunt had removed the blade, Brook sat and stared at the book open on the longue. He'd noted it before—he generally saw everything—but he hadn't taken an interest in it. He'd supposed it was one of the novels ladies were always reading, but now he saw it was indeed the book he read when he couldn't fall asleep at night.

It was boring as hell, but she'd made more progress than he had.

Was she interested in history? He'd never imagined Lila was much of a reader. Perhaps he did not know her as well as he thought.

And why the devil did he care? He didn't need to know her. He only needed to keep her safe for a few more days.

Hunt dried his face and neck and then helped Brook dress in the clean clothing. "Is it still raining, Hunt?"

"Yes, sir. And it's dark." And because Hunt could see Brook still wasn't dissuaded, he added, "And cold."

"Beezle can't stay inside forever."

Hunt muttered something about dry weather, but Brook ignored it.

"We may very well catch him tonight."

An hour or so later, Brook and Hunt shooed a prostitute away and took up their old positions. The moll returned though, and Brook couldn't help but notice she was just a girl, wet and shivering. He reached into his pocket and pulled out several coins. "Half-crown for a bit of information."

"Go on," she said. "You call it information if you want. Come back here with me, and I'll give you *information*."

Brook nodded at Hunt and followed her, not because he wanted to take her against the wall, as she assumed, but because it would be better for her if she wasn't seen conversing with him.

In the light from a window above, he saw the girl lean against a wall and open her arms to him. Brook shook his head. "I meant what I said. I want information." He kept his voice low.

"You want me to snitch?"

"I'll pay you." He jingled the coins in his hand. "You answer my questions. That's all."

"I don't lift my skirt?"

"I won't touch you."

She stared at the wall, thinking it over. Without the mask of forced sensuality over her features, she looked young and vulnerable.

"You a Runner?"

"Of sorts."

"Who you after?"

"Beezle."

"Oh no." She shook her head and slid several inches away. "He'll slit my throat."

"Which is why we're not standing on the open street." He jingled the coins again, making sure she saw the crown. "You know where his flash ken is."

"I know it." Of course she did. She'd been standing across from it for the better part of the evening.

"Did you happen to see anyone go in or out?"

"I saw you and that tall one go and come back. I kept my eye on you."

"Good. Was anyone else watching me?"

She bit her lip, and Brook jingled the coins again.

"Might be someone followed you."

"Who?"

She shrugged. "Don't know."

"You're a clever girl. You know. Crown to jog your memory."

She glanced around. "If I was clever, I wouldn't be 'ere talking to you."

"Was it Beezle?"

She shook her head.

"Stub?"

Another shake.

"Racer?"

She hesitated.

"Damn it." Even Brook knew how Racer had a reputation for running through the congested streets as fast as a town hack. "Did he come back while I was away?"

She glanced behind her again and then gave a quick jerk of her head.

"And then what?"

Another look over her shoulder. "Give me the blunt."

"Tell me."

"The blunt first."

It went against every rule he had, but he gave her the crown plus a tanner. He'd have given it to her even if she hadn't told him a thing.

"Racer came back and him and the other one you said—"

"Stub?"

Quick shake of her head.

"Beezle."

"Them two set off. Next thing I know yer back."

"What did—" But he was speaking to himself. She was gone, and she'd watch for him and keep out of his way. She wouldn't want anyone to link her to him. Brook didn't want that either.

He returned to the corner, where Hunt looked wet and miserable. "Sir."

"Racer followed us then came back for Beezle. The two set out a little while ago," Brook said without preamble.

"Do we wait for them to come back?"

Brook studied the flash ken. Like the rest of the buildings around, it looked dark and empty. No one in Seven Dials had tallow or lamp oil to waste. Brook wanted to settle back, watch the building until Beezle returned, but he couldn't shake the feeling that he should go.

It wasn't the rain or the cold, although those two factors made the work difficult.

He felt as though he'd forgotten something.

"I have a bad feeling about this, Hunt."

"We weren't followed, sir." Hunt had a way of cutting to the point.

"Not from here to the flat," Brook said slowly, his thoughts locking into place as he spoke. "Even Racer isn't that fast. How did you go from the flat to Derring House? Walked?"

"Of course." Hunt didn't need to point out he didn't own a coach.

"Beezle knows Derring House." Bloody hell.

"You think Racer went to Derring House, saw me, and followed me back to the flat."

"I have a bad feeling, Hunt."

"I know your bad feelings, sir. I trust them too." He'd already started back the way they'd come.

Brook was right behind him. At the end of the street, Brook began to run.

Lila had left the bedroom when she heard Brook exit but only to retrieve the book on the Peloponnesian War. She assumed her husband would be gone for the rest of the night, possibly the rest of the week. That should have made her happy, and she told herself the reason she was unhappy was because she felt lonely.

She didn't mind solitude, but she'd had little of it in her life. After three days alone, she had begun to miss the company of others. Reading of the battles between Sparta and Athens comforted her—or at least put her problems into perspective.

And her biggest problem, at the moment, was Brook Derring. Of all the men in London, why did he have to be the one to rescue her? Why did he have to be the one to marry her? Protect her? Kiss her?

No, she would not think about that kiss.

She turned another page in the book and stared at the words, which had begun to resemble ancient Greek.

How could she *not* think of the kiss? Who kissed like that? There was nothing proper or dignified about the way Brook had kissed her.

She should have been appalled at having been treated so cavalierly. He'd yanked her against him. Like some conquering general, he'd captured her mouth with his and made her bend to his will.

The worst part was that he was right when he said she'd liked it.

She *had* liked it. She'd liked being pressed against his hard, bare chest. She liked the feel of his mouth on hers. She liked that he didn't kiss her like a gentleman.

She *wanted* to be taken.

Lila supposed that was what galled her the most. For years her father and mother had admonished her to *act like a lady*. Any small infraction, from slouching to stepping too loudly on the stairs, had been met with stern lectures and reprimands. Lila had strived to meet their high standards. She'd wanted to be just like her mother, who had behaved like a lady even as she took her dying breath.

Now she knew why her parents were so hard on her. They must have seen that she wasn't really a lady at all. Inside, she was no better than a harlot who liked... What was it the prostitutes had said? *A good poke*.

Perhaps she'd never be anything more to Brook than *a good poke*. After all, he hadn't treated her much better than a whore.

And that wasn't a fair assessment either. He could have deflowered her right there in the common room. He hadn't. He'd stopped, even when it was quite clear from one glance at him that he hadn't wanted to.

But he hadn't wanted her enough to make her his wife in truth.

And which was worse? That he did want her or that he didn't want her enough?

Her head had begun to pound, and she remembered why she hadn't wanted to think about that kiss. She lifted the book again, determined to focus on the page before her.

A moment later, she turned the page, hoping the tide turned and Sparta's Lysander did not prevail over Athens's navy, when she heard a quiet tap. She ignored it, going back to Lysander and his plan to lure

Athens into battle by sailing for Hellespont and the source of Athens's grain.

The tap sounded again, and she realized someone was knocking on the outer door. This time she set the book on the bed and went into the common room. Finnegan and the other guard usually called out when they were at the door. But perhaps this was Mrs. O'Dwyer, returning for her tray.

She stopped before the door and laid her hand on the lock. "Who is it?"

"Open the door, my lady."

It wasn't Mrs. O'Dwyer. It didn't sound like Finnegan either, but neither was she familiar enough with him to recognize his voice upon hearing it.

"Who is it?"

"Landlord."

"Mr. O'Dwyer?"

There was a pause. "Yes."

She turned the first lock, then paused. "Have you come for the dinner tray?"

"That's right."

She turned the second lock. She should open the third, but her fingers hesitated. She'd never met Mr. O'Dwyer. She assumed there was a Mr. O'Dwyer. How could she be certain this was he?

Of course, Finnegan and the other wouldn't have allowed him to come up if they didn't know him.

She undid the last lock and opened the door slightly. A man stood without, his face in shadow. "You are Mr. O'Dwyer?"

"That's right. Mrs. O'Dwyer sent me for the tray."

He didn't move forward, into the light spilling from

the doorway so she could see him. That wasn't all that bothered her. There was something…

"You don't have an accent."

"What's that?"

Mrs. O'Dwyer still had the thick accent of her homeland. This man sounded like he'd been born in London. "You're not Irish."

Panic seizing her heart, she slammed the door and fought to secure the locks. She wasn't fast enough. The latch lifted, and though she pushed against the door to keep it closed, the man on the other side was too strong.

He rammed against the door, and it flew open, causing her to stumble back. She managed to keep on her feet and fled for the bedroom. She slammed the door and secured the lock just as the intruder banged against it.

"Go away!" She peered around the room frantically. The lock was flimsy and wouldn't hold against the man's hammering.

"Open the door. No 'arm will come to ye."

"Liar," she muttered. Why had she sent that wardrobe to storage? She could have used it at that moment. Instead, she grabbed the edge of the dressing table and dragged it in front of the door. One of her fingernails broke at the quick, and she gasped with pain, but she yanked the furnishing until it rattled with every bang of the door.

Only then did she back up and suck the throbbing finger. The dressing table was too small and dainty. It wouldn't hold. She needed a weapon. A brush? The bottle of cologne? Oh, but if that exploded all over the room, the scent would make it practically uninhabitable.

Where were Finnegan and the other—why couldn't she ever remember his name?—when she needed them!

The door shook, and the wood around the lock splintered. Lila squeaked with fear. This was it. Now she would die. The door gave way, and the man pushed his face into the slivered opening. His cheeks were red from the effort, and he grunted to move the dressing table out of the way.

She recognized him. It was the same man who'd taken her that night. The same one who'd killed the gentleman, the MP.

She backed away and around the side of the bed, hoping to put some distance between herself, the door, and certain death. At that moment, she spotted the book, snatched it up, and threw it at the door.

She'd played catch with her brother a thousand times as a child, and all that practice finally paid off. The book cuffed the man on the chin, and he stumbled back and out of the door's slim opening. Lila ran back and tried to shove the door closed again. If she could find a way to wedge the dressing table in front of it—

But the door wouldn't close. The blasted book had landed in the opening. She bent to free it, and a hand caught hers.

Lila screamed. It was the sort of scream she knew would make her throat raw later, but she didn't care. She didn't think there would be a later.

The dressing table still blocked the door, and the man couldn't pull her through the opening without first moving the dressing table. She was wedged between the table and the door. She fought to free her hand, but his punishing grip on her fingers didn't slacken. They were deadlocked in a tug-of-war until the door shuddered from a punishing blow. Someone else—there were two of them!—had kicked the door. Lila screamed again and yanked her hand, only to have it pulled back.

The door crashed inward, and the dressing table toppled over, the contents shattering with an angry crash.

⚜

Brook heard the scream and began to run. He'd almost reached the building and was grateful for the rain because if the sky had been clear, St. James would have been crowded, and his progress would have been slowed. Now, with Hunt keeping stride, they burst into the building. The scene that greeted them was chaos.

The landlady was yelling. Her husband knelt beside one of the dead guards. And Lila—it had to be Lila—screamed just as what sounded like an entire china cabinet crashed to the ground.

Brook took the steps two at a time, ignoring the burning in his legs. He burst into his flat to find Racer pushing his way into the bedroom, and Beezle crouched on the floor, his hand locked around Lila's wrist. A large piece of furniture had overturned, blocking the doorway and preventing Lila from backing away from Beezle.

Racer turned and saw Brook, but Brook couldn't tear his gaze from Beezle's hand on Lila's wrist.

He would have seen Beezle locked away for a thousand crimes, but the crime of touching Lila—his wife—meant death. Racer charged him, and Brook knocked him aside like one might an annoying insect. Beezle saw him coming, hesitated a moment too long in releasing Lila, and Brook had his hands on Beezle's shoulders.

He yanked the arch rogue to his feet, slammed his fist into him, and followed him as he careened across the room. Blood from Beezle's broken nose splashed the walls and Lila's new rug. There would be more blood yet. He reached for Beezle again when Lila shouted.

The warning was enough for him to duck, and, with a sharp sting, Racer's blow grazed his side. Beezle was on his feet now, and Brook had no more ducked to avoid his fist than Racer caught him.

With a bloody sneer, Beezle slammed his fist into Brook's breadbasket, making him double over, gasping. Hunt thundered into the room, met Brook's gaze, and Brook looked to Lila, who had managed to rise from the floor. She stood with her hands pressed against her pale cheeks, her face caught in an expression of horror.

Hunt had made a career of obeying orders, and he went for Lila, ushering her back into the bedroom, where she might be safe.

With a curse, Beezle lifted a knee, connected with Brook's chin, then ordered Racer to release him.

"We're not through yet, Derring!" he yelled as he ran for the door.

Not even close to through, Brook thought. Still unable to speak, he jabbed at the door when Hunt raced from the bedroom. "After him," he wheezed. The room spun, and he pressed a hand to his burning flank.

But he knew it was too late.

Beezle was free, and he'd be back.

Eight

LILA HATED THE SILENCE EVEN MORE THAN SHE HATED the sounds of the fight. What did the silence mean? Had Brook lost? Had he won? Her back pressed against the bedroom wall, she squeezed her eyes shut. The door was broken, but Hunt had shoved it against the jambs to give her a measure of protection. It also prevented her from seeing out.

Finally, she heard footsteps and the low sound of a man's voice. Brook or Hunt? Or the other? No, he wouldn't have spoken quietly.

Unless he didn't want her to know he was coming for her.

The stench of the spilled perfume made her head spin, and a piece of broken mirror jabbed at her foot through her delicate slipper. Still, she didn't move.

"My lady?"

She thought it was Hunt. She knew Brook's voice by now, and this one was too refined to be one of the thugs.

"Yes?" she managed, her voice shaky.

"Sir Brook and I are coming in. Beezle is gone."

She felt her shoulders slump, and she would have crumpled to the floor had it not been covered with perfume and broken glass. The door slammed back against the wall, still blocking the doorway but leaving a wide enough gap for Hunt and Brook to enter.

Brook's jaw looked red and he stood hunched, hand pressed to his side, but otherwise he appeared unharmed.

"Are you hurt?" he asked, his voice low and quiet.

She thought about her broken nail and the glass digging into her foot. "No. But you are."

"Nothing serious. We have to go. Now. Tonight."

She looked from Hunt to Brook. Hunt's forehead was creased and his brow furrowed with worry. Brook's expression might have been carved from stone.

"Where?" she asked. "To Derring House?"

"No. Somewhere else. Away from London."

She didn't want to argue. Now that the threat was over, she wanted to cry. Over the years, she had become an expert at *not* crying. *I will not cry* had become a mantra. Not crying came easily, but she couldn't stop her body from shaking.

"Hunt, the blanket." Brook gestured toward the brown velvet coverlet, and Hunt pulled it off the bed, unseating several pillows, and handed it to Brook. One-handed, he wrapped it around her shoulders then pulled her away from the broken dressing table so she might sit on the floor.

"I'll look in on the O'Dwyers," Hunt said, darting into the common room and leaving them alone.

"Oh no. Are the O'Dwyers hurt?" she asked. Selfish of her not to have asked before. "I thought he"—she nodded toward the common room—"was

Mr. O'Dwyer. That's why I opened the door. But then he didn't sound Irish, and I tried to close it again."

Brook closed his large, warm hand around hers. She had the impulse to rub her cheek on it. She must have been more shaken than she realized.

"It's not your fault. Beezle's crony followed Hunt here. Then he went to fetch Beezle, who came for you."

"But the guards—?"

"Dead."

The shock of the word pulled her breath from her lungs. Finnegan, dead? Big, gruff Finnegan who hadn't complained once when she asked him to position the new furniture not once but half a dozen times? Dead, because of her.

"How?" she whispered.

"Slit their throats. He would have done the same to you. He *will* do the same to you if I don't take you away from here."

"But I thought—"

"I failed you," he interrupted, seeming to read her thoughts.

She'd thought she'd be safe here. She'd thought this would all be over in a matter of days. She hadn't truly been concerned. After all, she was the daughter of the powerful Duke of Lennox. No one could hurt her.

She'd been wrong.

"I won't take more chances. My family owns land, and there's a small gamekeeper's house—a cottage really—about a half day outside of London. It's in disrepair, but it's livable. The main advantage is that it's relatively secluded. We have a few tenants farming the land there, but there's not much of a village or anything else nearby."

In other words, no chance of refurbishment. She looked at her beautiful bedroom. She'd have to leave it all behind. They would go to this cottage, and they would be safe from Beezle.

"For how long?" she asked. "How long do we have to stay there? How can you arrest this Beezle if you're in the country with me?" She twisted her hand to catch his wrist and hold it. "Do not say you'll leave me there alone."

"No. At the moment, I'm a liability. I led Beezle to you, so I go too. I have men who will track Beezle for me, men who know the rookeries as well as he. They'll find him and send word when he's been taken. We'll be at the cottage a few days. A week at most."

A week with Brook in the middle of the countryside. Just the two of them. Alone…no. She would not think about that. And she wouldn't think about what Brook meant when he said the house was in "disrepair."

She would think about a week. Seven short days. It would pass quickly and easily.

Only a week. What could go wrong?

❧

"This is not a cottage," she said when she looked out of the carriage window at the structure before them. They'd traveled all night and most of the morning in a nondescript coach that desperately needed new springs. She had jounced so much, her head rattled.

Even Brook looked pale and wan, and the journey had obviously upset his stomach because he had his arm wrapped about it the entire journey. Hunt had driven them. He would be the only one who knew where they were and knew how to reach them. Lila would not be permitted to write to her friends—what few there were—or her family.

She would not attend her cousin Rose's wedding. No hardship in that. She'd never enjoyed weddings, as they took place much too early and were solemn, tiresome affairs—her own included. She did enjoy the wedding breakfast—again, not her own, but those of others—and she thought of all the wonderful delicacies she would have to forgo in this dilapidated, old building that had probably never even heard of a chocolate tart.

She glanced at Brook. "You said it was a cottage."

"I said it was in disrepair."

She'd thought that meant weeds had grown up in the garden and the ivy on the brick walls needed to be trimmed back. She'd imagined a stone structure with large, rectangular windows, flowers boxes bursting with color, and a pretty vista curving behind it where she could take long walks when the urge struck her.

Of course, the flower boxes had been a bit of fancy, considering this was the middle of winter. She hadn't been wrong about the stone. The house was constructed of stone, and that was the only reason it still stood. No ivy grew on the dirty exterior and the windows had been covered with wood that looked to be rotting away. She was not in the habit of examining a structure's roof, but she cautiously studied the one on this building, hoping against hope it did not leak.

The structure was tiny and only a single story. If it

boasted two bedrooms, she would be surprised, and the kitchen was almost certainly in a separate structure in the back.

Thinking of the kitchen made her stomach growl. She had not eaten the dinner Mrs. O'Dwyer had brought the night before—for which she blamed Brook—and now she wondered where the servants would bed.

A sense of dread covered her like a wet cloak. "Are the servants expecting us?"

Brook gifted her with a look that could only be described as disgust, which was all she needed to know.

No servants. No flower boxes. No charming cottage.

The conveyance rocked as Hunt jumped down from the box and came to open the door for them. She waited for Brook to alight first, but he waved her ahead. Slumped in the seat as he was, he did not look well at all.

Taking Hunt's hand, she stepped down, her slipper immediately sinking into mud. She was too slow to save her skirts, and the hem was also dipped in mud and grime. With some effort, she extricated her foot and navigated the field of sinkholes until she reached the door of the building. A light drizzle fell, and the gray clouds matched the gray of the stones before her. She waited for Hunt to open the door for her, but when he did not, she turned and noted he stood at the carriage, speaking to Brook, who remained inside.

Well, if they wished to remain outside in the cold and wet to hold their tête-à-tête, that was all well and good, but she was ready for a warm fire and a bed. *Please God, let there be both inside.*

She tried the door, found it locked, but when she pushed on it, it creaked open. Obviously the Derring family had not been concerned about intruders if the house was this poorly secured. She pushed the door open, pausing as the stale smell of an old fire and the musty scent of a place long since forgotten wafted over her. She'd smelled it before in rooms closed up for a season or so and once when she toured an ancient castle.

Lila stepped inside and had to force herself to continue. Without any light from the windows, the interior was dark, but not so dark that she could not see the bare wooden floors. Indeed, there was a great deal of floor to see, considering the only piece of furniture in the place was a scarred table with a broken chair at the head. The chair lolled drunkenly to one side as she stepped over the threshold and stifled the rising panic. She saw no bed or bedroom. The back door most likely opened to the path leading to the kitchen, separate to protect the main structure from fire.

Lila doubted the path would be covered, which meant every time either she or Brook made the journey to the kitchen, they would be subject to the elements. And it would be the two of them going to and fro since the place was not large enough for one person and certainly could not accommodate a staff. Was she expected to prepare her own meals? She'd never done anything more in the kitchen than make a request of the cook. She did not even know how to prepare tea.

Not that there would be any tea in the kitchen. How would they eat? She glanced at the cold, dark hearth. How would they keep warm? A fat drop of water plopped on the floor in front of her, joining its brothers in the puddle at her feet.

Lila whined softly and pressed the heels of her hands to her burning eyes. She would not cry. One week. Seven days. Could she live seven days without food or heat?

She turned at a shuffling sound in time to see Hunt ushering Brook inside. It took a moment for her to understand what she saw, but Hunt supported Brook, whose face was a mask of pain.

Lila quite forgot about the fire and the tea and rushed to Brook's other side. "What is wrong?"

His coat was not buttoned, and it gaped, giving her a view of the red stain on his light-colored waistcoat. She inhaled sharply.

"You're injured."

"Nothing serious." He'd said that before, but clearly it was quite serious if Hunt had to drag him inside.

"I saw blood."

"Dried now. It stopped bleeding a few hours ago," Hunt informed her.

She stared at him. Had he known all along his master was injured? Why had no one told her?

"But when did this happen? How?"

"Racer had a dagger. He meant to plunge it in me, but he only gave me a scratch."

"You're lucky, sir."

"Story of my life."

Hunt dragged Brook toward the back of the cottage. Lila hadn't paid much attention to it, but now she saw a moldy blanket hung, cordoning off a small area.

Hunt pushed it aside, revealing a sizable bed nestled in a nook. He shoved Brook against the wall for support, then disappeared back out the door. A moment later, he returned with two thin mattresses and clean linens. He unrolled the mattresses and took down the moldy blanket. Brook didn't wait for assistance. He lurched like a drunkard to the bed and lay down.

Wide-eyed, Lila stared from Hunt to Brook, who had curled into a ball and did not move.

"I'll fetch the luggage," Hunt said.

Lila stared at Brook's back for a moment then ran after Hunt. She caught up to him outside, where the drizzle had turned into a fine, wet mist. "Shouldn't we call for a doctor?"

Hunt paused and looked down at her politely. "There isn't a doctor anywhere nearby. He'll be fine after a day or two of rest."

"But surely he needs medicine."

"I offered him laudanum, but he won't take it." He reached into his coat and withdrew a flask. "He drank some whisky. You might pour some on the wound to make sure it doesn't fester."

Lila stepped back. "*I* should pour? What about you?"

"I have to return to London."

Lila stumbled backward as though punched. Her face must have mirrored her feeling of betrayal because Hunt's expression softened.

"I do apologize, my lady. Sir Brook was quite specific about his orders."

She wanted to grasp Hunt by the coat and implore him to stay. She wanted to ask what she was supposed to do with an injured man and no help. Instead, she straightened her shoulders and lifted her chin into the mist. She'd nursed her mother for two years while the duchess had coughed and wasted away from the consumption. She could nurse a strong man with a minor knife wound.

Of course, she'd had servants to help her at Blakesford. She'd called for tea or a tonic or warm water, and it had appeared. She would not have that luxury now.

Hunt trudged past her, his arms laden with the luggage. Brook had only allowed her to pack her valise. She'd had to leave most of her more formal gowns at the flat. She would definitely not need them. Even the peach one she still wore was far too fine for this place. She would have to see if Lizzy had packed any of the dresses she'd worn to tend her mother. Most of those had been from several seasons ago or in colors she didn't think suited her.

Hunt went back to the coach and made another trip inside, this time carrying a large basket. Lila eyed its progress, for it looked promising. When he returned, Hunt paused before her. "I'd stay longer, my lady, but I don't want the horses to stand."

She nodded. They'd only changed horses when necessary the night before, and these were probably tired and ready for a rest. Hunt would change them out at the first posting house on the return journey.

"The basket contains a bit of bread and cheese, some wine, and a few apples. It's all I could find on short notice."

"Thank you, Hunt." The mist on her face numbed her skin and her feelings of despair.

"I will be back as soon as I can to look in on you. If anything should happen…" Here he paused. He waited until her gaze locked on his. "Mr. and Mrs. Longmire are about a mile and some that way." He gestured toward the south. "Go to them and have Mr. Longmire ride to Derring House. I'll come and bring help."

Lila nodded, though how she was supposed to walk a mile and *some* in that direction and find the people she sought was beyond her. She might easily be lost and never find the Longmires. She might break her leg and die in the woods alone.

Not that there were many woods about. The land had been cleared for farming, and she imagined it pretty and green in the summer. Now the rolling hills were brown with dead vegetation. Still, she could make out patches of wooded areas in the distance, havens for deer and rabbit and fox.

"You'd best go inside now, my lady," Hunt said. "You'll catch a chill if you stay out here." He looked pointedly at her thin wrap and her thin dress. Lila had long ceased shivering with cold.

"I will, Hunt. Thank you."

His eyes widened with surprise at her words. She knew she was not supposed to thank servants. If one began thanking servants, one would be saying thank you all day and night. But he had done more than deliver a pot of tea and she was grateful. She would have been more grateful if he could have stayed, but she watched as he climbed back up in the box and called to the horses to begin a slow walk back the way they'd come.

Lila turned and, with a shaky breath, trudged to the house.

❧

Her first task was to look in on Brook. He hadn't moved from where Hunt had left him. She watched his back, saw his breaths come regularly, and decided he was asleep, not dead. She spotted the basket Hunt had carried on the table, but she was too cold to sit down and examine its contents. She wished she had thought to ask him to start a fire in the hearth, but she supposed she could do it. The servants did it every day. How hard could it be?

Lila crouched and examined the hearth. She wished the windows had not been boarded over for she would have welcomed a bit of light, gray as it was, from outdoors. Gradually, her eyes adjusted to the gloom inside the room. The hearth had been swept clean of ashes. Inside, a sooty iron grate stood bare, in want of kindling. She looked about and spotted a poker leaning against the stones but no wood. She didn't dare to hope there would be coal.

She stood and turned around, searching the room for wood. But of course, that would be kept outside. And so she went out into the wet and the cold again and glanced over the front of the building.

No firewood.

Nothing for it but to circle the house. She lifted her skirts, ruined now by the mud and the persistent mist, and rounded the side of the cottage. She startled a blackbird into flight but didn't spot any wood. But of course the kindling would be in the back, near the kitchen. She should have thought of that and saved herself this trek around the house. Her feet were wet and cold, her slippers caked with mud, and her fingers felt stiff where they held her wrap closed. Finally, she spotted the kitchen building. Oh, she did not want to look too closely at it for it appeared in even worse condition than the main structure. Stacked against it was a neat pile of chopped wood.

And staring into the pile was a ginger-and-white cat.

The cat looked back at her, flicked its tail, and went back to hunting the wood. The fur on the cat's back was raised slightly, and the creature looked ready to pounce. Lila had no way to know if the cat was friendly or not, but she was grateful for its appearance, as that meant mice and rats were less likely to have gained a foothold.

Lila bent, attempting to determine what the cat hunted, but she didn't spot anything. And then with admirable speed and grace, the cat dove for an opening in the kindling pile. For a moment, only her orange rump and striped tail were visible, and then she emerged, a limp, scrawny mouse in her mouth.

She shook the mouse once more as though in triumph and, head held high, trotted off with the prize.

"Lovely," Lila muttered. Making enough noise to scare any more mice deeper into the woodpile, Lila approached and lifted three medium-sized logs from the top. They were wet, of course, but she discovered those just below were slightly drier. She pulled those out, glad for her gloves as the splinters dug into her skin even through the leather, and tucked the wood under her arm. They snagged her wrap and the silk of her dress, but she shivered with cold and was beyond caring.

Balancing the logs under her arm, she tried the door. It was locked, and she couldn't budge it with a firm nudge. Cursing, she walked back around the house and entered through the front. Lila dropped the wood on top of the grate and then stood back, slumping because she realized she had no means to light the fire.

She would not cry, though she was hungry, weary, and cold. She would not cry, though her feet were nigh frozen and her fingers stiff. She would not cry, even though she could speak three languages, ride with aplomb, embroider, sing, play the pianoforte, and no servant she knew had half as many accomplishments. But every servant she knew could light a fire. She was not stupid—at least she hadn't thought so until now.

And then it came to her: a tinderbox. That was what she needed. But where to find a tinderbox? She searched the basket and blessed Hunt profusely, for not only had he packed food, but he'd packed a tinderbox and the book on the Peloponnesian War. As the cottage didn't seem to hold any others, Lysander and his Spartans would keep her company for the week.

She knew how to use a tinderbox and deftly brought it to the hearth and withdrew the steel, flint, and matches. She struck the steel and flint together above the wood and blew on the sparks, but the wood was too damp even to smoke.

Lila had the urge to throw the box and its contents into the hearth and give up, but she gritted her teeth and clutched the box tightly. She needed something dry and flammable. Perhaps if she started a fire, it might grow hot enough to ignite the wood. Even damp wood burned if given enough fuel. With a sigh, she lifted her skirts and untied her petticoats. A quick look assured her Brook had not moved, and when she bent again, laying the petticoat near the hearth, she felt not only lighter but hopeful.

Once again, she struck steel and flint together. It took several frustrating attempts, but she finally produced a small flame and lit one of the sulfur matches. She quickly set the rest of the petticoat on fire and pushed it under the wood in the hearth. She was well aware wet wood tended to smoke quite a bit, and she opened the back door to clear the smoke from what she hoped would soon be a roaring fire in the hearth.

As she watched, the petticoat turned black and curled inward. Lila twisted her hands together and prayed the wood caught on fire. Otherwise she would have accomplished no more than losing her petticoat, which had added at least another layer to her thin skirts. With a pop and hiss, one of the logs began to smoke. She moved aside, coughing at the black clouds rising from the hearth, but she could see the red of the fire and let out a sigh of relief. She might suffocate, but at least she would be warm.

She reached her hands out to warm them and closed her eyes.

"Are you bloody trying to kill us?"

Lila swung around. Brook sat, hand on his side, glaring at her.

"I thought you were sleeping."

"How can I sleep with you going in and out and banging firewood on every hard surface you can find?" He coughed and waved the smoke away. "Wet firewood, I might add. We'll suffocate for sure."

Lila clenched her cold hands in front of her. "I'm

terribly sorry to wake you. If you were so annoyed, you might have risen and helped me."

His bloodshot eyes narrowed. "Where's Hunt?"

"He went back to London."

"Of course he did." He placed his palms flat on the mattress and pushed himself up, wincing at the obvious pain the movement caused.

Lila started to go to him then hesitated. He did not look as though he welcomed any assistance—hers or anyone's.

"What do you mean? He said you told him to return to Town."

Brook leaned a shoulder against the wall on one side of the bed. "I told him to see you settled first. But there's nothing he detests more than playing nursemaid."

"Do you need a nursemaid?"

"No." He pushed away from the wall and walked gingerly to the broken chair at the table. Lila held her breath when he sat on it, half-afraid all would crash to the floor. The chair creaked but held.

"I would open the door farther so we don't expire, but it might be better if you did it."

It was an order. She recognized one when she heard it, but, since it was nicely given, she did as he asked. "If I could open the windows, that might help."

"I'll take the boards off those that haven't broken as soon as I'm able. I'll also bring some kindling inside. It might dry out better that way."

"Is there anything I can do?" She gestured to the dried blood visible on his waistcoat. "For the wound?"

He snorted. "Are you better at nursing than starting fires?"

She knew it was a rhetorical question, but she answered all the same. "Yes, actually. I've never started a fire in a hearth before, but I nursed my mother almost every day when she was ill with consumption."

His dark gaze met hers and held. Something flickered there and then he looked toward the open door and the smoke curling out into the damp afternoon. "I apologize."

"No need." More proof he still saw her as the same spoiled debutante. That was fine. They had one week together, six more days when this one had ended. She didn't care what he thought of her.

But she did care if he caught a fever and died. She had no faith she could find these Longmires, and she didn't want to have to dig a grave by herself.

"You should at least allow me to look at the wound and perhaps clean it."

"I can clean it if you help me with this coat."

That was fine with her. She'd given her mother any number of baths with warm water and a cloth, but she did not think doing so for Brook would be quite the same thing.

"Very well. I'll help you with the coat and then go to the kitchen to look for a bowl and a pot to heat the water."

Again she saw a flicker in his eyes, which she thought might be surprise. Then he stood, and she moved behind him and tugged on the coat's tightly fitted shoulders. Brook had a broad back, which she knew because she had seen it unclothed, but she hadn't realized quite how broad until she had to undress him. Under her fingertips, his body was warm and solid.

She worried for a moment perhaps he was too warm, but it was only the contrast between her cold, bare fingers and his warmly covered skin.

As she worked, she tried very hard not to notice the way his muscles felt under her fingertips or the scent of bergamot in his hair and clothes. It helped that she did not have to face him. If she'd had to look into his eyes and perform this task, she would have blushed to the roots of her hair.

The coat's damp wool felt heavy and intractable, but she finally managed to coax it off one arm and then the other. He only hissed in one breath, when she jerked a bit too hard and must have wrenched his injured side.

Finally, she laid the coat on the table, though she thought it was probably beyond salvaging. The entire right side was stiff with dried blood. The rust-colored stain on his waistcoat looked rather gruesome, but at least it was old blood and not fresh.

He'd managed to unbutton the waistcoat but he struggled to remove it and not flex the wound. Lila slid one side off and then the other. Next came the cravat, limp and damp, which he tossed on the floor. She could see the back of his neck now, bronze and smooth, but dotted with fine, blond hair that darkened as it grew thicker at the trim line.

Had the fire finally warmed the room? She suddenly felt rather flushed.

"I'll just go to the kitchen for that bowl." She backed away.

"If you'll wait one more moment." He turned slightly, and she noted he had the buttons at the throat of the linen shirt open and was working on the fasten-ings at his cuffs. "I'm not sure I can draw this over my head."

Lila blew out a breath. This was exactly what she'd been wanting to avoid—the sight of his bare chest. And now it seemed she would have a close and personal view.

She watched him struggle for a moment to lift his hands and tug the shirt over his head, but when he winced, she stepped forward. There was nothing at all interesting about removing a shirt, she told herself. It was the act of a nursemaid. That was all.

She squared herself with him, careful not to look him directly in the eye, and rose on tiptoe, reaching for the open neck to try and pull it for him. He had to bend his head, and the shirt caught, and when he bent to help her, he grunted in pain.

"Try it from the hem," he said, straightening slowly.

Lila's gaze lowered. The shirt's hem was still tucked neatly into his breeches. She had not really wanted to put her hands anywhere too close to the lower half of him—or the upper half, for that matter—but it seemed that couldn't be avoided now.

If it couldn't be avoided, she might as well do it quickly. Lila cleared her throat and reached for his waist, hesitated, closed her hands, and grasped the fabric just above the waistband. She tugged it out, keeping her gaze firmly on a point somewhere in the middle of his rib cage. That seemed a very innocuous spot. When she had the shirt free, she slipped her hands under and carefully raised the material to reveal the bronze skin she remembered quite well.

As her hands slid higher, she inadvertently brushed his uninjured left flank, and the accompanying jolt caused both of them to jump. Lila accidentally dropped the shirt's material, and if she hadn't been a lady, she would have sworn.

Now she'd have to begin again.

"I'm terribly sorry," she murmured.

"It's fine." His voice was tight and sharp. He was almost certainly wishing this were over as much as she.

She began again, and this time when she touched him, she gritted her teeth and continued onward. She had to raise her gaze higher and higher to avoid seeing the bare flesh, until finally she stared at his shirt-covered head. Unfortunately, when she finally had it off him, she was staring into his eyes. They were dark brown as it was, but now they looked even larger and darker. The fire had finally ceased smoking quite as much, and the light reflected red and orange on his skin.

He had lovely skin, not at all pale and pasty as she might have expected with his coloring. She supposed it was because he spent so much time outdoors. Her gaze lowered to his taut chest. He certainly did not spend his days idly.

Her gaze caught on the crimson splash of blood, and she couldn't resist stepping back to assess the wound. As he'd said, it was not serious. It didn't appear deep, but it was long and had bled quite freely. She was relieved to see it didn't look infected, though as for that, she had no real gauge with which to measure.

Brook shifted slightly, and she realized she'd been staring at his chest—his wound, she corrected—for several moments. Lila straightened quickly and moved back.

"I'll just go to the kitchen."

He said something in return, but she was already out the door, the cold mist cooling her heated face.

Nine

As soon as she was out the door, Brook pressed his palms to the table and took several deep breaths. He didn't know which throbbed more—the wound or his raging erection. How was he supposed to remain unaffected when Lila undressed him? He knew she hadn't intended to trail her fingers up his chest as she removed his shirt, but even the innocent touch had made his flesh harden with need.

He must control his reaction to her. After he'd kissed her, she'd made it quite clear she didn't welcome his advances. Even had she welcomed them, he didn't want her. Therein lay the solution. He needed to remind himself what a cold bitch she really was. Yes, she needed him now, but she was still spoiled and haughty as ever.

Remembering the night he'd proposed to her was certain to cool his ardor. It seemed he'd been a different man then, young and foolishly optimistic and hopelessly in love.

If nothing else, he remembered how infatuated he'd been. The week he'd decided to ask her to be his wife, he'd strolled about London with an idiotic grin on his face. He'd thought of nothing but her—imagined their children, their wedding, growing old together.

And bedding her.

Even then he wasn't so innocent that he hadn't thought of that aspect of marriage. He'd wanted her in his bed, though he would hardly have known what to do with her when he had her there.

He'd know what to do now. Of course, the irony was that he didn't want her now. His body wanted her, but that was the normal reaction of any man to a woman undressing him. Brook knew what really lay beneath her lovely exterior, and he wanted nothing to do with it. He'd been a fool once. He could blame it on youth, but he wasn't a boy now. He wouldn't make that mistake again.

When she finally returned with a bowl and a pot, he had his body under control. It wasn't very gentle-manly, but he'd laid out the bread and cheese and eaten a fair share of it. Hunger only made the feeling of light-headedness worse. He saw her gaze flick to the food on the table, but she didn't remark on his less-than-chivalrous act.

"Where is the well? I'll fetch water to heat."

He could hardly imagine her fetching water in the silky dress she wore. Wrinkled and dirty now, it was still far more appropriate for a drawing room than any sort of useful activity. Then again, he wouldn't have believed he'd ever see her hunching before a hearth with flint and steel.

He rather liked the idea of her doing something useful for a change. At the same time, it went against everything he'd ever been taught. "I should do that."

"You can't," she snapped. "Where is it?"

"To the left of the kitchen," he answered and watched her go back into the rain and cold. Finally she returned, lugging a bucket of water. Brook wondered what her tittering friends would think of her if they could see her now. She poured water into the pot, then dragged it near the fire to warm. There was probably some sort of rack in the kitchen with hooks for that sort of thing, but he wasn't so much an arse as to suggest she make another trek outside to search for it.

Finally, she rose and, with hands on hips, looked about the room. She seemed to spot what she wanted and headed for a small cupboard near the bed where Hunt had placed the clean linens he'd brought from London. He couldn't help but watch her. She moved as efficiently as any housekeeper he'd ever seen, only she was far lovelier, even with soot on her chin and leaves clinging to her hem.

She opened the cupboard and withdrew a stack of linens. She cocked her head and studied the mattresses as though they were a complicated mathematical equation. Then she went to work making up the bed. It was a far cry from perfect, but it would do.

Then she went to the mantel and took down a flask Brook hadn't noticed before.

He'd been too busy watching her.

"Hunt says we should pour this on the wound." She set the flask and a small towel in front of him.

"That will hurt."

"It will, won't it?" She took the bowl, bringing it

to the heated pot to collect warm water. Brook would have preferred to clean the blood with water and leave the rest alone, but he also knew the dangers of infection. Better that he suffered the sharp sting of the whisky now than die of fever in a few days.

Gritting his teeth, he pulled the cap off the flask. Brook braced one hand on the table and allowed a small measure of whisky to trickle over the wound. The burn slammed into him, crumpling his knees. He dug his fingers into the table. "God's teeth that hurts."

"It does look painful," Lila said in that ennui-filled voice. If she found all this so tedious, he would be happy to make it more interesting. She just needed to step a little closer so he could wrap his fingers around her skinny neck.

"You'd better douse it again," she said.

He glared at her from between slitted eyes.

"You don't want it to become infected."

"Stubble it."

Her brows rose in surprise. He doubted anyone had said that to her before. She'd hear a lot more than that if she insisted on being *helpful*. Before he could think too much, he doused the wound again, this time biting back what threatened to be a rather womanish scream. In his experience, it was always the shallow cuts that hurt like the devil.

He slammed the flask on the table and gripped it with both hands, head down and breathing fast. From the corner of his gray vision, he saw her lift the flask and cap it, then reach for the rag and water.

"Do sit down before you fall."

He sat, feeling the chair creak under his weight.

When he opened his eyes again, Lila knelt beside him. She dipped the towel in the water and dragged it lightly over the blood on his side. She avoided the wound, cleaning above and below it. When the water had turned red, she threw it out and fetched more. Then she proceeded to wipe the rest of the blood away.

Her touch was light but confident. She had not lied when she'd said she'd done this before. The question was why she had tended her mother when a servant or a nurse could have done it. Perhaps she'd loved her mother. Surely even a cold-hearted woman like Lila had to love someone.

"I need to..." When she trailed off, he glanced down. Her fingers hesitated at his waistband. Some of the blood had seeped into the top of the breeches and onto his hip.

"Go ahead."

She hesitated, seeming unsure what to do. Finally, she pushed the material down, exposing his waist. Apparently, that didn't uncover all of the blood because she tugged the breeches farther down until his hip bone was bared.

"Would it be easier if I took them off?"

"No!"

He'd only been half-joking, but her horrified tone made him smile even amidst the pain. Now he wanted to discard the breeches just to shock her.

Carefully, she wiped the rest of the blood away. The sting in his side subsided enough that he could focus on her kneeling in front of him. He must be a cruel, vindictive man because he rather liked seeing her kneeling before him.

"If we rip your shirt into strips, we can use it as bandages. I don't think you'll be able to wear it again at any rate."

"Fine." He reached for it.

"You do have another?"

He barely stifled a smile. Perhaps his bare chest affected her more than he'd realized. "If Hunt has done his job, I do."

He ripped the clean portions of the shirt into several shorter strips and one longer strip to tie about his middle and keep the others in place. She watched him, biting her lip. When he finished, she shook her head and quickly looked away, a flush rising on her cheeks. He would have paid ten pounds to know what she'd been thinking at that moment.

Was it possible the high and mighty Lady Lillian-Anne, daughter of the Duke of Lennox, was attracted to lowly Brook Derring? Not *Lord* Derring, mind you. Only Sir Derring.

How mortifying.

"I hate to say this," she began, not sounding at all like she hated to say whatever it was she would, "but I think you must treat the wound one more time."

"It's clean. Just bandage it." He held the strips of what had been his linen shirt out to her.

"Excuse me, but I have a better viewpoint than you. It needs one more cleaning."

He glanced down, but damn if she wasn't right. He couldn't see the wound clearly because of where it lay on his flank. His gaze met hers. "You only want to torture me."

She smiled sweetly. "Why would I want to do that? You saved my life."

"Because you hate all of this, and though you realize it's not reasonable, you still blame me for it."

She cocked her head, considering. He noted that though they'd been traveling all night and some of the day, and she'd been doing manual labor around the cottage, her hair was still perfectly coiffed. Except for the smudge of soot on her chin, her face was still perfectly lovely. Her dress had seen better days, but considering his own clothes were in shreds, hers had held up nicely.

"I suppose there's some truth in that. But I resent the implication that I'm the sort of person who enjoys hurting others."

"So you aren't looking forward to applying that whisky to my wound?"

"Oh, I am. Apparently, my kindness does not extend to you."

"It wouldn't." He stood, grasped the table. "Very well. On my count. One—"

The whisky trickled over the wound, bringing fire with it. "Hell's fire, woman! You were supposed to wait until three."

She calmly capped the flask. "Better to do it quickly."

His vision wavered with the waves of red-hot pain. He was dimly aware that she threw the dirty water out and washed her hands in the clean. He sat back down again, the scent of sweet flowers surrounding him as she bandaged him a bit tighter than he would have liked.

Bloody hell, but he would pay her back for this. In spades.

She moved away, and he was thankful for the momentary reprieve. And then she pressed the bottle of wine to his lips and ordered him to drink.

It was good wine, a full red wine that had been aged for several years. He drank a hearty measure and then allowed her to help him to his feet and lead him to the bed.

Under other circumstances, he would have been quite pleased to have an attractive woman take him to her bed. At the moment, all he wanted was sleep. She helped him onto the sheets that smelled sweet and freshly laundered, and covered him with a thick blanket.

Brook thought about telling her thank you. Instead, he closed his eyes and fell into blackness.

He dreamed. It seemed he spent hours in dreams where he chased Beezle, but the arch rogue continued to slip from his fingers. Brook navigated the warrens of Seven Dials almost as well as Gideon—or whatever the hell his name was now. He turned blind corners, entered dark cellars, stumbled through fetid, rat-infested alleys. But Beezle remained always out of reach.

And then he staggered out of the darkness and into the glittering lights of a ball. He wasn't dressed for it in his boots and trousers. He couldn't possibly dance in boots. Had Beezle led him here?

The guests circled the dance floor, where an *L* had been chalked, surrounded by curling vines, wrapping around sword hilts where lions balanced.

The symbols of the Duke of Lennox. He knew this ball. It was the Lennox Ball, the night he'd proposed to Lila.

The dance began, and she was one of the first on the floor, led by some foreign prince or other. Brook knew how this night would turn out, but he couldn't seem to stop his younger self from admiring her. She was impossibly beautiful under the glitter of a thousand candles reflected off the crystal chandeliers. Her white silk gown shimmered with silver embellishments, and silver ribbon threaded through her thick, dark hair. Her pale skin was creamy in the lights, her full lips red.

She was the picture of a perfect lady, except for those lips. They were too sensual. She had either been told this or was aware of it because she quite often kept them pressed together. At the moment, she'd forgotten. His gaze strayed to her figure. The cut of the dress was extremely proper and modest. The daughter of the Duke of Lennox would not dare to possess a body either too thin or too full. She was perfectly proportioned, her movements in the voluminous skirts hinting at just a bit of curve to her hips.

How he'd wanted her.

He forced the dream away from that ball, that night, and then he was in his flat, lying on the bed with the brown velvet coverlet.

"Derring. Sir Brook."

He opened his eyes, and Lila stood before him, her hair down about her waist, wearing only a thin chemise. He reached out, caught the ribbon of the chemise and tugged. The bodice opened, revealing the swells of her breasts, but when it should have fallen off her shoulders, it remained firmly in place, denying him the sight of her body.

He would never have her. Even when she was

lawfully his to take, she would always remain out of reach.

"Brook."

Her voice again. Taunting him. Ever out of reach. Ever prim and aloof.

"Brook, wake up. Someone is here."

He opened his eyes, and he wasn't in the bed in his flat but in the cold cottage. The light streaming through the cracks in the boards covering the windows told him it was mid-morning. Lila stood before him. Her hair was down, but she wore a thick cotton wrapper over what appeared to be an extremely virginal night rail.

He frowned at the ugly white nightgown.

"Brook." This time she touched his forearm, and he knew he wasn't dreaming. Her hand felt cold and small, not at all like he would have imagined it in a dream. "I heard a horse and cart. I haven't opened the door to see who it is, but someone is outside."

He sat with no small amount of effort. Every muscle in his back and legs hurt, and his side sent throbbing waves of heat through him. But he winced and bore it until both feet touched the floor.

"It isn't Beezle," he said. "He wouldn't come with a cart."

"Then who is it?"

"Let's find out." He stood, wobbled, gained his footing.

"Brook! You can't open the door without clothing."

He looked down. He still wore his ruined breeches, but he was bare chested. He grabbed a thin blanket, wrapped it around his shoulders, then went to his valise and reached for his pistol. He took a moment to prime it, add powder and ball, then tucked it under the blanket so it would not be visible.

And then he opened the door.

An older woman sat with the horse's reins in her lap. Her eyes widened at the sight of him, wrapped only in a blanket. Her gaze drifted over what could be seen of his bare shoulders and the top of his chest, then down to his bare calves and feet. He felt Lila's warmth behind him and could imagine how that must look.

He could use appearances to his advantage.

"I'm so sorry to disturb you, Lord Dane."

Brook shook his head. "I'm not Dane. I'm his brother."

"Sir Brook." The woman nodded her head, dipping her dun-colored bonnet. The rain had ceased, but there was still a chill in the air, and she'd wrapped a tattered shawl about her shoulders. "I'm certain you don't remember me. I'm Mrs. Spencer. Mr. Spencer"—she glanced heavenward—"God rest his soul, and I live just down the road."

The Longmires were the closest farm to the cottage, which meant *just down the road* measured at least two or three miles.

"You must forgive me for not inviting you inside, Mrs. Spencer. We just arrived, and I'm afraid we are still settling in."

"Did you come to hunt?" Her gaze flicked to Lila, still standing behind him. She didn't believe for a moment he came to hunt. No one had hunted here since his late father, and that had been many, many years ago. The hunting lodge had been demolished and this gamekeeper's cottage all that remained from that time.

"No. Lady Derring and I are here on our honeymoon."

Mrs. Spencer's eyes widened. "Oh, how wonderful!"

Her explanation drowned out Lila's protest. "I am Lady Lillian-Anne."

Brook grabbed her by the shoulders and hauled her beside him. "Not a word," he muttered.

She elbowed him in the side—his injured side—which hurt like the devil, but he managed to keep his smile in place.

"Let me be the first from the town to wish you happy. In fact"—she lifted a basket that had been sitting at her feet—"I brought you some of my famous sponge cake as well as bread and soup."

"Thank you. This is quite unexpected."

"Mr. Spencer—God rest his soul—and I were, er, *are* fond of the Derring family. The best landlords, that's what Mr. Spencer—God rest his soul—always said."

"And how long has Mr. Spencer been gone?" Brook asked.

"Oh, about ten years now. We were lucky to have three strong sons who farm the land for us. Your mother, the countess, sent a lovely note of condolence. Would you like to read it?" She reached for her reticule. Obviously, she carried the note with her at all times.

"Perhaps later. Lady Derring and I should dress. If you will give me a moment to pull on my boots, I'll fetch the basket." Brook hastened Lila inside and closed the door slightly. He could see Mrs. Spencer peering inside from her perch on the cart's box.

He spotted his boots and crossed to them. "Stay inside," he ordered Lila.

"I'm happy to, but I am not Lady Derring."

He swung around. "The hell you're not."

She flung her arm out emphatically. "I'm the daughter of a duke, and my title——"

Brook grasped her wrist and yanked her close. He did not want either of their voices to carry. "I don't bloody care who the devil your father is, but you can wager your life the local farmers will. And if you give them something to talk about, the news might carry to London on the next market day. Right now, the last thing we need is Beezle knowing where we're hiding." His gaze cut to the crack in the door and Mrs. Spencer's craning her neck to peek inside. "Understand, *Lady Derring*?"

"Yes," Lila hissed.

"Good. One more item for Mrs. Spencer's benefit." He cupped the back of her neck and brought his lips to hers. Lila flinched and stiffened, but he held her firmly, wrapping his other arm about her waist and murmuring against her lips, "Play your part, Lady Derring."

She glared at him but put her arms around his neck, at least giving the impression of returning his embrace. He brushed his lips over hers, which certainly would have been enough to convince Mrs. Spencer, if she had doubts, but it wasn't quite enough for Brook.

Even though she wore a wrapper and nightgown, the material was thin and didn't conceal her lack of undergarments. She'd taken her stays off to sleep, and he felt the hard points of her nipples through the fabric. The sensation teased the bare skin of his chest, causing him to pull her closer.

He had no illusions that he'd aroused her. She was most likely cold, but whatever the reason, he couldn't help but want to feel her body pressed against his. The thin barrier of cotton was the best he could hope for.

Her lips parted slightly from the surprise contact, and he took advantage of the motion to kiss her lower lip and then to run his tongue lightly along her upper. Soft, plump lips that begged to be suckled, nibbled, kissed until swollen.

Lila's fingers dug into his shoulders, making him remember their audience. He gave her a playful flick of his tongue and slowly withdrew.

His mistake was glancing at her face. He'd thought she'd tightened her hands to compel him to release her, but her pink cheeks and dark eyes told him he'd misjudged.

She wanted him.

He would have lifted her and carried her straight to the bed had their audience not been watching. Instead, he stepped away, pulled on his boots, and dug in his valise for a clean shirt. When he was thus attired, he left Lila in the cottage and collected the basket.

Mrs. Spencer did not meet his eye, keeping her gaze on the sky. He thanked her and returned inside, leaving the basket on the table. Lila did not look at him, pretending to be busy stoking the fire. It was a hopeless cause. They needed more wood. The knife wound still hurt, but he felt better for the sleep and the healing that had come with that time. He'd check it later, but the bandages didn't show fresh blood, and he had no fever.

After he ate, he'd fetch wood and take a look around the cottage and kitchens. He told Lila this and she thanked him. Strange how often she thanked him, as though she actually appreciated his assistance and didn't expect it.

But he knew her kind, knew she'd grown up to expect others to jump to do her bidding. The minute he thought she'd changed was the minute he became the poor, besotted boy he'd been the night he'd proposed to her.

As there was only one chair, he used it and ate first, dividing all the food in half so she would have her own share. She could eat while he took care of seeing to firewood, fresh water, and the like. She managed not to glance in his direction once while he ate, a feat of some note considering the smallness of the room they shared. Was she angry at his insistence she call herself Lady Derring?

To hell with that. She *was* Lady Derring until he had the marriage annulled. She could hold on to her title all she wanted, but he'd call her Lady Derring every chance he had. It wouldn't hurt to bring her down a peg or three.

Or perhaps she was embarrassed by the kiss they'd shared. Undoubtedly, she hadn't meant to respond to him as she had. Perhaps she didn't hate him as much as she pretended.

He couldn't quite rid himself of that notion, and for the next several hours, it played in his mind as he hauled water, lay firewood out to dry in the sun, built a new fire, attempted to make the kitchen serviceable, and surveyed the property. It had been some time since he'd been there, and he wanted to know the lay of the land if he needed to leave quickly.

And all the while, he wondered what Lila would do if he kissed her again. For about an hour he told himself he didn't want to kiss her again, but even he couldn't convince himself of that lie. He did want to kiss her. He wanted her in his bed. He might not like her, but that didn't mean he wouldn't enjoy her.

That thought played in his head as he returned to the cottage and pushed open the back door. The fire still smoked, and Lila had left it partly open to give the smoke an outlet. He stood in the opening of the door, wondering where she'd gone, when he finally spotted a tattered quilt hung before the bed.

She'd meant it as a screen for privacy. He understood that immediately because she'd done a poor job of hanging it. If he'd been standing directly in front of it, he would have seen nothing. But from the side, she was clearly visible. She sat on the bed, one foot poised on the edge, pulling a silk stocking up and over her calf. His first thought was that silk stockings were entirely impractical for their situation. His second was that he'd like to feel the silk of that stocking against her skin and test which was softer.

She stretched her leg out, the skin white and nicely rounded, giving him a view of the inside of one thigh. He drew in a breath, wanting to go to her and slide the hem of her chemise higher so he might reveal all of that thigh and what lay at the apex.

Instead, he stepped back outside and pressed his back against the wall.

He had to grab hold of his desire. He didn't spy on women. He didn't kiss unwilling women. He couldn't control his thoughts or his erotic dreams, but he could control his actions.

Why should you?

The thought came unbidden, but with such clarity, Brook couldn't ignore it. Why shouldn't he have her? She was his wife. She legally belonged to him. This was no sham marriage. They'd said the vows. He'd signed the license, and her father had agreed to the contract terms.

They might plan an annulment, but that would only mean the marriage hadn't happened in the eyes of the law. Everyone else would know it had occurred. He wouldn't ruin her if he took her to his bed. No one would assume he hadn't.

And who was to say she'd be unwilling to kiss him if he attempted it again? He knew what desire looked like, and she might not have wanted to admit it, but she wanted him.

They were stuck there for the time being. Why shouldn't they make the best of the situation?

You want to teach her a lesson.

That was his conscience, and he couldn't argue with it. Yes, he wanted her as a man wants a woman, but he also wanted to punish her for the way she'd humiliated him in the past. What better way than to make her want him and then leave her desires unfulfilled, as she'd done all those years ago?

Could he do it? Hell yes. She was a virgin. What

did she know of the pleasures between men and women? What if he could make her love him, and then, once he had her affections, toss them aside as she'd done to him?

Cruel and callous, this sort of behavior. But hadn't she done the same to him? And he wouldn't force anything on her. He wouldn't make her any promises, wouldn't give her any lies. Her emotions, her body, her affections were her own to give.

Brook considered he'd spent far too much time amidst the morally corrupt if this was the sort of scheme he contemplated.

A better man would act the gentleman and vow not to use his worldly experience to seduce an innocent. A gentleman would not touch a lady he had no intention of honoring—permanently—with his name.

As Brook pushed away from the wall and stepped back into the cottage, he had to admit, he was no gentleman.

Ten

LILA HADN'T BEEN ABLE TO DRESS PROPERLY. SHE HAD no lady's maid to help with her stays, and her dresses didn't fit quite right without them. She couldn't even don one of her gowns without assistance. All of them had fastenings in the back or needed pins, and she couldn't quite place the materials in the appropriate places.

Her peach gown had been the only one she could put on by herself, and now it was past repair. She'd slept in her stays at the flat in London, but she couldn't stand them for another night, especially when she'd had to sleep on a quilt in front of the fire. She was uncomfortable enough on the floor. She didn't need the undergarments making her more so.

She'd spent half the night hating Brook Derring for taking the bed and half worrying he'd grow feverish and die, leaving her all alone. She supposed she might have shared the bed with him, for the sake of warmth if not comfort, but she hadn't been able to swallow her pride and climb in beside him.

She might also have asked him to help her dress.

Once again, her pride prevented it. Not to mention her modesty. She didn't want him ogling her. Although, if the truth be told, she actually thought she might rather enjoy a bit of ogling from him. She hadn't expected to enjoy his kisses or the sight of him half-dressed quite as much as she had. Who was to say she wouldn't have enjoyed more of his attentions?

Of course, she would never know because after he kissed her this morning—all a show for Mrs. Spencer—he hadn't so much as looked her way. It might have been the pelisse she wore over her ill-fitting gown. It might have been that she had not remembered hairpins and could do nothing other than plait her hair so it did not hang in her face.

It might have been that he hated her.

She could hardly blame him. She'd treated him abominably, but would he hold that against her for the rest of her life? She'd been eighteen and foolish.

Now she was five and twenty, and probably just as foolish, if in a different way. She couldn't quite stop herself from watching him under lowered lashes and wondering just when she might have another chance to see him without his shirt.

Not that it would matter if she did see him thus. He'd made it quite clear he didn't like her and could barely stand to be in the same room with her. He'd spent most of the day outside, clearly happy to keep his own company rather than share hers.

Finally, the sun had dipped low, and she laid out the remains of Mrs. Spencer's basket for the evening meal. Only one of them could eat at the table, and he had taken a seat before the fire. She brought him a bowl of broth and a slice of bread, but when she turned to take her own seat at the table, he surprised her.

"Sit with me by the fire."

She could hardly object. The wood had dried and didn't smoke, and the night was cold. The fire was warm and cheery.

She nodded and moved to join him, her heart beating a little faster at the chance to be close to him.

He watched her, his dark eyes cool and assessing. "I thought you'd refuse."

She'd been smoothing her skirts down, but now she looked up quickly. "Why?"

"I didn't think you'd want to sit on the floor."

"Oh." She looked down at it. At one time she might have found the notion appalling. But she'd done far worse, not even counting the tasks she'd performed the past day or so. "I don't mind."

His eyes narrowed. "Not at all?"

She took a bite of bread. "I could be more comfortable, but at least it's warm," she finally said because he seemed to expect a response.

They ate in silence for a few minutes, Lila searching her brain for some topic of conversation. She'd always been witty and garrulous, though never so much as to be considered forward. But now she found she could not think of a single topic of conversation that would not sound completely inane.

Finally, she settled on the weather. "Do you think it will rain tomorrow?" she asked at the same time he said, "I have a proposition for you."

She shifted with astonishment. "Pardon?"

"You asked about rain?"

She nodded but gestured to him to go on. "No, please, you first."

"Ladies first. And to answer your question, I saw rain clouds in the distance tonight. I think we'll see rain tonight into the morning."

"Oh."

"You seem disappointed."

"I had hoped to go for a walk tomorrow. I thought I might look for berries or something else we might eat."

"Berries? In the middle of winter?"

"Oh, I hadn't thought of that. I suppose I want something to do. I've all but finished the book on the Peloponnesian War."

He frowned at her. "Is it that interesting, or are you merely that desperate?"

She smiled. "Both, I suppose."

He gave her a slight smile, and she realized this was the first time they'd had a pleasant conversation in seven years.

"Well, we must eat. If Mrs. Spencer does not come to our rescue again, I will walk to the posting house. It's a couple hours' walk, but if the weather is not too bad by afternoon, I could be back by dinner."

She took another bite of bread. "Thank you."

His head jerked up, startling her.

"Stop thanking me." His brows lowered in anger.

"I'm sorry," she said automatically, confused by his sudden explosion.

He rose abruptly, forcing her to look up at him. "And don't apologize. You won't think me deserving of it when you hear what I have to say."

A tremor of unease rippled through her. The bread tasted stale in her mouth, and she set it down. "You're leaving me."

The look he gave her was one of astonishment. "No."

She sighed in relief.

"You don't want me to leave?" he asked carefully.

"No."

He crossed his arms over his chest. He'd never bothered with a waistcoat or cravat, and he'd removed his coat when he was inside for the night. In the firelight, she could see hints of his skin through the fine lawn.

"Then you enjoy my company."

"I…" He'd been little company the past few days, but she supposed someone was better than no one.

"Might I propose a way for you to enjoy my company more?"

"Of course."

He looked away and into the fire. "You are so innocent."

She had no idea what he meant by that. He didn't seem inclined to enlighten her. "I thought we might look for a deck of cards," she said. "I'm rather good at piquet."

He gave her a cocky smile that had her heart fluttering. She pressed a hand to her belly to quell the butterflies there.

"I don't want to play cards with you. What I propose is rather more…intimate."

"I don't understand."

"No, you don't. I shall have to be clear."

Lila didn't know why this admission should make

her shiver, cause her breath to come short. She had no reason to worry.

Did she?

"What I want, Lila, is to take you to bed."

Her hand went to her throat, and she thought for a moment she'd misunderstood. And then his gaze traveled lightly over her body—what little she imagined he could see of it—and she knew she had understood perfectly.

"Sir—"

"Don't call me sir, and don't go missish and formal."

She rose, hastily pulling her pelisse closed protectively. "I don't know how else to respond to such a...a..."

"Request?" he supplied. "This isn't rape I suggest. You may say no."

"N—"

He held up a hand. "Hear me out first."

"There's nothing to hear, not if you are proposing what I think you are."

He moved toward her, like a predator stalking his prey. "Oh, I am proposing exactly what you think. More than you imagine, I'm sure."

"I don't want to hear this." She turned, but he grasped her arm and turned her gently back. Only a finger or two touched her flesh. Most of his hand caught her pelisse, but that feel of skin on skin made her crave more.

She knew if he did not withdraw the request, she would not say no.

"First of all, I would point out we are married. What I propose is not immoral. It's not fornication."

She felt heat rise in her cheeks. This sort of conversation would never have been remotely appropriate just a few days ago. Except, of course, now she was married. He had a point there. He was allowed to talk thus to her, and she didn't have to blush like a virgin.

Only, she *was* a virgin!

His hand slid down her arm to capture her wrist lightly. She inhaled sharply but didn't pull her hand away. "No rejoinder?"

"I…"

But his thumb began to move in slow circles on her wrist, and she forgot what she had wanted to say.

"Very well, here's what you should point out. We don't intend to stay married."

His thumb continued its gentle circles, and heat spread from her wrist up her arm. "Are you arguing against your own point?"

"I'm no rake trying to take advantage of you."

She looked down at his hand, where his thumb had moved to her palm and now stroked the sensitive flesh lightly.

He gave her a cocky grin. "I'm not a rake. I didn't say I was a saint."

His thumb made a tiny circle in the center of her palm, and the light touch both tickled and aroused. Lila attempted to gather her thoughts. "As to your point"—the circle widened, and her entire body tightened—"your point…"

"The annulment."

"Right."

His thumb moved to her fingers, stroking each.

"I cannot argue your point because annulment or no, everyone will assume I—you—we—"

"That I deflowered you?"

"Oh, how I detest that phrase."

He lifted her fingers to his lips and kissed the pads one by one. Lila felt the room spin.

"No, you are no fragile flower. I won't pluck you unless you want to be plucked."

"Good Lord that's an awful metaphor."

He grinned. "It is, isn't it? But you understand my meaning."

She couldn't quite tear her gaze from his lips as he kissed another of her fingers, the tip of his tongue reaching out to flick the end. The room felt quite warm now, far warmer than simply the heat of the fire in the hearth. And her heart pounded in her chest, her body tense and seemingly poised to flee or... What was the alternative? Surrender?

"Another point you might argue," he said, "is that our actions might produce a child."

She closed her fingers before he could continue to kiss them. "You really have thought about this."

"Of course. I'm not an impulsive man."

No, she could see that now. And why did that make him so much more dangerous?

"There are ways to prevent children, of course."

Her eyes widened. "How?"

"I won't bore you with details."

Lila huffed. Surely he would know the subject was far from tedious to her. Everything he said surprised and fascinated her. She had almost forgotten to be appalled.

"Suffice it to say, I don't have the means with me. We may still enjoy each other without risking conception, but I know I'll want more." His eyes darkened, something she had not thought possible. "I will leave the decision with you, but if you decide to risk it and there is a child, know that I will accept him or her as mine."

"And when we part, the child will be yours. You could cut me out of his or her life," she said.

"True. Another point to consider."

"Then it would seem the honorable thing to do is to refrain from activities that would produce a child."

"That's your choice," he said. "But I will take you to bed, Lila. It might not be tonight, but it will be soon."

She finally tugged her hand out of his grasp. "What makes you so certain? You won't force me, and you've given me ample reason to refuse."

"I give you reasons to refuse because I don't cheat. When I win, I win fairly."

"Then I suppose you've lost." She crossed her arms over her pelisse.

"Oh, I don't think so. I haven't played my final card."

She ignored the flutter of anticipation in her belly. "What's that?"

"I'll have you because you want me."

Lila blew out a breath of indignation. "No, I don't!"

He gave her a disappointed frown. "I was honest with you. Am I not to receive the same courtesy?"

"But I am being honest. I don't love you."

He held up a hand. "Love and desire are two very different things. I don't love you, but I desire you. Perhaps you aren't certain what you feel for me. Perhaps there hasn't been enough desire in your life for you to be able to pinpoint the emotion." He'd moved toward her again, and she backed up until she was against the table and could move no farther.

"Or perhaps I just don't feel desire for you."

"I've seen it in your eyes after I kiss you. You want more."

She shook her head, but she knew she lied. She did want more of his kisses, more of his caresses. And what sort of woman did that make her when he pointedly told her he didn't love her? Lila didn't love him either, but she knew she was perilously close to the edge of that dangerous emotion. He was a difficult man *not* to love. He'd saved her numerous times, risked his life for her, and sacrificed for her. Not to mention, he was all the things he claimed—honest, thoughtful, honorable.

And she very much liked the look of him without his shirt.

If she allowed him into her bed—well, *his* bed— how could she stop herself from falling in love with him? And Lila knew he would never, never fall in love with her. He still hated her for what had happened between them in the past.

"I think this is a bad idea. Not because I don't want you." She held up a hand, placing it between them. "But because I do."

"Why not give in to that desire?" he asked, taking her hand in his warm one. "You are a woman with needs and desires like any woman. Why not indulge them?"

His dark eyes locked on hers, and he released her hand and ran his fingers up to her shoulders and over to the ties of her pelisse.

"Because..."

He flicked the ties and the garment opened.

"Because you might enjoy what I do to you?"

He pushed the pelisse off her shoulders, his gaze dipping down to the front of her gown. Could he see she wore no stays? Her hard nipples chafed against her chemise.

Because she might never want him to stop.

"You can retain your misplaced virtue, but it's for no one's value but your own." His hands skimmed over her bare collarbone. "In the eyes of the world, your virtue is long gone. You've lost it without the pleasure."

His fingers on her skin were so warm, so light. His touched persuaded her, never demanded.

"And you're so certain you can give me pleasure."

His fingers halted. "I've never been more certain of anything."

"Care to wager on that?"

What was she doing? This was madness. She did not want to further involve her emotions! On the other hand, what was more impersonal than a wager? She'd always enjoyed gambling, but she never felt elation at her wins or devastation at her losses. Why should this be any different? It was a game, nothing more. If she thought of it as nothing more than a game, her heart would be safe.

Either that or his touch had so affected her, she was willing to create any excuse to give in. She rather feared this was the case but refused to dwell on the possibility.

"Would I wager that I can give you pleasure? Name the stakes and terms."

"It's for me to define pleasure."

"A given, as long as you are honest."

"You may not do anything that will produce a child."

"Accepted. What else?"

Should she be blushing? She rather thought she should be. But she was too excited to blush, too feverish with eagerness.

"You will stop if I ask."

He frowned at her. "That goes without saying, but you won't ask me to stop."

Her breath hitched. "If I do—"

"I will cease immediately."

She bit her lip, trying to think of more terms. Brook stood patiently, seeming content to wait her out. "You will never mention this wager to anyone," she said, thinking of the infamous betting books at White's club.

"Madam, do not insult me."

"Fine. That's all I can think of." She took a shaky breath. "What now?"

But he didn't pounce on her as she expected. "What sort of wager has only terms and no stakes?"

That was right. She had to set the stakes.

"If I win…" What did she want? More than she wanted Brook to kiss her again. More than she wanted to be safe from this Beezle. Security. Safety. A life where she would not be sent from one relative to another like an ugly family heirloom. "If I win, there's no annulment."

For the first time since she had met him again, his face registered genuine shock. His mouth opened slightly, and he leaned away from her.

The fire crackled in the long silence. Lila had

ample time to reconsider what she'd said. She could withdraw the words. But she wouldn't. She hadn't even known this was what she wanted, not until the words had come out of her mouth. But now that she'd said them, she knew she wanted it more than anything else she had ever wanted, save for her mother to live.

"I'm not certain I understand," Brook finally said, his words slow and deliberate.

"You understand."

"Indulge me. If I am unable to give you pleasure, you want to *remain* married to me?"

"Yes."

He ran a hand through his hair, clearly puzzled. "I am not one of those men who think women mysterious creatures, but I will admit you have me mystified."

"Do you need to understand them to agree?"

"No." He gave her his attention again, and the feeling was heady. When Brook focused on her, she felt it in every fiber of her being. "I agree. If I fail to pleasure you—by your honest admission—then I will not pursue annulment."

"Very good. Then those are the stakes." She glanced at the bed, wondering if she should go to it or if he would lead her there. How long would this take? How long until she would be safe from this ruinous annulment?

His finger caught her chin and dragged her gaze back to him. "Those are only half the stakes, my lady. There's the question of what prize I receive if I win."

She jerked her chin away. "I should think that

is obvious. If you win, you are free to rid yourself of me."

"I'm free to do that without agreeing to the wager. What do I receive if I do agree?"

"And win."

He inclined his head, ever the gentleman although they were wagering over bedsport.

Lila hadn't considered this aspect of the agreement. She had no idea what to grant him. "What do you want?"

"This is your wager. You set the terms and the stakes. I won't have you agree to something you can't stomach."

Frustrated, she paced away from him. "This would be easier if you didn't act so much the gentleman."

He laughed, and she whipped around at the sound. "Don't worry, *wife*, I won't play the gentleman much longer."

Lila shivered. He meant he wouldn't behave like a gentleman when he took her to bed. The thought terrified and excited her equally.

"But I always honor my bets." He took a seat in the chair. "Take your time, if you like. We have all night."

She didn't want to take her time. She wanted this over and done. She couldn't stand the anticipation of what he might or might not do to her. Couldn't stand having him look at her with that knowing look. She wanted to know too.

And yes, if she was being honest, she wanted him to kiss her again.

"I don't need more time. If you win, I will…" She

had no idea what she had that she could give him. He didn't want money. He didn't seem to care for status or power. The only thing he seemed to want was her. "I will do whatever you want."

His brows rose. "Would you like to qualify that?"

Lord, he really did not cheat. She had left herself vulnerable, and he wouldn't even take advantage of that. How would she not fall in love with him?

"Yes. I will do whatever you want within reason."

"Too vague."

"Are you a barrister?"

He laughed. "No, but I know far too many of them. Might I make a suggestion, which you are free to take or reject or modify?"

"Of course."

"You might agree to do whatever I want for one night."

Oh, but that sounded incredibly wicked. She hadn't considered that he might want a carnal favor from her. She had meant he might ask her to collect wood or heat water. He wanted none of those things, of course. He wanted her.

"One night is a long time," she said, trying not to imagine his naked chest on the bed beneath her.

"Time is relative, but now you are thinking along the correct lines."

She considered for several moments, choosing and discarding several wicked, wicked—in her opinion, at least—options. Finally, she decided it did not matter. She did not intend to lose.

"I will grant you one request."

"Any request?"

She sensed danger, but he was a gentleman. He would not take advantage of her. "Yes. One request. Anything you ask."

"Very well." He rose. "I give you my word that I shall adhere to the conditions set forth."

"I also agree. Is that all then? Do we sign papers or shake hands?"

"A gentleman's word is his bond, but if you prefer to see this in writing—"

How mortifying! "No. That is not necessary. I trust you."

"Good. You'll need to trust me."

"I will?"

"Absolutely. Because now is when I stop acting the gentleman."

"Oh."

Nothing overt about him changed. His face didn't turn demonic. He didn't sprout horns or a forked tail. Instead, he walked to the bed and sat, calmly removing his boots. Then he looked up at her, his eyes dark with what even she recognized as desire.

"Lila, take off your clothes."

Eleven

If her startled gasp and choked "I beg your pardon" were any indication, he'd shocked her. If all went as planned, he'd shock her further before the night was over.

"Come here, Lila."

"Why?" she asked, eyes wary.

If he told her plainly, she'd probably recommence negotiations. He had no doubt she'd fulfill her end of the bargain, but she liked everything on her terms.

"So we might have a conversation without yelling across the room." The room was far too small for any yelling to be necessary, but Lila seemed to accept this response. She crossed to him, standing primly before him.

Brook was surprised at how much he liked her primness. It made him want to strip it away, layer by layer, like he might a high-necked dress. He'd never tangled with an innocent before, but he didn't feel particularly guilty. He hadn't deceived her or been dishonest. She'd agreed to the arrangement and even set the terms. His motives weren't particularly honorable, but he would honor the terms of the agreement. If she conceived a child, he would care for it. If she didn't experience pleasure, he would not petition for an annulment.

And wasn't that an interesting request? Why would she want to stay married to him, especially when she had made it quite clear the first time he'd proposed marriage she wouldn't marry him even if he were the last man on earth.

Had her feelings toward him changed? More likely she worried what the *ton* would say about an annulment.

Brook took her hand in his, a small gesture that caused her to pull back from him. Her ice-cold hand tensed in his.

"You're cold."

"I'm actually quite warm, thank you. I will leave my clothing on."

"If you wish."

He'd have her undressed before the night was through, but he wouldn't force the issue. She'd want him to take her dress off.

He moved to the side, making room for her on the bed. "Sit beside me."

"I would prefer to stand."

"Very well." He brought her hand to his lips and kissed her knuckles. "I won't hurt you, you know. If you don't enjoy something, you may ask me to stop."

"I do wish you'd stop talking so much. The more you talk, the more nervous I feel. Just do whatever it is you want to do already."

He opened her hand and kissed the inside of her palm, feeling her shiver. "So you're a romantic, I take it."

She laughed, and her hand relaxed slightly. He brushed his lips over the tender skin of the heel of her hand, tracing a path to her wrist.

"I suppose I don't know much about romance. I know it stems from love. You don't love me, and I...I don't love you."

He raised his gaze to her face, interested in her hesitation. Why had she stumbled over that admission? Did she hate him more than he thought or like him more than she wished?

He pressed his lips to her wrist, feeling the rapid tap of her pulse.

"I do wish you would stop that," she said.

"Stop what?" he asked, darting his tongue out to taste her skin. It tasted like smoke from the hearth and something unique that could only be her. "Be specific."

"Stop doing that with your mouth."

Brook pulled back. "You don't enjoy it?"

"I...it makes me feel...uncomfortable."

"Warm?" He ran his hands up her arms.

"Yes."

"Short of breath?" He stood and ran his hands down her back to rest on her waist. She had a small waist. He ached to move his fingers lower and explore the curve of her hips. All in time.

"Yes, exactly." She tilted her head to look up at him.

"Like you want something but aren't quite sure what?"

She nodded.

Brook bent and placed his mouth beside her ear. She tried to pull away, but he held her in place. He allowed his breath to tease her skin, felt her shiver.

"I know what you want," he whispered in her ear. He kissed the tender skin of her jaw just below her earlobe.

She exhaled softly and swayed toward him.

"I know the name for what you feel." He kissed her earlobe.

"What is that?" Her voice was breathless, and he didn't think she realized her hands had come up to clutch his chest.

"Arousal." He allowed his lips to trail over the curve of her jaw, moving one hand from her waist to the small of her back. Gently, he pulled her body against his, then touched his lips to hers.

The kiss was chaste and light, a kiss designed to calm her. She'd been kissed like this before. If he had to guess, he would have said half a dozen men had stolen a kiss like this from her on a moonlit terrace or behind a potted plant at a ball. He'd kissed her like this once upon a time.

He pressed light kisses over her lips until she relaxed against him. She didn't fear this. Neither did it fire her blood, but that would come soon enough. Brook allowed his lips to linger a little longer, press more firmly. She responded tentatively, her own lips moving against his.

She was comfortable, and that had to change.

He pulled back slightly. Her eyes were closed, her face tilted up to his. Deliberately, he lowered his mouth to hers and traced the seam of her lips with his tongue. Her eyes snapped open.

"What are you doing?"

"Kissing you."

"With your tongue?"

He raised a brow. "You've never been kissed like that before?"

"I…"

"It's very French, quite fashionable these days."

"Oh."

Brook almost smiled. Trust Lila to want to be in fashion, whether that meant her clothing or the way she kissed.

"May I continue?" he asked. "You haven't told me to stop."

Her lips pursed, but she nodded. "I suppose."

He began again, not because he felt the need to proceed in a particular order but because she would not be expecting it. As he predicted, when he repeated the light, familiar kisses, she relaxed again. She even leaned into him, her body asking for what her mind did not even know she wanted.

He traced her lips with the tip of his tongue, nudging them open until they softened and parted. He kissed her more deeply and with more passion until her hands fisted on the lawn of his shirt.

He tasted her, his tongue dipping just inside her lips to sample what she offered. Her body stiffened again, then relaxed when he kept his attentions light and controlled. Brook hadn't expected to struggle with his control, but the taste of her aroused him more than he'd expected. She tasted of the wine they'd drunk and the bread they'd feasted on, but beneath that was the taste of her—of Lila.

He hadn't expected the sensuality or the richness of her. Those full lips teased him, inviting him to take more when he knew she would balk if he moved too quickly. But he wanted more. He wanted all of her. Desperately.

And when she touched the tip of her tongue to his, a quick tentative taste, he almost lost all control. He broke the kiss and rested his forehead on hers, catching his breath. His erection strained at the fall of his trousers, his blood thundering in his ears and his body begging for release.

"Have I done something wrong?" she asked when he didn't resume kissing her.

They stood locked in an embrace, their heads touching, his lips only a few inches from hers.

"No. You're perfect," he said and meant it.

"But when I kissed you in the French style, did I do it wrong?"

He smiled, even as thunder rumbled in the distance. Oh, if she were intent of playing the student, he could definitely play the instructor.

"You did it exactly right. You aroused me, and I had to pause to gain control."

She nudged her head up, looking into his eyes. "Why? I thought you…that we…"

"Tonight is for you, Lila," he said. "For your pleasure. Not mine."

"You don't want anything?"

He kissed her lips again because he couldn't resist. "I want everything, but I'm in no hurry. And besides, there's a wager to win."

She turned her head. "Wouldn't want to be saddled with me for life."

He made no answer. He did not intend to lose the

wager or to stay married to her, but she had set the terms of the bet.

"I hate to disappoint you, sir, but you will lose. I will admit kissing you is quite nice, but then again, so is a playing a piano sonata or chatting over embroidery with friends."

Brook laughed. "I must say, my lovemaking has never been compared to embroidery before."

"I enjoy embroidery."

"I'm sure you do," Brook said. "In the morning, I'll ask again how the two compare."

This time he gave her no prelude, no gentle, soft kisses. Instead, he took her mouth hard and possessively. She might have protested had he allowed it, but he kissed her deeply, kissed her until her legs gave way and she moaned. He lowered her onto the bed, positioning his knees on either side of her thighs. His hand cupped the back of her head, his fingers tangled in the silky mass of her dark hair, his mouth tasting that erotic mix of wine and Lila.

And when he was breathless and feverish with want, she wrapped her hands around his neck and kissed him back. She proved a cunning pupil, her mouth and lips taking his as completely as he'd taken hers. What she lacked in skill and finesse, she made up for in passion.

Brook was hard-pressed not to toss her skirts and take her hard and fast.

He'd lose the wager, of course, but at this point he hardly cared.

He pulled away, dipped his mouth to taste the skin of her neck, the hollow beneath her jaw. She smelled sweet and tempting, the scent of lily of the valley clinging to her skin. He flicked a tongue out, tasting her, ratcheting up his need, although he'd resolved not to succumb to it. She arched at his attentions, but he ignored her upthrust breasts. He would have liked to bare them, kiss them, taste the hard points he could see through the thin layers she wore. Instead, he linked his fingers with hers and pressed her hands to the pillow beside her head.

He kissed her again, suckling her full lips, her tongue, giving and taking until her fingers tightened on his and he knew she wanted more. Brook shifted and nudged her legs apart, fitting one of his between them. He kissed his way down to her collarbone and over the swells of her breasts. He might have removed the dress easily and kissed her bare flesh if he'd thought she'd allow him to undress her. Brook didn't want to give her that much time to think.

Instead, he moved his lips over the silk of her bodice, learning the shape of her breasts with his mouth. He kissed the underside and moved his lips closer to the center, watching as the outline of the hard peaks of her nipples became more visible. Finally, he closed his lips on the fabric over her nipple, sucking both fabric and flesh.

Lila's hands, still grasping his, tightened as though she held on with everything she had.

"Are you—" She paused and sucked in a breath. "Are you certain this is proper?"

He moved to her other breast and repeated the action, in no hurry to answer her question. She blew out another quick breath, and he heard the moan she tried to suppress.

"Proper? I should think not. Pleasurable? Definitely."

"I think"—he took her silk-covered nipple gently between his teeth—"I—oh… I—I think we should only do what is proper." The last word came out as a weak cry.

He raised his head. "You should have noted that in the terms then. No renegotiation at this point, I'm afraid."

"But—"

"I'll release your hands now. I'd appreciate it if you unfastened the bodice of your dress. Then I could kiss your bare flesh, which would be even more improper."

"I most certainly will not."

He released her hands, having to all but pull his fingers free of her tight grip.

"Now what are you about?" Lila asked.

"I need my hands." He nudged his knee higher, toward the apex of her thighs.

"Why?" she squeaked, pretending she didn't notice how close he was to her core.

"To touch you, of course."

He reached down and slid the hem of her dress up past her ankles and around her calves. His hand met with silk stocking rather than bare flesh. Another man, one who did not enjoy anticipation as much as he, would have been disappointed.

His fingers touched her knee, and she jerked.

"Where do you plan to touch me?" she asked through clenched teeth.

He brought his knee higher, pressing it lightly against the heat of her core. "Nowhere proper, you can be sure."

"Sir Brook, I must insist we discuss this."

He moved his knee slightly against her heat. He imagined she was wet for him. If not, she would be soon.

"You will forgive me if I put off our discussion until a more convenient time." He slid his hand higher, cupping her thigh. "I am occupied at present."

He lifted his knee and used his hand to slide her skirts higher until he could see the tie of her garter and, just above, the pale skin of her bare thigh. Brook couldn't resist. He bent and kissed that skin, feeling her flesh pebble in response.

He pushed her skirts higher, and she caught them with her hands. Even with all her protestations, she hadn't used them to stop him. Now she would prevent him from seeing her. He would respect that. Instead, he bent to kiss the exposed flesh of her thigh again, opening his mouth to taste her soft flesh. He moved steadily inward, his head between her legs and his mouth on her inner thigh.

Her hands were white where they clutched the material she held, and he moved lower instead of higher, kissing the side of her knee, raising her knee, and kissing the back of it until she shivered.

He moved higher again, taking his time, trailing his lips over her skin with varying degrees of pressure until he learned which made her shift beneath him and which made her skin explode in gooseflesh. Gently, his knee nudged her legs wider, and his lips moved higher. She didn't release her skirts, but he made small forays beneath them, learning the landscape by the feel of his lips.

He could smell her arousal, knew she was ready for

him. His body reacted to it, straining against the tethers he'd imposed. Brook was a disciplined man and a patient lover, but he was having more difficulty curbing his urges with Lila than he could remember experiencing before. He hadn't expected this reaction to an innocent, one who clutched at her modesty and did absolutely nothing to entice him. He'd never been particularly attracted to innocence, but he found hers quite disarming.

Now he would disarm her. His lips moved higher and higher until her legs trembled where his cheek pressed against the warm flesh. Her skirts loosened, and when he kissed his way back to her knee, her fingers had moved to clutch the bedclothes beneath her. Brook didn't think it was a conscious choice. Her eyes were closed, her chest rising and falling rapidly.

He could give her pleasure if she allowed it. Slowly, he pushed her skirts higher, baring inch after inch of creamy flesh to his gaze. Her legs weren't particularly long. She wasn't a tall woman. As was everything else about her, Lila's height was ideal, neither too tall nor too short. But her legs were round and soft and between them lay ebony curls the same color as her hair. He could just see the pink of her sex, was desperate to part her and see all of it.

Instead, he kissed the flesh of her belly and her inner thighs, of her hip bone and the juncture of leg and pelvis. Lila trembled more, her breath coming in loud gasps and her hands clutched as though she were in agony.

Brook slid his hands up her thighs, parting them until the pink of her flesh was revealed to him. "Beautiful," he murmured. The light of the fire was hardly enough for him to see her as clearly as he would have liked, but it did not diminish his appreciation.

"This is mortifying," she murmured.

"By all means, you may ask me to stop at any time."

He believed she was past that point, but just in case, he bent and pressed his lips to her tender flesh. Her hips rose slightly off the bed, and her body tightened like a violin string. "You might tell me not to kiss you there," he said. Then he bent and licked a circular path around her core. "Or not to lick you there."

In response, she moaned and, though he held her legs open, her resistance all but fled.

He bent to taste her, dipping his tongue inside her. She was wet and tight, and his cock throbbed at the thought of entering that glove-like sheath.

Brook clutched at his control. "You might tell me not to taste you or to lick this small nub here."

He did just that, licking her lightly and quickly and pulling back.

Lila let out a small moan, and her hips arched.

"More?" he asked.

Her eyes were shut, and she refused to look at him.

"I'll take that as a yes."

He licked her again, this time working the nub with his tongue, conscious of how sensitive she was, and keeping his ministrations light and tender. She panted as his tongue worked her, her hips moving in an unconscious rhythm.

"Let yourself go, Lila," he murmured against her swelling flesh. "Let me give you this."

"No," she grit out. "I don't want to lose."

"You only lose when you deny yourself."

He bent again, and this time showed no mercy. His tongue stroked and flicked, inching her closer and closer to climax with a patience that few men had. Finally, she cried out, and her body rose, pressing hard against his mouth. She shuddered as his tongue continued to work her, drawing out every last ounce of pleasure until she collapsed back with a muffled cry.

He had won the wager; even she could not deny the force of the pleasure he'd given her. But Brook wanted more of her. For a brief moment, she'd wanted him, wanted his mouth, his tongue, his hands on her. He wanted to feel her desire, her need for him again.

Knowing she was not as sensitive now, he was rougher, pushing her legs apart and using a finger to trace her sex. She jerked at the feel of his hands on her, her delicate flesh contracting. When he brushed a thumb over that nub, she jumped in response.

"No. No more," she moaned, but he wasn't through yet. He moved his thumb over that small bud until she stopped fighting and opened her legs for him. Her eyes were an impossible shade of gold when she gazed at him. They shined as though they were liquid.

Brook bent again, taking her with his mouth, this time rougher. This time he suckled her, lashed her, laved at her inflamed flesh. His finger teased her entrance, not diving inside but tracing it and teasing the flesh. When he felt the first stirrings of her orgasm, he replaced tongue with the rasp of his thumb and watched her face.

She'd always been beautiful. He'd known few women as lovely as she. But in the throes of passion, she was truly ravishing. Her color was high, her skin glowed, her hair tangled about her like a dark halo. Her reddened lips opened, and she cried out at the same time he felt her jerk against him.

Brook would have given anything if, at that moment, she had opened her eyes and looked at him.

That was when he knew he was in danger.

Lila had lost. And she had not even lost quietly and with dignity. She had lost loudly and lustily. Good Lord, but the second time, she'd *wanted* to lose.

She was vaguely aware of her husband—though he would not be that for long now that she'd lost—settling beside her. She could feel his eyes on her as he smoothed the hair back from her brow. She could not look at him. She was too embarrassed at the way she'd reacted to his touch.

She wanted to slink away and bury her head under a mountain of pillows and blankets. Unfortunately, the cottage did not boast such a mountain. Perhaps if she pretended she was asleep, but how could she sleep with her skirts thrown up to her waist?

She pushed them down to cover her legs.

"Lila," he said.

"I do hope you will not gloat over your victory." She kept her eyes squeezed shut.

"A gentleman never gloats."

She opened her eyes and pinned him with them. "You, sir, are no gentleman."

Instead of being suitably chastised, he grinned. "You, my lady, would be bored to tears if I were a gentleman in bed. You would wonder what all the fanfare was about. I trust now you know the difference between my lovemaking and embroidery."

"Please do not say anymore." She could feel her cheeks flaming.

She'd tried to cover her blush with her hands, but he drew them back, holding them lightly in his own. "Your reaction was perfectly normal. Your body experienced what it was designed to experience. You won't go to hell for an orgasm."

"But I behaved like a savage." Her eyes were tightly shut, and she felt tears threatening to spill. She could not allow that.

"You behaved like a passionate woman. You completely undid me."

She opened her eyes. "What do you mean?"

"I mean"—he stroked her cheek with a tenderness she hadn't expected—"I didn't know under all that prissy and prudish loveliness, there was a ravishing beauty."

Now her cheeks flamed again. She'd received compliments for as long as she could remember, but this one was somehow different. More intimate, more meaningful.

"So that was not a sin?"

"Pleasure is not a sin."

"Yes, but…the way…what I mean to say is, do all married people do that?"

He opened his mouth to respond and then paused to consider. The look in his eyes rather reminded her of a startled stag she'd once come upon when she'd been walking in the woods at Blakesford.

"I can't say what other married people do. I'm not

in their bedrooms, thank God. I will say cunnilingus, which is what it's called, is not a secret."

"Oh, but I thought you said it was French. That sounds Latin."

He looked as though he might have discussed it further, then shook his head. "Might we discuss linguistics later?"

"Of course. I want to put on my night rail before I sleep."

"I didn't say we would sleep. Not yet, at any rate."

Lila stared at him, at the slow, wicked grin that parted his lips. She had new respect for those lips, for the skills he wielded with them.

And then it occurred to her that she had lost the wager. Not only did that mean he retained the right to petition for annulment, but it also meant he had won. She'd told him he could make one request of her, and now she would have to pay the forfeit. A small thrill of anticipation skittered through her. What would he ask her to do? Would it be something truly scandalous? Something she must do because to refuse would mean forfeiting the wager.

"Forgive me." She sat and pushed her hair back. "I owe you a prize. What is it you request?"

He gazed at her for a long, long moment. "I find I don't wish to claim my prize quite yet."

"Oh. Then when will you—"

"You would like to know that, wouldn't you? That would ruin the anticipation."

"At least tell me what you want."

"And calm your nerves? I don't think so. I like you on edge."

She scowled at him and jumped to her feet. "You're a horrid man."

"That's just what the king said when he dubbed me Sir Brook."

"The king obviously made a grave error. Please at least attempt to behave as a gentleman and give me privacy so I might dress in my nightgown."

"Very well. I'll step outside for a few moments before the rain begins to fall."

He closed the door behind him, and she sat on the bed, head in her hands. She'd made a grave error. She could hardly be blamed, as she'd been wholly ignorant of what Brook could make her feel. She'd never even imagined some of the things he'd done to her. She didn't even want to imagine them now or she'd start blushing all over again.

But what was she to do now that she'd lost the wager? He'd annul the marriage and then she'd be back under the protection of her father and Vile Valencia. It wasn't so much that she wanted to be Brook's wife. She wanted away from her stepmother.

Except that now that she'd been kissed by Brook—in multiple places—she rather thought she did want to remain his wife. Was that the sort of thing he'd do to her every night if she was his wife? And why was she even considering allowing him to repeat what he'd just done to her? She couldn't agree to let him touch her again if this would only end in annulment. She shouldn't want a man to touch her who didn't love her.

Lila realized she'd been sitting on the bed too long and rose to change from her dress to her nightgown. She did her ablutions and quickly climbed into the bed, pulling the coverlet up to her chin. She scooted all the way to the wall so Brook would have plenty of room. He'd been gone longer than she thought, and she hoped he might believe she had fallen asleep when he returned. She closed her eyes and tried to look as though she were sleeping.

The patter of rain on the roof and the roll of distant thunder kept her awake, and as the minutes passed, she began to wonder if Brook would return at all.

What if Beezle had lain in wait and caught him?

What if he didn't want to see her again and preferred to sleep outside?

Did he hate her enough to sleep in the rain?

Suddenly the door burst open, and Lila was so surprised she forgot to pretend she was sleeping.

Brook carried something small and wriggling in his arms. At first she thought it was a rat, but when he set it down, she realized it was the ginger cat she'd seen the day before and two tiny kittens.

"Oh!" She forgot she was only half-dressed or that she was supposed to be sleeping. Lila couldn't resist running to examine the mother and kittens. The mother eyed her warily, licking her wet fur and smoothing it down. The kittens, whose eyes were barely opened, cuddled close to their mother, who licked them as well.

"She has kittens." Lila crouched down to examine them. "Where did you find them?"

Brook didn't respond right away, and when she looked up at him, he quickly looked away. "She was moving them into the shelter of the woodpile. I'm not sure where she had them before."

"Are you certain there were only two?" Lila held her hand out to the mother cat, who sniffed it carefully then went back to washing.

"I waited to see if she'd go back for more. She didn't."

Lila lifted one of the kittens, who mewed immediately. The mother cat raised her head, but must have decided Lila was not a threat because she went back to smoothing her fur. Lila petted the kitten until it purred and closed its eyes, drowsing. It was absolutely precious—a ginger cat like its mother but with white stripes.

"This is a strange time of year for birthing kittens. I saw her with a mouse or rat the other day, but we should see if we have anything to give her to eat."

Brook nodded. "I'll look in Mrs. Spencer's basket."

While he rummaged for food, Lila found an old blanket and laid it near the fire. She placed the sleeping kitten on it, and the mother soon followed. Soon, all three were curled up together. She'd always wanted a cat or dog when she'd been a child. Her father and mother had forbid it. She'd had a pony, but she couldn't bring a pony inside or curl up with it at night. Lila glanced at Brook.

"Why did you bring them inside?"

He shrugged, pouring broth from the pot into a small saucer. "There's a storm coming. I wouldn't want to be out in it."

No one would, but most men she knew would not have cared if an animal was out in a storm. "I'm glad you brought them in. We'll all be safe and cozy together."

He gave her an odd look and set the saucer before the mother cat, who lapped up the broth eagerly.

"I rather thought you might object," he said, discarding his damp coat and running his fingers through his wet hair. Lila had to force her gaze away from him. When she looked at him, she couldn't help but think of what he'd been doing to her just a few minutes ago, and all the heat and mortification rose to her cheeks again.

"Me? Why?" She rose and moved back toward the bed. The cottage, which had seemed perfectly comfortable a few minutes before, now seemed far too small. Brook was not a large man, neither in stature nor behavior, but his presence made her feel small and vulnerable. She was suddenly conscious that she wasn't wearing her robe and that her nightshift did not hide as much as she would have liked.

She stepped behind the curtain she'd rigged in front of the bed for privacy but hesitated to slide into the sheets. She didn't want to give him the wrong impression.

"Most women do not like animal hair on their clothing."

"My mother was like that, but I always wanted a pet."

"You surprise me."

If he'd told her he was a pirate, his words would not have shocked her more. He was actually beginning to see her differently. She'd finally done something outside of the little box within which he'd placed her. Perhaps he might see her as more than the spoiled duke's daughter she'd been when they met.

He sat to remove his boots, setting them carefully on the floor so that the mud did not soil the wood. Lila tensed, knowing he would come to bed soon. She wasn't quite ready to sleep beside him. Neither did she want to insist he sleep on the floor. He was still healing from the knife wound—an injury he'd incurred to save her. He needed rest.

Neither did she want to sleep on the floor again.

"I think I shall go to sleep now," she said, making a show of yawning and climbing into bed.

"I'll be there in a moment."

Lila paused in the act of pulling the covers around her. Did he think she waited for him? "I am certain I will be asleep before you lie down."

A shadow fell over her, and she turned from the wall. He stood over the bed, his shirt off. Thank God he still wore his breeches.

"Are you nervous about my coming to bed with you?"

"No. I must say, I feel it is a bit *overly* intimate, but after what has already happened tonight, there isn't much else you can do to me."

She heard him chuckle softly right before the bed dipped as he climbed in beside her. "Oh, my little innocent. You do make it so entertaining to prove you wrong."

Twelve

THE HEAT OF HIS BODY SETTLED BESIDE HER, AND Lila resisted the urge to curve toward it. Instead, she huddled on her side of the bed, waiting for him to pounce.

He didn't.

He hissed in a breath, making a sound of pain, and then lay still.

Oh, how could she pretend to sleep if he was in pain? She turned toward him, propping herself up on her elbow. "Are you well?"

He'd pulled the curtain mostly closed, shielding the bed from much of the firelight. Outside, lightning flashed. The storm was still miles away, but for an instant the room flickered brighter. His face looked grim and set in marble.

"Fine. I moved too quickly."

Lila sat, concerned. "You didn't open the wound again, did you?"

"No. In my haste to join you in bed, I forgot my injury. It was a twinge. Nothing more."

He wasn't the sort of man to hiss in pain at a *twinge*.

If he opened the wound, she'd better clean and bandage it again.

"Let me see." She tugged at the coverlet.

He held it in place. "Lila. I'm fine."

"Let me see."

He released the coverlet, and she drew it down. She couldn't see anything in the dark and reached over him to draw the curtain back and allow more firelight. Across the room, the mother cat raised her head to peer at her curiously, then lowered it again and went back to sleep.

Brook hissed in another breath, and Lila glanced down at him. Her unbound hair trailed over his chest. He certainly didn't welcome the sensation.

"I beg your pardon," he said.

Now that she had more light, she settled on her knees and studied the bandage. It looked clean and dry. The wound hadn't started bleeding again. She plucked at the binding, peering underneath. She saw no sign of infection. It seemed to be healing quickly.

"Satisfied?" Brook asked.

"Yes." Now was the time she should pull her hand away and cover him with the sheets again. She should lie back down and resist his advances, thereby preserving some of her modesty and dignity.

Her hand lingered though, her fingers hovering just above the bronze flesh of his chest. Her skin looked pasty beside his gold-tinged chest. "How is it your skin is so tanned?" she asked.

"I believe we have Mediterranean blood somewhere in our family line," he told her. "One of my ancestors couldn't resist the allure of a Moroccan princess. Or so the legend goes."

"Really?" She glanced at his face. His eyes, always so dark and mysterious, were locked on hers.

"That's the rumor. Of course, it might also be because Northbridge boasts the best swimming hole in all of England. I've been known to swim there for hours in the summer."

She almost asked if he swam nude but closed her mouth before the impertinent question might be voiced. "And here I thought you spent all of your time chasing thieves and murderers in Spitalfields."

"I would, but my mother insists I visit her on occasion. I'm certain you understand."

She didn't. Her mother had been dead these past five years, and neither her father nor her stepmother requested or seemed to want her company. They sent her away more often than not. She doubted they even wondered where she was at the moment or what she was doing. No one would miss her if she were to disappear and never return. Her father might be put out, but he wouldn't really mourn. He had his heir and an adorable young daughter to dote upon.

Her relatives would be relieved they no longer had to accommodate her when her father sent her away. The debutantes and unmarried misses would rejoice, eager to take her place on the social staircase. She had no real friends, having only ever used other girls to achieve her own ends. And when her mother became ill, and Lila wanted a friend, no one came to call except to gloat over her misfortune.

Men were not friends but prizes to be won.

Her brother might miss her. Colin and she had always felt affection for each other. He protected her, chaperoned her, warned her away from men of dubious character, and chastised her for the worst of her bad behavior. But he also had his own life and interests. He wouldn't mourn her long.

She looked down again, at the hard flesh just below her hand. Even her own husband didn't want her. He could not wait to end this marriage and be free of her.

"Will you ever touch me, or are you to torment me all night?" Brook asked.

Her eyes locked on his again. His mouth curved roguishly, but his eyes were dark and intense with desire. Her gaze drifted down to the waistband of his trousers, which he'd most likely kept on to avoid terrifying her. She was not experienced in such things, but she could see the bulge in them, an indication, even she knew, of arousal.

"You want me to touch you?" Lila asked.

"Must I beg?"

She almost laughed. She couldn't imagine him begging.

"I did that once. I won't do it again."

She recoiled slightly as the memory slammed into her. He had begged for her hand in marriage, and she'd been so callous, so unsympathetic. No, the man Brook Derring was now would never beg. And the Lady Lila Pevensy—Derring—she was now would never turn her nose up if he did.

This wasn't the time for apologies. He wanted her to touch him, and she lowered her hand until her fingers brushed against the smooth skin of his side. He didn't react, seemed not to breathe as she slid her hand up toward his nipple. It puckered and hardened as her finger traced it.

Her hand skated over the firm muscle to the other side, learning the texture and feel of him. Where she was soft, he was firm and solid. Her fingers crept lower, toward his belly button. His chest had very little hair, but a line of golden hair began there and delved lower. She traced it, pushing back the coverlet as she did.

His hand caught her wrist in a viselike grip.

"Not yet."

She blinked at him, almost as though wakened from a dream. She'd been so intent upon exploring his body, she'd forgotten she should have been demure and shy. "I thought you wanted me to touch you."

"More than you know. But you were unwittingly making promises you don't intend to keep."

He referred to coitus, of course. By touching him so close to his…to that organ, she implied she wanted to consummate the marriage. She wanted no part of that, not when it would only end in annulment. Not when it was only her body he wanted.

He sat, and she shrank back. She'd forgotten they were in bed together. His injury made her forget how virile and powerful he was. "And now it's my turn to touch you."

"But you touched me earlier." The words were out before she could stop them, and her face instantly flamed.

"I want to touch you again."

He brushed the back of his knuckles over her cheek, trailing them down toward her chest.

"Why?" She had to duck her head, allow her hair to slide forward and shield her before she could go on.

"What I mean to say is, you took no pleasure of your own before. Did you?"

He pushed her hair back and cupped her face. Lila was surprised by the tenderness of the gesture. It was almost as though he cared about her.

"It gave me pleasure to watch you climax." He leaned forward and kissed her lightly on the lips. "I want to see it again."

And Lila desperately wanted him to touch her again. Her skin felt so warm where his hands met her cheeks. His touch was so light, so gentle. And yet she knew it could be demanding and forceful.

"And this time will you…" She did not know how to say it.

"I'd like to," he said, kissing one side of her lips. "But I don't think you're ready for that yet." He kissed the other. "And as I've said, I'm a patient man."

His hands dropped from her face to land lightly on her shoulders. Beneath the thin nightgown, her skin burned with his touch. He slid one finger inside the scalloped edge of the bodice and slid it to the center, where he played with the ribbon she'd knotted to keep the gown closed.

She took a shaky breath and looked at his face. All of his attention was focused on that white ribbon. Slowly, he traced the tail of the ribbon until he held it between two fingers. One quick pull, and it would come loose. Instead, he tugged ever so gently so the bow she'd made came undone fraction by tiny fraction.

Lila held her breath, unable to move or even to speak. She knew when the material parted, she would be exposed to him. She couldn't seem to tell him to stop. Her breasts felt heavy and full. Her nipples rose, hard and sensitive against the soft material. It was as though her body betrayed her and begged for his touch, even as her mind told her that if she allowed this, she would risk falling in love with him.

He was handsome, unselfish, brave, kind, and intelligent. She had no defenses against a man like that. The more she gave of her body to him, the more she risked giving her heart completely.

The knot popped loose and the material at her shoulders immediately sagged. It would have slid down, but she quickly caught it, holding it in place over her breasts. He didn't pull her hands away. Instead, he respected her right to cover herself and moved to push her thick hair off her shoulders. His fingers combed through it, twisting it around his hand until she had to raise her chin. Holding her in place, he bent and kissed her. His lips were tender, searching. He kissed her as though she were his lover, not the woman he'd despised the last seven years. When he urged her lips open, she parted for him, unable to resist kissing him in return.

A frisson of heat raced through her when their tongues tangled. His mouth slanted over hers, his tongue mating with hers, stroking hers, exploring her. And she never wanted him to stop. In that moment, she wanted to give herself to him. Though part of her rebelled against the vulnerability of the act, she opened her fingers and released the material of the nightgown. It slid off her shoulders and caught on the swells of her breasts.

Brook continued to kiss her, and she was his willing

prisoner, held in place by his hand in her hair. His grip was firm but not painful, just enough to show her he was in control.

Finally, he drew away. The hand in her hair held still, but his other traced the bare skin of her shoulder.

"You're like a marble statue," he murmured. "So white and perfect."

"So cold," she said with a trace of bitterness in her voice.

"Not at the moment. At the moment, your skin is hot and alive. Shall I taste the heat of it?"

Surely the question was rhetorical, but she couldn't stop the yes tumbling from her lips. He arched her neck back farther and pressed his lips to her shoulder. His mouth was warm and wet, and she shivered at the feel of it on her skin. He explored every inch of her shoulder with his lips and tongue, sliding into the valley of her collarbone and tracing the slope of her neck. Lila was all but panting. She had not known the skin of her shoulder could be so incredibly sensitive.

His lips lowered, kissing a path from the skin of her neck to the swells of her breasts. Her flesh burned with each slow, delicious kiss he placed. He must have heard her heart pounding as his tongue delved in the valley between her breasts, barely covered now by the thin material.

And then he took the edge of the nightgown between his teeth and pulled it lower until she felt the cool air on her breast and nipple. He groaned softly, looking at her far longer than was comfortable. Her hair was wrapped about his fist, but now he released it and used his other hand to slide the nightgown from her other breast.

She had the impulse to raise her hands and cover herself, but just as she moved to do so, he growled low in his throat, a very satisfied sound.

"Do you know how many times I've pictured you like this? Your hair down, your breasts bare, your skin warm to the touch?"

"No," she whispered. She'd never considered that he thought of her in that way at all. Had he imagined her like this when he'd asked her to marry him that night at the ball, or was it something he'd thought of since they'd come to the cottage?

"More times than I will admit," he said, glancing up at her with a small smile. "And yet"—he reached out, running the back of his hand along the side of her breast until he caressed the plump underside—"you are more perfect than I could have imagined."

His hand closed on her flesh, one thumb rubbing lightly over her nipple. Lila inhaled sharply at the sensation, a sharp jolt of pleasure radiating through her body. Thunder rumbled again, and the flash of lighting—closer now—lit up the sky outside.

"You like that?" he asked, his thumb circling the hard flesh.

Lila couldn't answer, didn't want to answer, didn't want to think about what he did to her.

"Let's see if you like this." He bent his head so she saw only the top of his hair. She felt his warm breath on the skin of her breasts and then something light flick across her nipple. She jerked, and when she settled, it happened again. His tongue, wet and skilled, circled her hard point, laving it until she was all but mad with the desire for more of his touch.

Just when she would have cried out from frustration, he took her nipple in his mouth, sucking hard on it and rolling the bud over his tongue. Lila moaned and arched, offering her other breast for the same treatment.

He obliged her, using his thumb on her well-used flesh, now swollen from his lips. When he pushed her back on the bed and came down on top of her, his arms braced on either side, she didn't protest. Outside, the rain pattered on the roof, and the wind lashed at the boards on the windows. Inside, Lila was wrapped in her own storm.

He didn't love her, but she could only describe what he did to her with hands and mouth as loving. He was gentle and thorough, responding to every mewl, every tensing of her body, every quick gasp. She wanted the pleasure he'd given her before again and again. His knee parted her thighs and pressed against her core so he rocked against her, and she, wanton now and beyond caring, moved her hips in the rhythm he showed her.

Finally, with a curse, he drew back and yanked her nightgown down to her belly. He lifted her hips and stripped it from her, leaving her naked before his gaze. He still wore his trousers, and her gaze dipped to the hard bulge where his manhood pressed against the material. Would he take her now?

"Not yet," he murmured, notching her chin up so she looked into his eyes. They were so dark, she was almost lost in them. His knee nudged her legs open, and that she resisted. She was already so exposed. Lila felt herself blush at this removal of her last vestige of modesty.

"Let me see you, Lila," he murmured, kissing her lips, then her chin, then her cleavage. "You're so beautiful."

She didn't know whether to believe him or not, but she couldn't resist the way his hands stroked her thighs or the way his mouth moved against her skin. She allowed him to part her legs, then closed her eyes as his gaze dropped and he looked at her *there*.

He looked for what seemed a long time before his fingers inched higher, touching the sensitive flesh just where she most needed him. He parted her folds and pressed one finger against her opening. She could feel the wetness there, was embarrassed by it, but he made no comment, merely circled her, teasing her, and coming closer and closer to the bud she desperately wanted him to stroke.

She opened her eyes and met his gaze. What she really wanted, she realized with horror, was for him to put his mouth on her again. But instead of complying, he continued to tease her with light touches, all the while watching her face for her reaction.

Lila closed her eyes again, squeezing them tightly, forcing herself to say the words. "Your mouth," she whispered. "Please."

He made no response, his fingers still stroking her, creating a slow building heat that made her want to squirm. Finally she opened her eyes and looked at him.

"You're killing me," he said, his voice rough. "I want you almost more than I can take."

"Yes," she said, understanding what he meant. Her entire body hummed, and she felt more alive than she ever had. And yet it wasn't enough. There was still more, still something she reached for.

"You want my mouth on you? You'll have it, but first I want to slip inside you."

She frowned, uncertain of his meaning until his finger drifted down and slid inside her.

"Oh," she moaned, not expecting the way her body clenched around that single finger or the way she pushed against it, wanting him to move deeper inside her. Instead, he slid out, then back in again. Lila's breath came in loud moans as he continued his torment, skating up to glide the wet finger against that small, sensitive nub. But just as her body strained for release, he inched back inside her, this time with two fingers. Lila's hips arched, and his thumb circled the wet nub.

She was dizzy, her head spinning. There was nothing but Brook—his eyes, his hands, his presence. She never wanted this to stop, and yet she all but sobbed with the need for release. When he finally pressed her toward it, she could hear herself murmur, "Yes, yes."

"Look at me, Lila," he told her. "I want you to see me when you come."

She opened her eyes, her gaze on his. With his hard body burnished by the firelight and lit up by flashes of lightning, his muscles tense from the control he exerted, and his eyes dark with desire, he was nothing short of a Greek god. She would have done anything he asked at that moment.

His thumb pressed against her, and her hips bucked. With a scream, she fell into pleasure, fell into his dark eyes, fell into oblivion.

Even in her stupor, she could see the way his eyes warmed, the way he relished her pleasure as he might his own. Lila, who had for years rarely thought of anyone but herself, wanted to give this back to him. She wanted to give Brook the pleasure he'd given her.

The waves of sensation began to recede, and Lila relaxed slightly. But Brook surprised her by bending. With one of her legs crooked over his shoulder, opening her wider to him, he pressed his mouth against her.

His tongue entered her, stroking the spot his fingers had made sensitive. Lila called his name, arched for him. Even as her body resisted the onslaught of more sensation, she welcomed it. And then when she thought she could not take more, his lips found that delicate bud, and he teased and licked and sucked until, with a cry that rivaled the booms of thunder, she tumbled over the precipice once again.

Thirteen

SHE SLEPT. SHE'D ALL BUT SOBBED OUT HIS NAME
before her eyes had closed and she'd drifted to sleep,
sated and spent. She hadn't bothered to pull the covers
around her body, which suited him just fine. She had
the most perfect body he had ever seen.

Her legs were shapely, her hips flared, her breasts
fit perfectly into his hands. She had pale pink nipples
that darkened to dusky rose when he stroked and
licked them. The dark hair between her legs parted
to reveal skin the color of a delicate orchid. He could
have admired her all night, but that would not ease
the throbbing in his cock. Instead, he covered her and
brushed her hair back from her forehead.

Then he rose and walked to the one-paned window,
letting the cool air seeping through the glass subdue the
worst of his ardor. The storm that raged outside was
expected. The feelings churning inside were not.

He hadn't expected to want her so much. He'd had
beautiful women in his bed before. After he'd been
knighted, he'd had quite a few beautiful women in his
bed. He'd become more selective in his bed partners

after he'd rescued the brother of Viscount Chesham and became a hero. He did not relish being used by women seeking to gain status or entertain with gossip.

Lila was beautiful, but no more so than other women he'd known. And yet he struggled to contain the desire he felt for her more than he'd ever had to with any other woman. Was it her innocence? Those wide eyes and that furious blush?

He wanted to be gentle with her but could not resist making her scream with need for him. She'd sobbed his name before falling asleep.

His name.

He'd liked the sound of it on her lips more than he liked to admit. He'd liked the way she looked at him when she climaxed, like he was the only man in the world.

He didn't quite know what to make of this possessiveness. She was his wife, and that made her different. Brook had never thought much of the institution of marriage. His mother and father's marriage had not made the state of matrimony particularly alluring. Even as a child, it had been clear to him that his mother only tolerated his father out of a sense of duty.

His father had been an honorable man who had treated his wife with the respect owed to a countess, but he hadn't loved her. Brook had never once seen them so much as touch hands or exchange endearments, not even when they hadn't known he observed them. They were in private just as they were in public—cold, formal, and aloof. When Brook came of age, he'd often wondered if his father had a mistress. Dane and he had discussed it, and his older brother thought the earl had not. This was no surprise, coming from Dane, who almost never stepped outside the lines Society had set for him.

Brook often stepped outside the lines. And now, with Lila, Brook was uncertain where the lines had been drawn. He wanted her, but how much was too much? How much desire was dangerous when he knew she was the kind of woman who could so very easily crush him if she caught the first glimmer of softness?

But perhaps he was being unfair. He had changed. Why couldn't she also have changed? What if her recent actions—apologies, nursing him, cuddling stray kittens—were indications of who she really was? What if the spoiled, selfish girl had grown into a kind, thoughtful woman? If that was the case, might his desire evolve into something more?

Brook had turned away from the window to watch the rise and fall of her shoulders as she slept. Now he turned back, pushing the battle between his cock and his brain out of his mind for the moment.

Trees swayed in the wind and the rain poured down in sheets. Thunder shook the ground and lightning illuminated the fields beyond. He could sympathize with man or beast caught in the weather tonight. The wet roads and deep mud would keep his nosy neighbors away for the next few days.

Unfortunately, even if the weather had been ideal, he could not depend on his neighbors' charity. He hadn't had time to plan this escape and had been forced to leave without adequate provisions. With two, no—he glanced at the cats curled up by the fire, the mother watching him with one eye open—five mouths to feed, he would need to take action as soon as the rain cleared. He didn't like leaving Lila there alone, even for a few hours.

He could take her with him.

But he had no horse, and that would mean walking several miles. He could only imagine how volubly she might complain at being forced to walk any distance.

But if Beezle came when he was away, she'd be dead.

Ridiculous to believe Beezle would find them, could find them, but Brook had learned that sometimes the ridiculous was possible.

She woke before him in the morning. He felt her stir and her body stiffen when she realized he slept beside her. He wondered if the reaction was surprise or distaste. She was attracted to him. He could see that plainly enough, but then he would have sworn she'd been attracted to him, even in love with him, all those years ago.

And she'd broken his heart.

He could feel her patting the coverlet, searching for her nightgown. He could have told her it had fallen to the floor on the other side of the bed. Unfortunately, she would have to go around him to leave the bed, and if he didn't move, that meant she had little choice but to wait for him to wake or crawl over him.

She pushed the covers back and inched closer to him. Realizing she would have to go over him, she edged down the bed, so as to go over his legs. But just as she straddled him, he opened his eyes.

He must have enjoyed torture because the sight of her pained him. She was glorious with her tangled hair and her long, naked limbs. If she'd positioned herself a little higher on his body, he could have stripped the covers away and taken her. Brook was thankful for small mercies and for a moment to tamp down his lust.

But he wouldn't allow her to escape. Instead, he caught her around the waist before she could scamper away and settled her on top of his cock. Unfortunately, the coverlet was between their bodies, but her gasp of protest made it clear she felt him beneath her.

"Good morning," he said.

"Let go of me. I want my night rail."

"And I want you exactly as you are."

She moved her hands to cover herself, which made him smile considering what she'd allowed him to do the night before. She'd covered her breasts, and so he slid his hands up the silky skin of her thighs until she lowered her hands to cup the place between her legs. Brook moved one hand to her belly and watched the shiver ripple through her skin. Her nipples darkened to rose and hardened.

He slid his hand higher, fondling her full breast and plucking at her nipple.

"Stop," she whispered, her voice a plea. "I can't—I don't want this."

"Don't you?" He moved to her other breast, bringing the nipple to a hard point. "You don't want my touch or you don't want to want my touch?"

"I don't want to want it."

She hadn't lied, which he could appreciate.

"Then I'll stop," he said, removing his hands and slipping them around to her back. He took her hair in his hand and pulled her slowly down, until she was poised over him. Her breasts were inches from his lips, her nipples so close he could have darted his tongue out and touched them. He released her hair.

"Walk away, if that's what you want." His lips brushed her breast as he spoke. "I won't stop you."

She hesitated, and he held his breath.

"But if you prefer to stay," he said after a long moment, "I will take your hard nipple into my mouth and suck it until you cry out with need. Then I'll slip my hands between your legs, into that slick, hot place, and stroke you until you come apart. Your choice."

She still hesitated. Then she rocked back, and he thought she would dash away. Instead, her mouth came down on his, the kiss so hot and unexpected, all the breath was knocked out of him. He kissed her back, his hands in her hair, her bare flesh brushing against the skin of his chest. She kissed his lips, his jaw, his neck. Brook clenched the bedclothes to keep from flipping her over and taking her when her small tongue tickled his ear.

She was an excellent student, and she'd soon become the teacher if he didn't take control.

Hands on the swell of her hips, he slid her body over the hardness of his cock until he could feast on her breasts. When his hands slid down to cup her between the legs, she was his.

He did exactly as he'd promised and was rewarded when she arched above him, riding his fingers with abandon. She was more seductive than the highest-paid courtesan, and Brook knew he would struggle to give her up.

Sometime later, they'd dressed and broken their fast with the last of the bread from Mrs. Spencer's basket.

They'd given the last bit of broth to the mother cat, who had escaped outside with her kittens, probably to hunt for mice or birds. A chill wind blew, but the rain had gone and the sun shone from a cloudless sky. Brook couldn't have asked for a clearer sign that he should travel to the posting house.

After he'd helped Lila—who had turned shy and quiet again—dress, he'd gone to the hook where her pelisse hung and handed it to her.

"You'll need this and a bonnet." He glanced at her valise, stowed in one corner. "If you have boots or a scarf, put that on too."

She set down the cup of lukewarm tea she'd made earlier. It was truly horrible, but he'd drunk it quickly and made a mental note to take charge of any cooking from then on.

"Why?"

Brook donned his greatcoat, turning the collar up and feeling about in his pockets for gloves.

"We haven't any provisions. I must go to the posting house and buy what we need."

Lila stood. "But we haven't a horse."

"We'll walk."

Lila sank back down. "Exactly how far is the posting house?"

Brook shrugged. "Far enough. We'd better leave now if we want to be back before dark."

"I remember that posting house," Lila said, lifting the teacup once again and holding it close. "It was at least six miles. I am no great walker. You shall have to go without me."

Brook placed his hands on the table and bent close.

He'd been prepared for this, and he understood her reservations. He would have left her behind if he could.

"Put on your pelisse, your bonnet, and your gloves, and be ready to depart in five minutes."

Far from being intimidated by his threatening pose, Lila appeared annoyed. She set the cup down with a thunk and rose to face him. "No."

With that, she sauntered toward the fire, holding her hands out for warmth. Oh, what he wouldn't have given to walk away and let her fend for herself for a few days. That would teach her to tell him no. Knowing Lila, he'd return and she'd have the entire cottage refurbished and a full staff at her beck and call.

He couldn't take the risk Beezle might come for her. He couldn't risk that a vagrant might spot the cottage and seek shelter from a rain shower. She was unprotected there, and he would not leave her. Nor would he stay. As an investigator, he often discovered useful information just listening to others talk. If anything or anyone unusual had been seen in the area, the locals would remark upon it. A visit to the posting house was his best chance of finding out if Beezle or anyone else who might prove dangerous was in the area.

Brook would have preferred to stay indoors and woo Lila back to bed, but he hadn't stayed alive in the most dangerous holes of London by doing what he wanted instead of what he should. His side had healed, the food was all but gone, and the weather had cleared.

It was time.

He'd been silent for several minutes, and Lila

peeked at him over her shoulder. She undoubtedly thought her display of pique had dissuaded him. Quite the opposite.

"Darling wife," he said before she could turn back to the fire.

Her back stiffened and she rounded on him. "Do not call me that."

"You misunderstand." He spread his hands as though in supplication. "This is not a request I make of you; it's an order." He placed his hat on his head. "We will leave in"—he made a show of checking his pocket watch—"three minutes now. Either don your warmer clothing, or I'll drag you out in that."

"You wouldn't dare." Her eyes flashed amber fire.

Brook crossed his arms over his chest. "Two minutes."

Lila stared at him for a long moment. He would hate forcing her to walk six miles in this cold in only a thin muslin day dress, but he would do it. She would see it as further proof that he was a brute. Brook saw no need or reason to prove his strength or power to a woman. But he would protect her, even from herself.

Finally, just as he poised to move, she stomped across the wood floor and yanked her pelisse from the table where it lay. She shrugged it on and took her time fastening it. By his reckoning, her time was up, but he gave her a little leeway as she pulled on gloves, a bonnet, a scarf, and half boots. Closer to ten minutes had passed when she was finally ready, but Brook offered his arm magnanimously.

Lila walked right past him and out the door.

Brook smiled. He did like her sometimes. He really did.

The wind cut through her pelisse and her dress, and straight to her bones. Lila tried to keep her head down so the top of her bonnet took the worst of it, but her ears still ached from the cold. Her fingers, which she'd tucked inside her pelisse, felt numb and frozen. Her feet were the worst of all. The rain had left muddy puddles everywhere, and she could not avoid stepping in many of them. Consequently, her feet had been wet and stiff shortly after they'd set out.

Everything from her toes to her back to her red nose hurt. She had no idea how long they'd been walking or how much farther they had to go. She simply followed Brook.

For his part, her husband didn't look troubled at all by the wind or the wet. His feet must also have been icy, his face windburned, but he showed no sign of flagging. Lila wouldn't ever admit it to him, but his resoluteness fueled her own. If he could go on, so could she. If he did not make complaint, neither would she.

The fact that her teeth chattered and her jaw had locked closed certainly aided in her efforts to quell any grumbles that rose to her lips. Unfortunately, she'd been thinking about her cold toes and how much she hated Brook Derring and not looking where she walked. Too late, she saw the small hole in front of her. Her foot slid into it, and she overcompensated in her efforts not to lose her balance. Lila fell forward, catching herself on her hands and crying out when her wrist buckled in protest.

Brook swept her up immediately, enveloping her in

his warmth and checking her ankle for signs of injury, as though she were a small child.

"Where does it hurt?" he demanded. Then, before she could answer, he made a sound of disgust. "If you needed to rest, you should have said so. I knew you were too quiet."

"Perhaps you would have been happier if I'd complained incessantly."

His dark eyes pierced her. "There is a difference between complaint and request." He put his warm hand around her ankle. "Does this hurt?"

"No. My ankle is fine." Cold but fine. "It's my wrist." She offered it to him with a small wince. She did not think it was broken, but the pain had not subsided.

"Take off your glove," he said. Then, "Here, allow me."

But when he tried to pry it off, she hissed and recoiled.

"Damn it," he swore.

"Let me try," she said, tugging gingerly on one of the fingers.

"No. I can't do anything about it out here. Better to press on and examine it at the posting house. Can you walk?"

Lila realized she'd been perched on his lap as he knelt on the road. She started to scramble up, and he settled his hands on her hips to hold her steady. As soon as she stood, she shied away. She did not want to feel his hands on her. She did not want to remember the wanton things they'd done together.

"My ankle is fine," she said, testing her weight on it. "How much farther to the posting house?"

"Not more than a mile now."

Lila wanted to cry. A mile yet to go, and she was already so weary. But she blinked the tears away and started forward. Brook walked beside her, his hawk-like gaze on her.

She wanted to rail at him, to blame him for the ache in her wrist, but she could see in the furrow of his brow, he already blamed himself. "I would not have brought you if I could have been certain you would be safe at the cottage."

Why he still called that tiny hut a *cottage* was beyond her.

"Yes, I can see why you would worry. There are any number of creaky boards and rusty nails that might cause me injury."

"You know my concern is more serious than that. If Beezle were to find you—"

"Beezle find me? Good Lord, I don't even know where I am," Lila said. "Surely a thief from London's rookeries can't know."

"You make a mistake when you underestimate the rabble. Beezle wouldn't be an arch rogue if he didn't have cunning and boldness. We already know he has contacts in Parliament. Even if Beezle doesn't have the resources to trace us here, you can be sure the members of Parliament do."

Lila's boot caught on a rock and she stumbled— not enough to fall, but Brook's arm went around her nonetheless. She might have shrugged it off if it hadn't been warm. At that moment, she would have rubbed shoulders with the devil himself if it meant more warmth.

"If there is a member of Parliament who ordered

this Fitzsimmons dead, why is he worried about me? I saw the murder, but I didn't see him. Even if I can identify Beezle, I don't know who he works for."

"You are a loose end. A man with political ambitions, a man capable of ordering the murder of another, will not want a loose end."

"And so I hide away forever? Even when this Beezle is caught, you cannot be certain he will reveal his employer."

"He's no snitch," Brook conceded. "But I've been known to persuade other closed-mouthed rooks to tell me their secrets."

Lila peered at him curiously. "How do you do that? Or do I not want to know?"

"Incentives." His gaze remained on the road before them. Lila didn't ask him to elaborate. She didn't need to. Hadn't he persuaded her to join him in bed with incentives? He was obviously a man who knew how to get what he wanted. The worst of it was that she almost believed, for a time, it was what she wanted too. Although, how any woman wouldn't want Brook Derring to kiss her, touch her, was a mystery to Lila.

She hadn't known she could feel the way he made her feel. It wasn't just the physical pleasure, although that was certainly part of it. But he made her feel as though she were the most desirable woman in the world. He looked at her, touched her, as though he wanted her more than…well, more than anything else. More than air or water or life.

It was ridiculous, a figment of her imagination. She'd allowed her emotions to cloud her other senses, just as she had when she'd been a child and read love poems and the Arthurian legends with their romance between Guinevere and Lancelot. Upon discovering Lila devouring the story of Arthur for a third night in a row, her governess had pointed out that Lancelot and Guinevere's love had not ended well.

The lesson seemed to be that strong emotions only caused trouble.

Lila believed that more than ever. She had to rein in her emotions for Brook Derring or she would fall helplessly in love with him. The problem was she did not know how to prevent doing so. If he would only act like an overbearing tyrant—as he had that morning when he'd threatened to drag her out in only her dress—she might be able to hate him.

But he insisted on catching her when she fell, rescuing small kittens, and kissing her senseless. Even when he was overbearing, it was for a good reason. He wanted to protect her. Lila was no Guinevere, but even Lila's defenses could not withstand that sort of assault.

The worst of it—as though all of this wasn't bad enough—was that he did not seem to care. He didn't catch her or protect her because he was in love with her. He did it because it was the sort of man he was. She'd wanted to believe it was out of a sense of duty, but how did duty account for the mother cat and the kittens? How did duty account for the fact that he'd covered her up last night so she wouldn't grow cold while she slept?

Dratted man. If only he still loved her a little!

But, of course, she'd ruined that. Just as she'd ruined everything else in her life. She'd alienated every friend she'd ever had. She'd thought herself better than every man who ever proposed. And Lila had angered her mother by spending too much, snubbing her friends, and refusing to marry the man her mother had chosen for her.

And then her mother had died.

Lila had realized, too late, that life was fleeting. She'd understood only at the end of her mother's life that kindness and compassion were more valuable than beauty or cutting wit. When one lay on a deathbed, no one cared if you'd been a diamond of the first water or turned down a half-dozen marriage proposals. If you had no friends, no love, you died alone.

Lila's mother had not died alone. Lila had not left her side, and Colin had come as often as he could.

But her father had stayed away. Lila had wanted to believe it was because his wife's illness tore at his heart. Later she came to realize he had already been courting his next bride. He'd never loved his duchess. Their marriage had been an alliance between two great families, nothing more.

Lila had vowed, at first, never to marry. It was a ridiculous vow because after her year of mourning, she wasn't invited to any of the Season's events anyway. All of her "friends" from the past had married, and the new crop of debutantes could have cared less about her. Her father's choice to marry again when his old duchess was barely in the grave had created something of a scandal, which meant the Duke of Lennox was not at the top of many guest lists.

Her father hadn't cared. He had a new duchess to keep him busy.

Lila was the one who had suffered. She'd been lonely and made desperately unhappy by her father's new marriage. She hadn't bothered to hide her dislike of her stepmother, and she'd been exiled.

Now, against all odds, she found herself married to one of the men she'd rejected. Only he didn't want her any longer, and she was in very real danger of being either killed or set aside via annulment.

Lila wasn't certain which option was worse.

Lila raised her head at the sound of hoofbeats. On the road ahead, a coach charged toward them. Brook pulled her to the side of the road, using his body to shield her from mud spatters. He raised his hat to the coachman and walked on.

When the posting house came into sight, Lila wanted to sag with relief. Her injured wrist shot streaks of white-hot pain up her arm, and her hand felt heavy and swollen. Brook maneuvered her through the muddy yard of the posting house, with its strong smell of horse manure, and into the warm common room. The heat was almost stifling after the brisk breeze of the last couple hours. Brook spoke with the proprietor and requested the use of a private room. Finally, she was able to sit by the fire and warm her shivering body.

The proprietor promised to return with tea and cakes, then left them alone. Brook took the seat beside Lila.

"Let me see your wrist."

Lila hesitated, wanting to keep it close and protected, but she finally lay in on the table.

Brook pushed up the sleeve of her pelisse and pressed lightly at the top of her glove. She hissed in pain.

"Bloody hell."

"I beg your pardon!"

"I'd like to see if you don't curse when we have to pull that glove off. That wrist is either badly sprained or broken."

Lila glanced down at her glove. The fabric had stretched slightly to accommodate her swollen wrist. She'd always had slender, graceful wrists. The sudden doubling in size alarmed her.

"Would you like me to do it, or would you rather have a go?"

Lila considered the glove and said, "I'll do it."

With her good hand, she tugged on the fingers, wincing when her wrist protested at even the slightest movement. She paused when the pain threatened to make her sob and closed her eyes. She was exhausted from walking in the cold on an almost-empty stomach and now by the effort of removing the glove. Finally, she pried the glove off and dropped it on the table. Brook took her hand in his, twisting it this way and that.

"Forgive me," he said, pressing his fingers against the swollen flesh lightly then turning her wrist to and fro.

Lila bit her lip to stifle the cry of pain, but it was bearable. Brook did not mean to hurt her. He flinched when she made a sound of distress, and his touch was as gentle as if she was a Sevres vase.

"It's not broken," he declared finally. "At least I don't think it is. If it is, the fracture is small."

"It certainly hurts as though it's been broken."

He glanced up at her with a wry smile. "Have you ever broken a bone?"

"No."

"An expert then. It hurts because you've sprained it. Badly. I'll need to ask the proprietor for linen strips to bandage it. The less you move it, the better, for the next few days."

Lila nodded, wishing she'd injured her left wrist instead of her right. Eating or sipping tea with her weaker left hand would be difficult.

"I inquired after a gig and a horse so the postboy might drive us back, but the gig has a broken axle and that carriage that passed us took the last of the fresh horses. I'll ask if the proprietor has a room available."

"Rooms?" Lila felt as though a wash of sun spread over her. She might sleep in a comfortable bed tonight and dine on real food. Perhaps the posting house had a hip bath she might make use of.

"Room. We only need one."

He would insist on one room. But did he do so in order to protect her or because he wanted her close?

"While we're here, you'll need to stay out of sight. I'd prefer to go back to the cottage tonight, but I'd be a brute to make you walk back when you're in so much pain."

Lila bit back the retort that he was a brute most of the time anyway. She would accept this kindness graciously. Perhaps they might even stay at the posting house until this Beezle was caught and his employer ferreted out. She would never have seen a posting house as anything other than a brief stop on a journey, but compared to the hovel in which Brook had hidden her, the accommodations here were luxurious.

"Oh." Lila frowned in concern.

"You don't want to stay?"

"I do," she said. "I just thought about the mother cat and her kittens. I hope they aren't too cold or hungry tonight."

Brook stared at her, the fire making his dark eyes look like polished mahogany. "You are concerned about the cats?"

When he put it that way, it seemed rather silly. "I...I suppose they will be fine."

Brook sat back and crossed his arms over his chest. He regarded her so long she began to squirm. Thankfully, they were interrupted by a quick knock at the door when the proprietor, who Brook called Mr. Nicholson, brought hot tea and a plate of small sandwiches and cakes. Brook inquired after a room, and the proprietor assured them his finest was available—did any innkeeper ever possess a room *not* his finest?—and hurried away to bid the maids to make it ready for the couple.

Lila reached for the teapot with her left hand and grasped it rather awkwardly. To her surprise, Brook waved her away and poured the tea himself, inquiring whether she wanted milk or sugar. She took neither and wasted no time blowing on the tea and sipping it.

If her mother looked down on her from heaven right then, she would have been most displeased at seeing her daughter blow on tea like a common scullery maid. Lila was too hungry to care. After she sipped the hot tea, she snatched a cake and took a large bite. It was so delicious, she finished it off with another bite and reached for a second.

Lord, but how she had missed these small civilities.

Brook was either not as hungry as she or had better manners because he took his time choosing a sandwich and waited for his tea to cool before sipping it. Lila knew he watched her with those hawk-like eyes, but she didn't care. It wasn't as though, after what he'd done to her the night before, he had any remaining illusions about her being a proper lady.

She'd reached for a third cake and was about to begin nibbling it when Brook rose to pour her more tea. "I left the kitchen door open," he said.

"What?" Lila asked, around a mouthful of food. She could all but hear her mother's voice, urging her not to speak with her mouth full and to say *pardon*.

"For the cats," he said, raising the teapot. "If they grow cold or it rains, the kitchen building is open. It won't have a fire, but at least they'll be inside." He glanced down at the plate. "You've eaten all the cakes."

She stared at him, in her shock, unable to apologize.

"I'll call for more." He went to the door, and she swallowed the lump of cake. She couldn't taste it anymore. She couldn't even feel the pain of her sprained wrist. Her head spun and her heart thudded.

Long before she'd ever considered the cats, he'd thought to leave the kitchen open for them. He hadn't thought her silly for mentioning the mother cat and kittens. He probably wondered why her thoughts turned to them so belatedly.

As Lila watched Brook speak with the proprietor, his head bent so he might look the man in the eye, with his broad shoulders shielding her from view, one thing became perfectly clear.

She was in love with Brook Derring.

Fourteen

BROOK HAD VOWED TO LEAVE LILA ALONE THAT NIGHT. He'd sit in the common room, listen to the talk of travelers and locals alike, and return to the bed chamber when she was almost certainly already asleep. Her wrist pained her, and the walk had almost done her in. He hadn't thought about how little she'd eaten in the days before they'd arrived at the cottage and in the days since they'd been there.

Of course, she'd never complained of hunger. She actually complained very little, which was rather unexpected. He thought she'd be quite vocal about everything and everyone—including him—being quite beneath her.

That was the Lila he remembered.

He didn't know this Lila who blinked back tears when injured, who worried over stray cats, and who flushed like a pink rose when he touched her.

He didn't need to know that Lila. In fact, he thought a bit of distance wise. Unfortunately, that was before he heard her request hot water and a hip bath from the maid. Now, instead of listening to the conversation of the two men who were passing through on their way from London to Bridgwater, he was thinking about Lila, wet and naked.

He imagined walking in on her, seeing her rise from the bath, the water sluicing off the pale pink tips of those gorgeous breasts. He would touch her there then allow his hand to skim down to the dip of her waist and out to the flare of her hip.

And then… If he didn't stop imagining what he would do next, he would embarrass himself here in the common room. Brook sipped his ale and focused on the acrid taste of it. It was truly awful, and he had a passing acquaintance with bad ale from his time in the gin shops of Tooley Street.

"Rumor is," one of the Londoners said, causing Brook to glance his way, "the Bow Street Runners have been hard at work ferreting out the rabble down in Covent Garden."

"I saw it myself," the other, a stout man with wispy reddish hair, concurred. "I know an abbess in Covent Garden, and I paid her a call the other night. Half the men in the streets was in an uproar, making for this hidey-hole or other so the Runners wouldn't catch them."

"The Runners go too far when a respectable man can't have a bit of fun," his companion said amiably.

Brook did not think visiting an abbess—the name for the owner of a bawdy house—would qualify as a respectable activity in most quarters, but the description of the chaos in what was most likely Seven Dials or somewhere nearby interested him.

Beezle was the arch rogue there. If the Runners

had caught him, chaos might certainly ensue as other rogues vied for the top position. On the other hand, he'd watched the Runners chase after their shadows more than once. Beezle had a dozen hidey-holes. He could wait the men out.

"My question," piped up the redhead, "is where the devil is Sir Brook? Fitzsimmons, that MP, was buried a few days ago and guards posted to keep the Resurrection Men away. Derring was said to be after the murderer, but now he's all but disappeared and his Runners are running amok."

Both men laughed at this play on words. Brook sipped his ale. He was commonly thought to be a part of the Bow Street Runners, but though he often worked with them, he did not work for them. He was an investigator and quite independent of Bow Street.

"I heard he got himself leg-shackled and retired to the country for a bit 'o sport. If you know what I mean." This from the man Brook could not see clearly.

Brook might have rolled his eyes and moved to another table to overhear other conversations, but one small fact bothered him. Although his marriage was not a secret, he had thought his departure from London done covertly. If these two knew he had left London for the country, who else knew?

The most likely place for him to flee was Northbridge Abbey, his family's estate. Marlowe and Dane were there with their young children. Although Brook knew Marlowe could more than handle herself, he worried about what might happen if Beezle took the family by surprise. He immediately requested foolscap and quill so he might pen a quick note of warning that could be sent on the next mail coach headed in that direction.

Where else might Beezle look? The Derring family had land all over the countryside. Much of it was in the north and west country. Those estates took several days to reach. Only Northbridge and this relatively rustic land his father had used for hunting and farming were close.

Brook closed his hand around the quill. Beezle would never find him here.

Still, he had a bad feeling.

The common room was all but empty by the time Brook made his way to the bedchamber he shared with Lila. It was late, and he moved quietly so as not to wake her when he entered. The room was dark, but he spotted movement by the fire. Lila turned to look at him, her long, raven hair flowing down her back and ending in curls at her waist. She wore her chemise, a simple garment she could don by herself. It was also a thin garment, being made of high-quality linen.

Brook could easily see the lines of her body outlined by the firelight.

He paused in the doorway, catching sight of her, and then slowly closed and locked the door.

"I tarried too long in the bath," she said by way of explanation. "My hair is still drying."

"I thought you'd be asleep."

She nodded. "I wondered if you were waiting so you would not have to speak with me."

Brook paused in the process of crossing the room. "Why do you think I don't want to speak with you?"

She looked back at the fire, running a hand through

her thick hair to test its dampness. Brook sat on the bed and removed his boots.

"It's obvious you don't like me," she said after a long silence. "I know why."

Why did her statement send guilt hurtling through him? "It's not as though you like me," he said in defense. "This marriage isn't a love match."

"It wasn't, no."

He rose and took a step toward her, then stood rooted in place. He didn't understand her. He'd never understood women like her.

"I do wish you would talk about it," she said. "I'd like to have it out and not leave it standing between us like a great, invisible wall."

Brook raked a hand over the stubble on his cheek in frustration. "And I wish you would say something that made sense. Talk about what?"

She looked up at him, her eyes the color of hard amber. "The night you proposed to me."

Pain lanced through him, tinged with embarrassment. It shocked him that he could still suffer pain over the events of that night. He thought he was long past caring.

But for an instant, he felt like a youth of four and twenty again—naive and hopeful and so incredibly foolish.

"What is there to say? I proposed. You said no." He lifted a glass from the table and filled it with wine.

As he sipped, Lila stroked her hair again, and he followed the progress of her pale fingers on the dark tresses. "I don't remember it quite that way. As I recall, you asked me to run away with you. Did you think I'd agree to that?"

The old anger rose in him again. He squeezed the wineglass, then threw it against the wall, watching as the glass exploded and red wine ran down the wood panels in rivulets.

He took a deep breath and scrubbed his fingers over his eyes. "I apologize."

"No, I apologize." She rose, seeming uncertain what to do with her hands. He could see her move toward him then hesitate and clasp her hands in front of her. She obviously had no idea the fire made her chemise all but transparent.

Brook looked away. This was no time to let his lust get the better of him, especially when the lust was mixed with anger.

"Why do you apologize? You didn't throw anything."

"I apologize for my behavior in the past. I led you on," Lila said. "I knew you fancied me, and I let you believe I felt the same."

He'd known this. He'd realized it the night she'd finally rejected him, but hearing her say it from her lips drained his remaining anger. Perhaps that was what he'd wanted, what he'd needed all this time—an apology.

"Silence." She folded her hands under her breasts. "You don't forgive me."

He did not. "You think because you say *oops* I forgive and forget? Now I'm supposed to trust you? I should believe you have really changed?"

"You could give me a chance."

Brook ignored the way she glanced up at him from under her lashes, the look of vulnerability in her eyes. Better she be vulnerable than him.

"I was in love with you," he hissed, his voice so forceful she took a step back, although he hadn't moved closer to her. "I might have been young and foolish, but that didn't mean I couldn't fall in love."

She closed her eyes, regret making her features look pinched.

"Do you know the first time I fell in love with you?" he said.

She shook her head, though he hadn't needed nor wanted a response from her.

"The first ball of that Season. I hadn't wanted to go to any of the events. I would much rather have caroused with my friends from school or explored one of the rookeries. Even then I was intrigued by crime and punishment. I'd often spend hours at Old Bailey, watching the trials. Not because I received some perverse pleasure from others' misfortunes, but because I wanted to know how the investigators or the Runners had caught the thieves and murderers."

"Even then you knew who you were," she said, and he could see the admiration in the way she smiled at him. "You were not a man who wanted to attend balls. Why did you go?"

"My mother can be quite persuasive. She dragged both Dane and me to as many events as she could. After I saw you, I didn't need to be dragged."

Lila shook her head. "Brook, don't."

He moved closer to her, until he could smell the faint scent of flower-perfumed soap on her skin. "Why? Does it pain you when a man says he thought you were beautiful? I remember the dress you wore. How pathetic is that? It was gold silk with small red flowers and you had a scarlet ribbon wound through your hair. You danced every single dance. I wanted to ask you, but we hadn't been introduced. I rectified that the next night at the theater. Do you remember?"

She shook her head.

"It took quite a bit of maneuvering on my part to convince my mother to stop by the Duke of Lennox's box at the King's Theater. It took even longer for us to make it inside as it was stuffed with your suitors."

"Brook. Please—"

"I waited until it was my turn, and the smile you gave me made me float on air for a week. I'm sure it was the smile you gave every man, but I managed to convince myself it had been only for me. I convinced myself I was special to you."

She covered her face with her hands. "Why are you doing this?"

"You said you wanted to have it out. Isn't this what you wanted to hear? How I acted like a lovesick puppy, mooning over you? How I attended every single ball, hoping to secure a dance with you? How I thought of you day and night and planned our wedding and our marriage and even named our children?"

"No." Her voice sounded weak and futile.

"Then one night, it was perhaps the third time I'd danced with you, you called me *Mr. Derring*, and you made some comment I'm sure meant nothing to you."

"Don't tell me what it was." She turned, her back to him.

He took her by the shoulders and turned her around. "You wanted this. At least do me the courtesy of listening."

"While you humiliate yourself again? No!"

"What's the matter? You don't want to hear of my undying love and devotion?"

"I said I was sorry. Why are you torturing me?"

"Torturing *you*? Is that what I am doing? How cruel of me, not to consider your fragile feelings."

She looked away from him, and he shook her until her hair spilled over her shoulders.

"You said, 'Mr. Derring, tell me you shall run away with me. The Season has barely begun and already I'm so weary of the parade of balls and soirees and fetes.'"

She flinched as though hearing her words caused her pain. He knew how they sounded, how they had almost certainly sounded then—false and silly and spoiled. Only he'd been too much the clodpole to hear them that way. He'd thought she meant it.

"Do you remember the night when I first kissed you?" he asked.

"Of course."

"Finally something you do remember."

"I remember it was the Vanbrughs' ball, and you led me out into the garden."

"You did not protest."

She shook her head. "I liked the danger. I liked the possibility you might kiss me." She clasped his hands in hers. She was cold, despite having been in front of the fire; her hands were ice. "I might not have been in love with you, but that doesn't mean I didn't think you were handsome."

He laughed, a reaction she hadn't been expecting. Her eyes widened, and she tried to release his hands. He wouldn't let go.

"Is that what you've told yourself all these years?"

She shook her hands, still trying to free them. "No. Truth be told, I rarely ever gave you a second thought."

"Now that I believe," he said. "Finally, honesty from you. When I hear you admit to that, I can almost believe you've changed. But you did not kiss me that night because you found me handsome. You kissed me because you wanted to make Viscount Ware jealous. You knew he'd followed us out and wanted him to see me kiss you."

Her cheeks colored.

"Now let's see how honest you are."

"Fine. That's true. I'd forgotten Viscount Ware."

Brook cupped her chin. "Did he ever kiss you?"

Her eyes were round and large as she nodded.

"Better than me? Be honest."

Her brow furrowed. "Then or now?"

He released her chin with a laugh. "That answers the question."

"Brook, no one has ever kissed me the way you do now."

If she'd thought that admission would melt his heart, she was mistaken. "That's unfortunate for you. I've kissed many women and almost every one of them knows more of the art than you."

Pain flashed in her eyes, and he was instantly sorry. Hurting her would not curb his pain. He knew that, but he couldn't take the words back now.

"Then I had kissed precious few women and none like you. I don't know how I mustered the nerve even to dare to touch you. I was shaking like a new soldier who has had his first taste of battle. I wanted, so desperately, to kiss you perfectly, to show you how I felt without words."

"Please." She was begging him now.

"I was out of breath after the kiss, my head spinning as though I'd been waltzing, and I could hardly stop the words before they tumbled out. Do you remember what I said?"

She nodded, swiping at a tear with the back of her hand.

"I said, 'My dearest Lady Lila, I love you. More than my own life. If you will consent to become my wife, you will make me the happiest man in the world.'"

"It was a lovely proposal," she said. "Any woman would be lucky to have a man say such words to her. I mean that, Brook."

"You mean it now, but at the time the words meant nothing to you."

"You have to understand—"

"Understand? That you'd received a dozen such proposals? That it was all a game to you? That you were spoiled and selfish and vain? I understand, Lila. I could even forgive you all of that, but I can't forgive you for your answer."

"My answer? I never said yes! I never gave you leave to go to my father."

"Then what did you say?"

She pressed her lips together. "I don't remember."

"You said, 'Of course.'"

She shook her head. "No."

"Yes."

She let out a breath. "Then I said it to stop the proposal, not to agree to it. I probably wanted to go back inside and give Viscount Ware a chance to show his jealousy."

He inclined his head.

"Do you want me to feel ashamed of my behavior now? Fine. I am ashamed. Does that change anything? No. I cannot go back, Brook. If I could, I would."

"And what would you say?"

She paused for just a moment too long.

"Honesty. What would you say, Lila?"

"I would say yes!" She looked up at him, her eyes fierce and burning. "I know you don't believe me."

"I think the least you might have done is to tell me not to go to your father. I might have avoided that humiliation."

"And you blame me because you are not an earl? Even if I had said yes, my father would have said no. You are not titled. You had very little chance of ever inheriting a title."

"And now that my brother has a son, I have even less chance."

"I don't care about that. I don't want a title."

"Oh, really? Didn't you tell me you were not *Lady Derring* just a few days ago?"

She didn't answer. What answer would she have made at any rate?

"I wasn't good enough for you then, and I'm not good enough for you now. I might have let it go after your father's refusal"—he went on before she could defend herself with what he knew would be weak excuses—"except you had asked me to run away with you. I supposed you knew all along your father would never consent to the marriage of his daughter to a lowly second son and that was why you had asked me to take you away."

She swiped another tear away. "I'm sorry. How many times must I say it?"

"You needn't ever say it. But you wanted to know why I won't forgive you. There aren't enough apologies in the world for what you did."

"I made a mistake."

He took her by the shoulders. "You laughed at me when I confessed my feelings. You *crushed* me."

"I didn't mean to."

"Oh, well, then that makes it all quite all right."

"No, what I mean is I didn't understand how you felt then. I'd never been in love. I didn't understand what it was, how it made you vulnerable."

"And you understand now?"

"Yes."

Her gaze met his, and his chest tightened unaccountably. The way she looked at him made him want to take her in his arms and kiss her until she cried out his name, even though at the moment he loathed her more than ever. He pulled on the loathing and tamped down the lust. Brook raised one eyebrow indifferently.

"And who was it you finally fell in love with? Or were there many?"

She laughed bitterly. "Only one man."

He crossed his arms over his chest. "I am all agog with curiosity. Who is the unfortunate man?"

She looked down, then raised her eyes until he saw the tears shimmer on her lashes. "You."

Brook took a step back. "Is that some sort of jest?"

"I wish it were. These last few days, I've fallen in love with you."

"Why?" The word sounded harsher than he'd intended.

"Do you think I want to fall in love with you, a man who hates me and with good reason? I didn't want to love you. I tried not to. I tried to fight it when you saved me from Seven Dials, when you married me, when you didn't scream at me even though I ruined your flat."

He laughed. "I wanted to scream."

"Then you should have! Perhaps that would have ended my infatuation. Instead you kissed me and fought Beezle for me and took me away to that hovel you call a cottage."

"Exactly! I'm no prince sweeping you away to a castle."

"And I'm not so shallow as to be swayed by a beautiful house—not anymore. If you didn't want me to love you, why did you take me to bed? Why did you touch me and make me feel things I'd never felt before? You made me want you, and then just when I was my most confused, my most muddled, you brought the damn cat inside!"

She covered her mouth as though she hadn't meant to utter the curse.

"The damn cat?"

Her cheeks turned redder.

"What does that cat have to do with anything?"

"It means you are not a brute. I wanted to think you callous and unfeeling, acting only out of lust. But you're not. You cared about that cat. You do have a heart."

"You can't start thinking that way." Brook paused. Had he just told her not to believe he had a heart? "It was only a cat."

"And kittens! And there are those children you wrote the letters about. The ones you saved from a life of thieving in Whitechapel or St. Giles."

Bloody hell. He'd forgotten about the children.

"And you've been knighted for bravery. Even I read about how you saved Viscount Chesham's brother from an opium den and reunited Lady Elizabeth with her parents. You're a hero."

"I can't deny I have my good points, but I have my bad too."

"Like what?" She put her hands on her hips.

"I was acting out of lust. I took advantage of your innocence when I took you to bed."

"I'm your wife, as you pointed out. You can't take advantage of me in that way."

"But I don't intend to stay married to you." He pointed a finger at her. "See?"

"And yet all you've done is give me pleasure. You haven't even been selfish enough to take your own. I'm still a virgin, for God's sake!" She frowned. "I am still a virgin?"

"Yes," he said through clenched teeth.

"Do you see why I've fallen in love with you?" She paced away, flinging an arm out as she spoke.

She was angry and beautiful, and he could still see through her chemise. And she loved him.

"This is perfect for you," she said. "You can have your revenge. You can treat me ill, crush me just as I crushed you."

"I would never do that."

She threw up her arms in frustration. "Of course not! That just makes me love you more!"

"Fine." He crossed to her and grabbed her hand, pulling her to the bed.

"What are you doing now?"

"Something reprehensible, something guaranteed to make you hate me." He lifted her into his arms and carried her the rest of the way to the bed.

Instead of struggling, she wrapped her arms around his neck. "I'll never hate you."

"We'll see." And he claimed her mouth with his.

Fifteen

LILA SANK INTO HIS HEAT AND THE VELVET SOFTNESS OF his lips. She adored his lips and the many, many ways he used them to bring her pleasure. His kisses were alternately light, then demanding. She never knew what to expect, and after the first few drugging kisses, she ceased attempting to anticipate, ceased thinking at all. Her mind drifted, and she allowed sensation to overtake her—the way his tongue slid in and out of her mouth, the way his teeth bit her lower lip lightly, the way the coverlet felt on her bare legs when he laid her down.

He came down on top of her, his weight braced on his elbows but his heat covering the length of her. She used her arms wrapped around his neck to pull him closer and urge his warmth to surround her. Her fingers slid through his close-cropped hair, liking the way the spikes of it felt on her sensitive flesh. She worked her way down and over his broad shoulders. She could feel the muscles underneath the lawn shirt he wore, hard flesh so different from her own.

Lila had always imagined herself married to a man

who would one day be a duke or marquess—a man who wielded great power politically. But those men seldom exerted themselves beyond the occasional shooting party. The man splayed over her was strong and honed from hard labor, respectable labor. This was a man who found the lost, who saved the damned.

Her hands skimmed down to his back, felt the way the muscles bunched and tensed with her touch. He liked her touch on him, which gave her hope. Maybe he didn't hate her quite as much as she'd supposed. Maybe he could even come to love her one day.

His hands grasped her arms and pulled them away from his back. He pushed her back on the bed, holding her locked into place. For a long moment, their gazes met in the firelit dark. His breathing was harsh and erratic but his grip was solid and strong. She could not have broken it even if she'd wanted to.

She didn't want to.

"You don't like me touching you?" she asked.

"I like it too much. If I'm to do this well, to do this right—"

Lila shook her head and closed her eyes. "No, no! I'm falling in love with you again. Do this badly and wrong."

He nodded solemnly, though she saw the way his mouth quirked with amusement. "Badly and wrong. I will do my best."

Careful of her injured wrist, he wrenched her arms over her head, pinning them with one hand at the edge of the bed. His other hand slid down her body, roughly ripping her chemise down to expose her upthrust breasts. Lila gasped, her body arching for him even as her mind protested that this was shocking and indecent.

He made a low groan deep in his throat and then he was kissing her again, not roughly but softly and tenderly. His hand came up to cup her cheek and his thumb smoothed over the heated flesh. He pulled back, rubbing his callused thumb over her swollen lips, parting her mouth and slipping inside.

He tasted of brandy and bergamot, and she flicked her tongue over the pad of his thumb. His eyes seemed to grow darker, and she lapped at him, circling the round digit, learning its texture.

"Suck," he murmured, his voice low and husky. The sound made her entire body tingle with awareness.

Lila did as he bid, sucking lightly on his thumb and then taking it deeper into her mouth and applying more pressure.

He pressed his body hard against her, and she could feel the evidence of his arousal at the junction of her thighs. He was stiff and hot, much like the thumb in her mouth.

Gradually, he withdrew his thumb, rubbing the wetness over her lips. "That is not the sort of thing a man should do with his wife," he muttered.

"Then it's reprehensible?"

"Oh, I can think of a dozen ways to make those skills you just honed very, *very* reprehensible."

"What does a man do with his wife?" she asked. Her nipples puckered at the scrape of the lawn on her flesh. "Show me."

He dipped his mouth and kissed the spot just below her jaw, tracing his tongue lightly over her skin until she shivered at the soft heat of his breath on her earlobe.

"Make it bad."

His teeth closed on her earlobe and he nibbled his way up until she shuddered when his breath teased her ear. "Very bad," he whispered.

He still held her hands imprisoned with one hand, while the other slid down her shoulder and between her breasts. Her skin quivered with anticipation as the trail continued down her belly, pushing the material of the chemise away until she was naked beneath him. His hand trailed back up, over her thigh, skimming the hair between her legs, making her stomach tense, and then finally closing on one breast. He kneaded her flesh until it felt heavy and full, and then his fingers plucked at the nipple until it was hard and throbbing.

He lowered his mouth, taking it gently into his mouth, teasing it as she'd teased his thumb, and then sucking gently at first and then harder until she cried out with desire. Her hands strained against their prison.

"I want to touch you," Lila said.

"Not yet."

He repeated his actions on her other breast, this time his sucking seemed to attach to an invisible cord that pulled between her legs. Her hips arched, pushing her pelvis against the hard length of him, wanting to feel the friction there, where she knew what the outcome would be.

Brook's mouth slid down her belly, exploring her until gooseflesh appeared. She couldn't help but strain in anticipation of the feel of his hot mouth on that secret part of her. Finally, he couldn't hold her hands any longer, and he released her, grasping her hips in a rough grip and angling them upward. His mouth skimmed her hip bone, moving slowly inward until she felt his breath tease the sensitive spot between her legs.

She parted her legs, needing him to touch her there, kiss her there.

"What do you want?" he murmured against the skin of her thigh.

She wrapped her hands in his hair and guided his mouth where she wanted it.

He shook his head. "Oh, no. Not this time. You must say it. Say what you want."

She inhaled sharply. He was making good on his promise to act the reprobate. How was she to say out loud what she was hardly willing to admit even in the darkest parts of her mind?

"Brook." Her voice sounded breathless with entreaty.

He nudged her legs wider with one stubbled cheek. "Say it, Lila."

"Your mouth," she whispered. "I want your hands and your mouth on me."

With a whispered curse, his mouth was on her. But the light touch of his tongue was gentle and teasing. She arched her hips higher, wanting more pressure, more heat, but he continued to tap at her center lightly while one finger played at her opening.

"I could tease you like this for hours," he said. "I could make you so senseless with need you'd reach down and pleasure yourself to escape the craving."

She shook her head. Touch herself while he watched? Never.

"That would be reprehensible." He sat and yanked his shirt over his head. Lila sucked in a breath at the sight of his glorious chest limned by the firelight. She couldn't stop her hands from sliding over that sleek skin, ending on the flat plane of his taut belly.

He lifted her hand and placed it over the bulge in his trousers. She tried to pull back even as her curiosity was roused. What did he look like? What would the flesh there feel like with her fingers wrapped around it?

"I could enter you fast and hard. Is that reprehensible enough for you? Would you hate me for taking you like a brute your first time?"

Lila nodded, though the idea excited her more than scared her. She wanted to feel him move inside her, wanted that hard length of him sliding in and out as his fingers had.

"You'd hate me, and that would be easier for both of us."

But instead of opening the fall of his trousers and doing as he threatened, he skimmed his hands under her bottom and raised her up. His mouth closed on her core again, teasing and tapping until she writhed against him. Her hands dug into his shoulders, and she heard the quick cries of passion filling the room. She should have been mortified that such sounds came from her mouth. Instead, Brook's fingers dug into the flesh of her bottom, urging her on.

Finally, with the delicacy of the first blooms of spring, she came apart. She unraveled like a coiled ribbon, opened like a rosebud. Every particle of her body let go, sinking into the oblivion of sensation.

If this was his definition of reprehensible, she would ban commendable deeds altogether.

She felt the bed shift, felt him move, and opened her eyes to see him push his trousers over his hips.

His bare hips.

Her gaze lowered, but in the darkness she could only make out the vague shape and form of his manhood. Her heart sped up as she realized what he would do now. She trembled with fear and anticipation. She wanted this.

Bending over her, his lips met hers again. This time when he pressed against her, there was no clothing between them. He felt like warm velvet against her entrance. The gentle pressure of him there made the delicate flesh throb. His hands cupped her breasts, brushed down over her waist and hips, lifted her until he was poised for entrance.

Her gaze met his, and she couldn't read his expression. This was his chance to make her hate him. She had heard the act could hurt the first time if the man was rough and uncaring. But she had also heard that a considerate husband would take care when he claimed his wife's virginity. If Brook loved her, even a little, he would not hurt her.

Slowly, he entered her, and she felt his thickness spreading her. He slipped back out, then in again, and that ribbon inside her coiled with need. The second time he entered her, he went slightly deeper, and she liked that, like the way he filled her. This was not bad at all. Perhaps he was a small man or perhaps the rumors of pain had been exaggerated.

He withdrew again, and she wrapped her legs around him, urging him to continue.

"Are you hurt?" he asked. He was the one who sounded as though he hurt. His voice was tense and low.

"No. It feels wonderful. More."

He entered her again, this time resting his forehead on hers. She saw his eyes were closed and his jaw clamped shut as though he concentrated intently. He pushed deeper, and her eyes widened. Perhaps she had been wrong about him. Perhaps he was not so small.

He rocked against her, obliterating the thought with the rush of sensation. She gasped and tried to move her hips to increase the pressure, but she was trapped by the weight of him, the feel of him inside her.

He withdrew again, entered again, and each time it seemed he filled her just a little bit more. The sensation was not pleasant, though she would not have described it as painful. Just as she began to feel discomfort, he'd rock against her and spirals of pleasure would unravel.

He withdrew again, and she wanted to cry out in frustration. Her body hummed with need, throbbed with the feel of him filling her. She wanted more, wanted him to rock against her again.

"Are you ready?" he asked.

Oh, she had been ready for an eternity. "Yes. Please, please." She was begging. She had never thought she would beg for anything.

He entered her again, not as completely, but when he rocked against her, she didn't care. This time his fingers slid between their bodies and he touched her, stroked her. She was ready, and at his first touch, she cried out with pleasure.

But with the pleasure came a sharp jolt of pain as Brook slid inside her, farther and farther, stretching her until a burning ache made her vision go dark and blurry. She gripped his shoulders tightly, half sobbing, half moaning with the last vestiges of pleasure.

He didn't move, but he breathed heavily, and now she realized it was not from arousal but from restraint. She'd thought those shallow thrusts the entire act, but she had not imagined she could be filled and stretched as she was now. It hurt. He was far too big for her to accommodate.

"Lila?" She heard the question in his voice, knew he asked if she was hurt.

"Don't you dare move," she whispered. "You are too big for this."

She thought she heard him laugh. If he was laughing at her, she would kill him.

"You fit me perfectly."

"No, I don't. Don't move or I *will* think you reprehensible."

He sounded as though he laughed again. "I have to move. Otherwise we'll be stuck like this forever."

"Then get out."

"Not yet, darling Lila. Give it a chance."

Darling. He'd called her *darling*. Did he mean it?

He withdrew but not all the way, sliding inside her again. She hissed at the pain.

"I'm sorry. I am trying to be careful, but you feel so damn good."

Withdraw and thrust. The next thrust was not quite so painful. It still felt strange and she too full, but it was not intolerable.

He moved faster, and she caught her breath because she could see how, if she wasn't still in some pain, the action might feel good.

"I'm sorry," he said, sounding as though he spoke through clenched teeth.

"Stop apologizing. It makes it difficult to hate you."

"Right. In that case, I'm not sorry." He groaned. "Not sorry at all." She felt his entire body tense. Beside her ear, his breathing sounded fast and ragged. Finally, he withdrew and rolled onto his back.

She pushed up, but he was already on his feet. "Don't move."

Lila lay back down. Why did he want her to lie still?

He padded away, then returned with a towel in one hand. He reached for her, and she squealed when she realized he planned to clean her between the legs.

"I can do that," she insisted.

He gave her a look of amusement. "It's not as though I haven't seen you there. And everywhere."

She took the towel from him and pressed it between her thighs. It came away tinged with pink. Lila blinked at the evidence of her lost virginity.

"It's normal," Brook said. She looked up, seeing only the shadow of him beside her. His backside was illuminated by the fire in the hearth, but she could not see his face or his expression. "Do you still hurt?"

She shook her head, surprised to find her throat too closed to enable her to speak.

"I'm told it will not hurt next time. Here." He dropped her chemise over her head and helped her pull it on. The feel of it was comforting, and when he knelt to help her tie the strings at the bodice, she allowed it.

If bedding her was supposed to make her fall out of love with him, he should have been less tender, less concerned. His attention and care made her heart swell with even greater love for him.

Which was foolish.

He didn't love her. He could never love her, not after what she'd done to him. He desired her, nothing more. The fact that he treated her so honorably served to show her what a fool she'd been when she'd refused to run away with him. He would have made her a wonderful husband. He would have cherished her and loved her. What were title and prestige compared to finding the one person who loved you and whom you could love in return?

Of course, she hadn't known what love was, what it felt like, how much she needed it, when he'd begged her to be his wife. She'd only known vanity and the heady feeling of being sought by so many men. She'd confused popularity with friendship, and when her mother fell ill and Lila had stepped away from public life for a time, she'd realized just how quickly popularity could fade and how few true friends she had.

The tally? Zero.

"You'd better climb under the covers before you catch cold. I'll join you in a moment."

Lila nodded and slid under the sheets, still warm from their bodies.

She hadn't deserved friends before. She hadn't deserved Brook Derring. She probably didn't deserve him now, but, oh, how she wanted him.

❧

Brook stepped behind the privacy screen and leaned one arm against the wall. He needed a moment to himself, a moment to gather his scattered thoughts. He rested his forehead on his arm and closed his eyes. The image of Lila, eyes closed and lips parted, rose in his mind. Brook quickly opened his eyes again.

She'd told him she loved him. What was he supposed to do with that information? Did he believe her? And if he did believe her, what then? It didn't change the past. It didn't mean he loved her or wanted to stay married to her. He'd married her to protect her and with the assurance it was a temporary union. He did not have to feel guilty for seeking an annulment when that had been agreed upon from the start.

He hadn't forced her to do anything. And he'd damn well made sure she enjoyed everything they did together. And still the thought that he'd ruined her wouldn't leave his mind.

She'd been an innocent.

He'd expected that. He would have been surprised if she'd never been kissed, never danced a little too close, never allowed a man's hands to stray a bit from what was strictly appropriate. But Lila was no rule breaker. She'd never let a man have her.

Until now.

Because she loved him.

She shouldn't love him. Not that that ever stopped anyone from falling in love. He should never have fallen in love with her all those years ago, but knowing that hadn't stopped him from doing so. His heart had hardened since then. He'd seen more of the world

after a week in the Saffron Hill rookery than many
men saw in a lifetime. Love was an emotion reserved
for those like Lila, privileged men and women with
the time and leisure to daydream. Love didn't feed a
hungry child or stave off the craving for gin or recover
the blunt lost at dice.

Love was a nice, if useless, emotion.

That didn't mean Brook hadn't felt anything when
he'd tumbled her. Perhaps it was because he had once
been in love with her that he'd felt more than he ever
remembered feeling when bedding a woman. Every
gasp, every breath, every moan seemed imprinted on
his brain. He'd wanted to give her more pleasure, even
if it meant his was not as great.

He could have taken her fast and hard. She'd been
ready for him, and she was no tiny, delicate flower. He
would have enjoyed her that way, especially after he'd
felt how tight and hot she'd been. He'd almost lost all
restraint then.

Instead, he'd been exceedingly careful and proceeded with the utmost care. He'd wanted everything
to be perfect for her.

Why the hell had he cared? She hadn't cared a
whit for his feelings when she'd crushed him with her
refusal to elope. And tonight, she'd encouraged him to
act the reprobate, to make her hate him.

So why hadn't he done it? He was perfectly capable
of all sorts of inexcusable acts. His thoughts swirled,
and when they settled, one remained.

He didn't want her to fall out of love with him.

Brook blew out a breath and pushed away from
the wall in disgust. What the devil was wrong with

him? He found a dry towel, dipped it in the basin of water, and washed the evidence of her virginity off his flesh. The cold water served to cool his ardor for her. Despite having had her just a few moments ago, he would have liked to take her again. He was a man of stamina and vigor, but usually his interest was not aroused for several hours after release. To want her when he'd just had her perplexed him.

Everything about her perplexed him. Beezle's capture and this whole affair could not end soon enough. Brook was ready for his old life back—long days and nights in his office on Bow Street, hours spent in the filth of St. Giles, time alone in his flat. This marriage could not end soon enough.

Brook splashed a handful of water on his face, then padded to the bed, where Lila lay. She didn't move, but he doubted she slept. He could all but hear her thinking. He climbed in beside her, her body heat reminding him how cold he'd acted, and he wondered what she thought about. He'd never once wondered what a woman thought about. He'd often wondered if his sister thought at all, but that was before she'd married Dorrington and ceased to be Brook's concern.

Since he would not stoop to asking her what she thought about, he did the next best thing. He pulled her into his arms and kissed her temple. "Go to sleep," he ordered. "Morning will be here soon enough, and it's a long walk back."

"Do we have to go back?" she asked with a yawn.

"There's the cat to think of," he said, only half joking.

"We should take her and the kittens back to London with us."

Wouldn't that be a cozy, domestic scene? What was next? Children?

He supposed that was possible now. She might be pregnant. He hadn't used any means to prevent pregnancy. Those were risky at best, but at least they were somewhat effective. He might have pulled out with Lila, lowered the chance she might conceive. Why hadn't he?

That was another issue he preferred not to examine too closely. Perhaps he'd best take his own suggestion and go to sleep.

"Brook?"

Her voice came to him through a haze, and he nuzzled closer to her. She was warm and soft in his arms. Her hair smelled of wildflowers.

"Go to sleep, Lila." He'd just drifted off and sleep tugged at him like an insistent toddler.

"I will. I just wanted to say thank you for telling me why you still hate me."

He sighed and opened his eyes. "I don't hate you. But, Lila, regardless of what happens between us, in bed or otherwise, we have no future. Understand that. There is no hope for you and me."

He heard her take a shaky breath.

"I don't say this to hurt you. I say it because it's the truth." And because he *didn't* want to hurt her. "I cannot love you, but I don't hate you."

"I'd understand if you did," she said after a long silence. "I know you didn't want my apologies. I know they change nothing, but sometimes we must say the things we feel because otherwise it may be too late."

He stared into the darkness.

"My mother has been gone for almost five years, and daily I still think of little bits of information I'd like to share with her. I have questions I wish I'd asked, conversations I wished we'd had."

"You never seemed overly fond of her when I first met you."

He could feel her shrug. "I suppose I wasn't. When she became ill, when I realized I would lose her, I wished we had been closer. I tried to make that up at the end, but I never truly could."

He pulled her closer, even as his mind screamed *danger*. Whispered confessions in the dark could lead down alleys he did not want to take. He'd revealed as much of his emotional life—all of it from his past—as he would. He did not want to know any more about her emotions. He did not want to see this soft, caring side of her.

"I'm sorry for your loss. I still think of my father at times." Which was true. Not because he missed the earl but because there were so many reminders of him at Derring House. He'd been an old man even when Brook had been young. Every tutor he and Dane had ever had talked incessantly of what would be expected when his brother became the earl. His father's death was almost accepted long before it ever occurred. He supposed losing his mother would have been more of a shock.

"That's right. You lost your father shortly after I—"

"Yes. It was another blow, but the two of them together made me the man I am today."

She turned in his arms, the silky skin of her belly sliding against him. "What do you mean?"

"It means I wanted an escape, and I found one. I escaped to St. Giles and Whitechapel and Holborn Hill. I found my true calling. If I'd married you, if my father had lived longer, I would never have become an inspector. I would never have been knighted."

"Speaking of which, why—"

He put a finger over her lips. They were petal soft and lush, begging to be kissed. He resisted, though his cock rose to attention in protest.

"That's a story for another time and not nearly as romantic as the ladies like to make it." He moved his finger away. "Now, go to sleep."

He closed his eyes, opening them again immediately when she snuggled up against his chest, her soft hair tickling his shoulder. Her mother's death truly had changed her. He would have to have been a stubborn fool not to see that. Now she apologized, she worried over kittens, she took an interest in someone besides herself.

She *loved* him.

But he could not go back. The Brook that had loved her had been a different person. That man was but a distant memory.

Lila pressed her cheek against his shoulder and curled into him. Their legs tangled at the ankles, and he tried very hard not to imagine lifting one of those legs and resting it over his hip. He could slide into her heat quite easily that way.

Not tonight.

Tonight, he would sleep. He closed his eyes and tried to settle his body, but where to put his hands? He shifted one under his head but the other kept falling over the lush curve of her hip. All too easy to cup her rounded bottom from that position.

His cock ached uncomfortably, and Brook gritted his teeth.

Lila's breathing slowed, and while he struggled to find a comfortable position, she was soon sleeping. Damn the woman, and damn his misguided sense of chivalry. If only his body would listen to his sense of honor.

The easiest way to avoid being stirred up by her was to turn his back to her. All he need do was push her off him and roll over. She didn't weigh much, and it would be easily accomplished. But all Brook did was think of moving her out of his arms. In the end, he couldn't tear himself away.

Sixteen

LILA'S WRIST LOOKED LIKE IT HAD BEEN RUN OVER BY a carriage wheel. By the next morning, her normally slender hand had swollen to twice its size, and her wrist was as thick as her palm. She could not even manage to fit a glove over the offensive-looking body part. She kept it tucked in her pelisse all through breakfast, which made for difficulty eating.

When she remembered to eat, that was.

Most of the time, she could not seem to keep her gaze from straying to her husband's face. He looked exactly as he had yesterday and the day before, although he'd shaved at the posting house and now the scruff from his chin was gone. She liked seeing the razor-sharp lines of his cheeks and jaw, but she kept expecting him to look different somehow. Of course, why should he? She was not the first woman he'd made love to. He'd not been a virgin. Besides, all of her peeks in the mirror had shown her that her own face looked exactly the same as it had last night.

No sign proclaiming her lost virtue had appeared on her forehead. No blood even stained the sheets where they'd slept the night before. Brook's quick attention with the towel had all but erased the evidence.

She wondered if she would be expunged from his thoughts as quickly once the annulment proceeded.

"Stay here," Brook said, interrupting her perusal. She quickly lowered her gaze and toyed with her porridge.

"Where are you going?"

"I asked the proprietor to acquire supplies for us. I want to see if he's done so. Keep the ice on your wrist. It will help with the swelling."

Obediently, she placed her wrist on the small block of ice she'd been given, but as soon as Brook was gone, she lifted it again. She knew ice was rare and expensive, even in the winter, but her wrist hurt more on the ice than off. She supposed she should have been thankful it was her wrist and not her ankle, although had it been her ankle, she might have been able to stay at the posting house another night. Lila did not look forward to the long, cold walk back to the hovel or the rustic conditions once they arrived.

She should have enjoyed her time there, as it would be over soon and she'd probably never see Brook again. She had been such a fool not to see his value when they'd first met. All she'd seen was a boy without a title or power or sense of style. Now she knew none of those attributes meant a man had any substance, any character. Brook was the sort of man who considered the needs of others before his own. It might not have been fashionable to chase down thieves in Spitalfields or search for missing people in Seven Dials, but he did it all the same. He genuinely cared about the welfare of others. How had she thought an intricately tied cravat comparable?

One day, Brook would fall in love with a woman, and when he did, he would love her with the sort of devotion and faithfulness Lila knew of only from novels. And to think, if she hadn't been such a fool, that woman might have been her. She'd probably grow old with only her memories of the time they'd spent together.

The door to the private room opened, and Lila quickly set her wrist on the ice again. But instead of Brook, a young woman with light brown hair and bright blue eyes stood in the doorway. Her hair had been pulled into a loose mass of curls, but much of it had come free and tumbled about her shoulders and her pale cheeks. She wore a bright blue redingote with ruffles and pleating down the front, and a matching bonnet hung from one gloved wrist. Lila knew immediately from the woman's dress, she was someone of wealth and importance.

But something about what way she stood, with one hand on her hip, belied that she was a lady.

"Are you Mrs. Brook Derring?" she asked.

Lila nodded, still staring at the woman. Her speech had been perfectly correct, but something about it did not sound quite right.

"And who are you?" Lila asked, rising.

The girl turned away from her. "Max, it's true! There was a wedding. Brook's wife is in here."

Booted footsteps rattled the boards beneath her feet and then a man stood behind the woman. He swept off his hat and gave Lila a ceremonious bow. Lila immediately curtsied.

"Forgive us for intruding, Mrs. Derring," he said, his speech that of a perfect nobleman.

"The proprietor said we might find you in here," the woman added. "We had to see this for ourselves."

"We should introduce ourselves," the man said, though Lila had already inferred who they were. The man was tall with brown hair and brown eyes. He and Brook were of a height, and though Brook's hair was lighter and his eyes darker, the resemblance was too strong to miss. This must be Lord Dane, the earl and Brook's brother.

"I am Lord Dane and this is my wife, Lady Dane. I believe you are now my sister by marriage."

"Yes," Lila finally managed. "I'm so pleased to meet you, my lord. My lady." She curtsied to each.

"You don't have to call me *my lady*," the countess said. "You can call me Marlowe."

"Marlowe?" Lila remembered the stories in the paper now. The earl had married a former thief. This must be she. "I'm Lad—Lillian-Anne, but everyone calls me Lila."

"A pleasure, Lila," the earl said. "You are the eldest daughter of the Duke of Lennox?"

"Yes. I believe we met years ago."

"I remember, my lady. You had quite the come out." Dane entered the room and looked about. "Where is my brother?"

"He went to speak with the proprietor about supplies. We're staying at the cottage nearby."

Dane's eyes widened. "What the deuce is he thinking taking you there?"

"You have a house nearby?" Marlowe asked.

"Not exactly." He pulled out a chair and gestured to his wife.

"No, thank you. My arse is sore from too much sitting as it is."

Lila coughed, but the earl didn't seem the least bit offended.

"I take it you do not know the reason for the marriage," Lila said.

"Is there a reason?" Dane asked with a quick look at her waist. "Besides the usual, that is."

"The dowager wrote to summon us to the wedding," Marlowe said. "That was the extent of the letter. She often does quite a lot of summoning and not much explaining."

"We were detained by heavy rains and flooding near Northbridge Abbey," Dane said, "or we would have come sooner."

"That's very kind of you," Lila said, "but one can hardly fault you, considering the abruptness of the wedding."

The earl nodded, obviously waiting for her to go on. Lila wondered where to begin and how much to reveal. The silence must have dragged on longer than the countess liked. Finally, she moved beside her husband. "Am I the only one wondering why the wedding had to occur so quickly?" she whispered loudly.

Lila laughed. The girl was gauche, but it seemed to come from a lack of guile. Lila found her oddly refreshing.

"We are waiting for Lady Lila to craft her response," Dane answered, making very little effort at sotto voce.

"Her response to what?" Brook asked coming in

behind his brother. "Don't tell me you've begun the inquisition already. I thought I was the inspector."

"Brook!" Marlowe flung herself at him, embracing him hard and with obvious ease. Lila wondered if she would ever feel as comfortable embracing her own husband.

Dane patted his brother on the shoulder and ruffled his hair, which seemed to annoy Brook and amuse Dane. "Where is Hunt?" the earl asked. "He's been lax in his duties."

"He's in London with Dorrington, watching Beezle."

"Beezle?" Marlowe parted the two men, shouldering herself between them. "Not the Beezle I know."

"The same. In fact, you're well met," Brook said, moving toward the table where Lila stood. "I'd like to ask you some questions, if you don't mind."

He indicated the chair Dane had pulled out earlier, but this time, instead of complaining about her backside, the countess sat. Lila sat as well, knowing the men could not do so until both ladies were seated.

Brook gave a succinct accounting of the events leading up to their marriage. Lila was curious to see whether he would mention his plans for annulment, but he said nothing of it, as though marrying a woman to protect her from a crime lord were an everyday occurrence in his life. Perhaps it was. She hadn't thought to ask if he'd been married before.

"Marlowe," he said after he'd finished with the summary, "I wondered if you could think back and recall any political men Beezle might have associated with—MPs or lords or the like."

Marlowe's brow furrowed and she lifted her thumb

to her mouth, then, realizing she had her gloves on, lowered it again.

Lila could not help but interrupt. "Forgive me for asking, but how do you know this Beezle? Was it from the time you were a…the time you lived in St. Giles?"

Marlowe smiled at her. "I do know I was a pick-pocket and a housebreaker. I've never pretended differently, and in this case, you're in luck. Beezle was part of my gang, the Covent Garden Cubs. I wouldn't call him a crony. We never liked each other much."

"And this is the same man who abducted me? Is that sort of thing common?"

"Not when I was in the gang, though I wouldn't put it past Beezle. He was never afraid of taking a risk, and abduction isn't anything new. Satin—he was the old arch rogue—abducted me. The difference is that I was a child. I can't see why they'd abduct a woman unless it's for ransom."

"That was my thought," Brook added. "There have been a few other instances of that sort of thing going on, but I couldn't tie them to Beezle."

"What is an arch rogue?" Lila asked.

"The prince prig," Marlowe answered. "The dimber-damber upright man."

"The leader," Dane supplied. "When I met Marlowe, Satin was the leader. He was hanged at Tyburn, and Beezle took his place in the gang."

"The Covent Garden Cubs are one of the most powerful gangs in London right now," Brook said. "Beezle took what Satin started and expanded it. There's nary a gin house or a bawd in Seven Dials who doesn't pay something to Beezle to keep trouble away."

"Beezle is the trouble, no doubt," Dane added.

"Considering he's mostly built upon what Satin began, I thought he might have retained some of his political contacts. Did you ever see Satin or Beezle with a Mr. Fitzsimmons, an MP?"

Marlowe looked down at the table. She tapped a finger in a staccato rhythm. Finally, she shook her head. "I don't remember any politicians, any swells at all to tell you the truth. Sure, the swells were bubbles—I mean, what's the word?" She looked at Dane.

"Victims?"

She rolled her eyes. "Right, but Satin would never have trusted a nob any more than he'd trust a pig." She looked at Brook. "Oops, sorry."

"I'm not a Bow Street Runner, but I suppose I qualify as a pig all the same."

"Yes, but you're the best sort of pig," she said, kissing his cheek and holding out her hand. In it, his gold pocket watch flashed. "Just keeping in practice," she said when he took it back.

"What about me?" Dane asked.

She kissed his cheek. "You are the best sort of nob."

Lila could see the love between husband and wife, between the entire family. It was obvious the trick of picking Brook's pocket was one the countess had done in the past. It had the feel of an inside joke. Lila's family had had their own, but that was before her mother had died.

"I'm sorry not to be more help, but a week away from the rookery is like a year, which means I've been gone decades. I will say that if I had yellow boys and was looking for someone to filch the daughter of a duke, Beezle would be an easy choice."

"But no one wanted me filched—er, abducted," Lila argued. "I was kidnapped for ransom."

"Beezle told you that?" Marlowe asked.

"No. He didn't tell me anything except I would be sorry I'd seen the murder."

"He would have killed you to rid himself of the witness. Unfortunately, if he'd filched you for ransom, that means he wouldn't be paid."

"That is unfortunate," Brook said, "but he didn't expect her to see. He thought she was locked in a cellar."

"I still don't think he would have killed her until after he had the blunt," Marlowe said.

Brook ran a hand though his hair. "I hadn't considered that angle. I don't know what Beezle was thinking because Dorrington found her before Beezle had a chance to kill her. Considering what she saw, I believe she's in danger."

"I agree," Marlowe said. "And you're right to hide out here. Beezle knows London better than his ugly mug, but he doesn't know the countryside. Still, I feel…" She looked at Dane, and he nodded.

"I'll take care of it."

Lila wondered how married people did that, how they managed to communicate without words. She and Brook could barely communicate with words.

"Take care of what?" Brook asked.

"Making the staff of Northbridge aware of a possible threat. I don't want anything to happen to Lyndon or Maxwell while we're away."

"Beezle is after Lila, not your sons," Brook said,

"but it's not a bad idea. One cannot be too careful when dealing with a man like Beezle."

"Should we continue on to London?" Dane asked. "The wedding is over and you and your new bride are not in Town."

"That's up to you." Brook folded his arms.

"What he means," Marlowe said, "is it won't be on his head when your mother flies into a rage because we haven't been to see her."

"I'm sure Susanna would like to see you too," Brook added.

"Yes, but I'm not scared of Susanna," Marlowe said, speaking of Brook's sister. "We're closer to London now than Northbridge, and I'd rather go on. If I have to sit in the carriage for much longer today, I won't be responsible for my actions."

Lila saw her chance. "Would it be a terrible imposition to drive Sir Brook and me back to the hovel—I mean, cottage? It's quite cold for a walk."

"Of course," Dane said, gallantly. "I wouldn't hear of you walking."

"You may well have to hear of it," Brook said, rising. "Mrs. Derring and I cannot accept your offer. We'll walk." He leveled his dark gaze on her, a silent warning not to disagree. But Lila was in no mood to be amenable. Her wrist ached, her feet were sore from the walk yesterday, and she wanted no part of the cold wind she could hear rattling the shutters.

If she was honest with herself, she wanted no part of this marriage. She might initially have seen it as an inconvenience, a matter to be socially overcome, but now it had become so much more. She'd fallen in love with Brook, and she couldn't forgive him or herself for that, especially when he made it quite clear he would never return her affections.

When he made it quite clear she was the reason he would never return her affections.

And now she'd met his brother and Dane's wife, and Lila liked them. She found the countess oddly charming and the earl gracious. They were just the sort of people she would want at her dining table or around her at the hearth on a cold winter night.

Of course, there was no chance of any real relationship with Dane and his wife. She'd be separated from Brook soon enough. And the loss of what might have been a wonderful friendship rankled Lila.

Everything about Brook and their marriage rankled in the cold light of day.

Lila burst out of her seat, her cheeks burning with anger and indignation at the unfairness of the entire situation. "You walk. I'll take the carriage ride."

Brook raised a brow. Clearly he thought she was acting daft. "It's better if the Earl of Dane's coach is not seen at the cottage," Brook argued with a patience she imagined he generally reserved for small children. "I chose that cottage because it's not widely associated with the Derring family."

"Do you think this Beezle has men watching the cottage?" Lila asked sweetly. She waited for his answer. When he shook his head, she added, "There, then he will never know." She nodded at Marlowe. "Even the countess said this Beezle doesn't know the countryside. It will take several hours to walk back, and it's freezing. Your brother's coach can have us there in a half hour or less."

"Perhaps we should step outside and leave you two to discuss this privately," Dane said, rising and moving toward the door. "Marlowe, come on."

"Why?" she asked, clearly much more interested in the argument than in politeness.

"No need," Lila said, "I've made up my mind. I will wait for you in the coach, my lord." Lila swept out of the room.

❧

Brook had half a mind to stomp after her and drag her out of the coach, but that would only amuse his brother and Marlowe more. Already, Marlowe had a hand over her mouth to hide her smile.

"Perhaps I will wait in the coach with Lady Lila," Marlowe said.

"Good idea," Dane said. "She seems so frail and helpless. Best not to leave her alone."

Marlowe followed Lila, and Brook raised a hand. "Not a word."

"I wouldn't dream of saying anything against your lovely wife. She's quite the breath of fresh air."

"That's something considering who you married," Brook muttered.

"I suppose I always assumed that having a hero for a brother meant your wife would worship the ground you walked on. Did I miss something, or does Lady Lila seem lacking in worshipfulness?"

Brook had the urge to tell his brother Lila *did* worship him. Well, she was in love with him, at any rate. But he refused to rise to the bait. "It's not your concern."

"I won't argue with you there. Do I remember correctly? Isn't she the girl you mooned over for an entire Season?"

"You do know I fight better than you," Brook said, a warning in his voice.

"When next you're in London, we'll test that at Gentleman Jackson's," Dane said, clapping him on the back. "I imagine you'll be ready to beat someone to a pulp."

Brook removed Dane's hand from his shoulder. "Let's go before Lila decides to leave without us."

"Then you accept my hospitality as well?" Dane said as the two moved through the common room.

"It's either that or leave my wife to her own devices while I walk back. I can't think which is worse."

❧

The next night and day were the longest of Brook's life. All the talk of London had made him yearn to be back. He itched to return to the work he knew waited for him there. Crime in London never took a holiday, and he couldn't afford one either.

Not that this was a holiday. It was work, and Lila made sure it felt like work. Ever since they'd alighted from Dane's coach and waved good-bye, she'd been surly and snappish. She'd said more to the mother cat and kittens than she had to him. He'd obviously done something to upset her, and he knew enough of women to determine it was more than suggesting they walk back when she preferred to ride.

He had his first hint that night when he made a comment about retiring to bed, and she informed him he had better not think of touching her. He hadn't actually been thinking of bedding her—oh, very well, he had been thinking of it. Not seriously. He imagined she was somewhat sore after the night at the posting house.

There were other things they might do, and perhaps if he gave her pleasure, she would cease scowling at him.

He thought about asking what he'd done to upset her, but he'd attempted that with his sister Susanna a few times. Susanna had only become angrier, retorting, "You mean you don't know?"

Brook had inferred it was better to pretend to know than to ask. Still, he thought as he lay beside Lila that night, she did not act like a woman in love with him. She had pushed herself as far away from him as she could, and though she pretended to sleep, he knew from her breathing that she was no more asleep than he.

Perhaps she did act like a woman in love after all—a woman whose love is unrequited. He'd been clear that he didn't love her anymore and had no intention of falling in love with her now. Perhaps it was better that she distance herself from him emotionally before he distanced them physically.

She was hurt, and he understood that. He knew all about misery and heartache, but telling himself that didn't ease the guilt he felt for causing her pain. Because he knew what the torment of unrequited love felt like, he also could sympathize with her suffering.

What could he to do alleviate it? He couldn't make himself fall in love with her, though the Lila he knew now would have been easy to love. She was as intelligent and witty as she'd always been, but now she was also kind. But what he'd felt for her was in the past. He wasn't that foolish, lovesick boy any longer.

On the second night, he was rather tired of the heavy silence in the cottage. The weather had been clear all the night before and that day, and they'd both taken advantage of it and spent time outdoors. He'd wandered the length of the property, telling her he wanted to make sure all was secure. Brook had no idea what she did.

Not much, he thought when he returned. The cottage was as untidy as it had been when he'd left in the morning. The bed was unmade, the floors not swept, and the breakfast dishes unwashed. He hadn't ordered her to do any of those chores, but she might have taken it upon herself as she had nothing else to do but read the bloody book on the Peloponnesian Wars, which she'd done all afternoon the previous day.

He understood she'd always had servants, but he was not one of them.

It was almost dark by the time he entered the cold cottage. He noted immediately the fire in the hearth had all but died out. He stoked it, seeing all the other evidence of Lila's laziness. He didn't see her anywhere though. He went back outside and found the mother cat staring at the kitchen building while her two kittens tumbled one over the other nearby.

"She's in there, eh?" he asked the cat, who blinked her green eyes at him in response.

He couldn't think why she'd have gone to the kitchens when he'd brought back bread, cold meat, cheese, soup, and tea from the posting house. She need only heat the tea and soup, and that could be done by the hearth in the cottage—if she didn't allow the fire to burn out.

He strode to the kitchen and pulled open the door, immediately waving a hand to clear the plume of black smoke that billowed out. "What the hell?"

Someone coughed, and he covered his nose with his sleeve and burst inside. "Lila?"

She coughed again. At least he thought it was her. He couldn't see her for the smoke filling the room.

"Lila!" he yelled.

"Here." Her voice was faint but strong enough for him to pinpoint. He followed it until he all but tripped over her. He bent and realized she crouched on the floor.

"What are you doing? Get up!"

"They say smoke rises," she said through coughs. "I thought if I bent down I could see through it to put out the fire."

Fire? Sweet God in Heaven, give him strength not to throttle her. He dragged her out of the kitchen and sucked in clean air. A quick look at her told him she was uninjured, and he turned to study the building. He didn't see any plumes of fire yet. He had to put it out before it engulfed the kitchen. The risk that it would also spread to the house was too great to chance.

Brook removed his coat, then, taking a deep breath, dashed back into the kitchen and groped his way through the black smoke. How the hell was he to find the fire when he couldn't see anything? He finally moved toward the ovens, expecting to be overwhelmed by the heat at any moment. The smoke was strongest in the ovens, and Brook waved the coat to clear it. More black clouds billowed from the oven, and he threw his coat over it, hoping to douse whatever fueled the fire.

Almost immediately, some of the smoke cleared. Brook used his boot to stomp on the soot and ashes, and crush the embers of whatever was burning. Satisfied the danger was over, he emerged, fetched a bucket of water from the well, and returned, dumping the water on the steaming debris in the oven. He left the hiss and steam behind and fell outside, gulping in air.

"Can you breathe?" Lila asked, coming to kneel beside him. "Is the fire out?"

He nodded. He couldn't breathe well enough to speak yet.

"I don't know what happened. I was attempting to warm the bread—"

"Warm the bread?" he wheezed. Why the devil did she want to warm the bread?

"I thought it might be a nice addition to dinner, especially after I knew you would be out in the cold, but I couldn't quite understand how the oven worked, and then I had to look for kindling. By the time I found some, it was already late, but I managed to start a fire. If I'd been thinking, I would have brought a spark from the fire in the cottage, but I didn't think of that until later."

Brook closed his eyes. Perhaps it had been better when he didn't know how she'd spent the day.

"I put the bread inside the oven, but then it began

to smoke. I tried to stoke the fire, but that didn't work. Before I knew it, the smoke was so thick I could barely see."

That must have been the point at which he arrived.

Brook wanted to be angry with her. The bread was obviously a lost cause now, and she'd almost set the kitchen building on fire. But how could she know the stove's chimney was probably blocked with old ash and the debris of leaves that had accumulated over the years? Any servant would have thought to clean the stove before cooking, but Lila, in all her ignorance, still did not understand where she'd erred.

She'd wanted him to have warm bread. How could he be angry with her for that?

"Come inside," he said, hoping she hadn't ruined all the foodstuffs and they'd have something to eat. He stood and offered his hand, pulling her to her feet. The cat and the kittens trotted in ahead of them, and Brook lit the few candles he'd bought at the posting house. Lila sat in the chair and pulled off her boots, dropping them in the middle of floor.

"I'm covered in soot and ash," she said, shaking out her hair—again, on the floor. He supposed she expected him to sweep that up. "I need to wash."

Brook crossed his arms. "I suppose you want me to fetch water from the well."

"I'll warm it for us."

It was the most she'd spoken to him in two days, and he had to admit washing the smell of smoke off with warm water did sound appealing. With a sigh, he headed for the door again. Before he opened it, he turned back. "Do not start a fire while I'm away."

She rolled her eyes.

Tired now, his muscles sore from the exertions in the kitchen, he drew water up from the well and hauled the bucket into the cottage. He carried it toward the fire. Unfortunately, he had to pass the table and chair, and he'd forgotten about Lila's boots. With the bucket obscuring his vision, he stumbled over one of the boots, dropped the bucket, and landed hard on one knee.

"Bloody hell!" he roared. "What the devil are your boots doing in the middle of the floor?"

"I'm sorry." She swept them up and moved them to a corner where his valise sat. "I'll move them."

Brook rubbed his knee and rose to his feet, eyeing the pool of water on the floor where some had splashed over the rim of the bucket. "Good, and while you're at it, sweep up this soot, mop this water, and wash the dishes. I'm not your servant."

As soon as the words were out of his mouth, he knew he'd gone too far. Lila's head rose, her brown eyes burning with the gold of the fire. Her hands settled on her hips.

"And I'm not *your* servant." She held up her bandaged wrist.

Damn, he'd forgotten her wrist. No wonder she hadn't done any of the chores. They would all have been difficult with injury. He was such a thoughtless arse.

"If you wanted me to do any of that, all you need do is ask, and I would have tried, but I don't take orders."

Now was the time to apologize. Brook did consider doing so. He really did. But his damn knee twinged in pain and he was hungry and his eyes burned from the smoke and he'd forgotten how beautiful she was when she was angry. His hunger for her rose in him like a dragon.

"That's too bad," he said, moving toward her, "because you need someone to give you orders. You have no idea how to survive without servants."

She didn't want him, he reminded himself. He couldn't give her what she did want. And yet he yearned to strip off the dress she wore, stroke her satiny skin, kiss her mouth until it was wet and swollen.

"And why should I? I'm doing the best I can." She marched up to him, jabbing the air between them with a smoke-gray finger. Then, seeming to notice the finger, she bent and washed her sooty hand in the water.

"You're doing your best to kill us."

"Insufferable man!" She rose, flicking water from her hand and into his face.

The icy water added fuel to his desire, sparking a smoldering anger. Whether he was angry at himself for still wanting her or angry at her juvenile actions, he wasn't sure. He also didn't care. He clenched his hands to avoid taking her by the arms and shaking her. She wanted to flick him with water? She'd receive the same in return.

"You want a bath?" He bent and lifted the bucket.

Her eyed widened as she realized his intent. "Don't you dare," she hissed.

He gave her a tight smile. "Here's your bath." And he dumped the bucket of icy water over her head.

Seventeen

LILA SHRIEKED AS THE COLD WATER CRASHED OVER her with all the force of a battle-ax. She tore the bucket out of his hands and upended it over his head, but the lout had left none for her. Lila threw the bucket on the floor, where it thudded harmlessly into a corner. The cats raised their heads and then went back to sleep.

Brook stared at her with a look of shock, as though he couldn't quite believe what he'd done.

"You," she said, beginning to shiver, "are no gentleman."

It was the worst insult she could think of, and yet he grinned, seemingly unoffended.

"Do you hate me yet?"

She wanted to say yes. She wanted to hate him. It would have been easier than the pain of regret and the hurt of anticipating being without him. But she didn't hate him.

"Hate you? After you save me from the burning kitchen and douse the fire like some sort of hero? Is that how you propose to make me hate you?" Her teeth chattered as she spoke, and she saw him start forward as if he might try to warm her.

With one look, she stopped him.

"And this?" he asked, gesturing to her dripping hair and gown.

She clenched her fists. "This is a start."

"Then allow me to finish."

She saw exactly what he meant to do in the flash of desire in his eyes. Before she could protest—as though she would have—he pulled her into his arms and pushed her back against the table. His mouth descended on hers, kissing her with a heat that dispelled every single shiver. Warmth, like a small candle flame, bloomed low in her belly, radiating out and making her tingle everywhere.

His savage mouth slanted over hers again and again, and she responded by clutching his hair in what she hoped was a painful grip and kissing him just as savagely back. When she nipped his lip, he pulled back, pointing a finger at her. "Behave, little vixen."

"If you don't have to behave, neither do I."

He glanced down at her wet clothing and swore. "Get that off before you catch cold. You're shaking."

She reached for the dress's fastenings, but her fingers were clumsy and numb. The pins and tapes eluded her awkward efforts.

"I'll do it," Brook said. But instead of delicately unfastening the white muslin day dress sprinkled with a pattern of purple flowers and greenery, he yanked it off her shoulders. Lila gasped when she heard the material rip.

"What are you doing?"

"Warming you," he said. He yanked the dress down and took her chemise with it. Her already-hard nipples puckered painfully, and when his gaze swept over her appreciatively, she felt a surge of desire so strong she almost moaned. Her dress hung in tatters around her waist, but Brook slid it down, leaving her nude but for her stockings.

Despite the fact that he'd removed the wet clothing, she didn't feel any warmer. His hand cupped her hip and moved upward, smoothing the gooseflesh away. When he reached her breasts, he paused and rubbed his large thumbs over the distended tips. Lila's head fell back, and she moaned.

"Do you know how angry you make me?" he asked, his voice gruff. "Demanding to be driven back in the coach." He tweaked a nipple, and she pressed against him, wanting more. "Refurbishing my flat." He tweaked the other nipple, and her breath caught at the sensation. "Setting the kitchen on fire."

His hand ran down her belly, cupping her between the legs. He stroked her, his finger sliding into her wetness. He pushed her back on the table, lifting her on top of it and pushing her legs apart. His finger moved in and out, while his thumb circled her sensitive nub.

"Do you know how angry you make me?" she said, her voice breathless. "At least the kitchen fire was an accident. The cold water was not."

"It served its purpose," he said with a wicked smile and a long look at her naked body.

"Not entirely." She reached for the fall of his trousers, flicked it open, and took his hard length in her hand.

Her hands were cold, and he inhaled sharply at the feel of her freezing fingers on his warm flesh. She'd had no opportunity to study him, hadn't seen much more than a glimpse of this part of him. His skin here was slightly darker, the root of his manhood nested in golden hair. The skin was smooth, though hard, and the tip pink and stretched tight until the skin was almost shiny.

Tentatively, she ran a hand up and down his shaft. His hot gaze met hers, and his hands settled heavily on her thighs.

"Careful," he said, voice husky.

She raised a brow.

"You're playing a dangerous game."

"I'm not afraid." She wasn't. She knew so little of men and their anatomy, but she could see in his face what she did aroused him. She varied her strokes and her pressure until his eyes went dark and his breathing quickened.

The head of his erection felt like velvet in her hands. She bent and touched her tongue to it, wondering if he would have the same reaction she did when he put his mouth on her.

Brook made a sound of protest and grasped her hair. But he didn't pull her head away. He seemed to want to, but there was obviously a war within him and he couldn't decide which side to choose.

"No proper wife would do this," she murmured against that velvet skin.

"No," he agreed.

She licked him again. "But you like it." She could tell from the way his manhood jumped in her hand that he did.

"God yes."

She swirled her tongue around the velvet tip, and he made a sound of pure masculine pleasure.

"And you like me," she said. "Admit it."

He paused, and for a moment, she thought he would contradict her.

"I do," he finally said. "More than I want to. More than I should."

"Yes." She knew what he meant. "I love you, despite all your insufferable behavior and constant heroics."

She swirled her tongue around him again. He didn't love her. Not yet, but she had to hope, didn't she? He'd hated her a few days ago, and now he liked her more than he had ever thought he would. Could that not turn into love?

He had given her so much pleasure, and she wanted to give some of that back to him. She ran a hand up and down the hard length of him. "Tell me what to do," she whispered. "I want to be the most improper of wives."

"Lila, you don't need to do this."

She glanced up at him. "I want to. I find I…" She gave him a small smile. "I find I rather like it."

He closed his eyes, and she could feel him pulse in her hands.

"Put your mouth on me, take me inside."

She did as he asked, tasting the slight salty flavor of his skin on her tongue. She drew him in as far as she could, unable to take all of him.

"In and out," he groaned.

She obeyed, finding a rhythm he seemed to like.

His hands gripped her shoulders, and his breathing sounded harsh and labored to her ears.

"Suck, Lila."

She did as he asked and was rewarded by a deep moan. She would have repeated it all, but he pulled her up.

"Did I do something wrong?" she asked in confusion.

"No." His voice was brusque and harsh, and he jerked her off the table and into his arms. Before she could wrap her arms around him and divest him of his shirt, he spun her around and bent her over the table.

Her breasts pressed against the smooth wood, still warm from the heat of her body. She turned her head to look at him as he stepped between her legs, kicking them open. Lila's mouth dropped as she realized how exposed he'd made her. His hand roved over the bare flesh of her bottom, settling between her legs.

Two fingers dipped inside her, and she couldn't stop her body from arching back at the pleasure of his touch. The movement brought her in contact with his manhood, the heat of the hard staff brushing against her. She pressed back harder, taking more of him inside her and rubbing against that hard flesh just outside.

"Give me strength," he muttered, sliding his fingers out and replacing them with the thick head of his manhood.

Lila stilled, realizing what he meant to do. Her eyes searched his face, which was flushed and tense with strain. Their gazes collided.

"I won't hurt you," he said.

She gasped as he pressed inside her, entering her a mere fraction but enough to awaken every single nerve. Need coiled in her belly, need for the fullness of him, while the tips of her sensitive breasts pebbled against the hard table. She dug her fingers into the wood as he gave her a little more of what she wanted.

He moved so slowly, so frustratingly slowly. She rocked back, trying to take more of him, but his hands caught her hips.

"Not yet."

"More," she moaned when he only gave her another inch.

"I don't want to hurt you," he said through what sounded like clenched teeth. "You are so bloody tight."

"Is that bad?"

"No, good. Very good. I can't keep hold of my control."

"Then let go." She wiggled her hips again as best she could with his hands holding her still. "You won't hurt me."

With a groan, he slid into her, filling her so fully and completely that she gasped. This sensation was completely different than what they'd done the other night. If that had been an invasion, this was a conquest.

And she loved it. Loved the push of him inside her and the slide of him as he withdrew. His hands on her hips moved her body, but she found the rhythm easily enough. She rose on tiptoes to take him deeper, and his hands on her hips clenched. Reaching forward, he took one of her breasts in his hand, fondling the hard nipple. The waves of pleasure flowed through her, each one crashing higher than the next. As his pace quickened, he seemed to swell inside her, and she couldn't stop the small mewls of pleasure from escaping her lips.

His fingers on her nipple were as relentless as his thrusts in and out of her. And then his other hand slid over her hip and between her legs to that place where they were joined. He found that sensitive bud and massaged it with the same insistent movements as her nipple. A crippling wave of pleasure crashed over her, making her legs wobble. She pressed her hands against the table for support as he rocked into her again, his fingers still playing her, bringing her higher and higher until she came apart with something between a sob and a scream.

And still he persisted, his fingers teasing and his hard length caressing every single sensitive spot. She had not thought she could climax again or climax harder, but the wave she rode crested, and her entire body felt as though white heat flowed through it. For a moment she was weightless, senseless, drugged by the pleasure, and then she felt the weight of his head on her shoulder blades.

Brook had felt her climax, the clench of her muscles making him lose all control. He'd managed to hold off long enough to prolong her pleasure, teasing it out of her, but her erotic cries of pleasure and the feel of the plump flesh of her bottom pushing urgently against him finally undid him.

He pumped into her, coming so hard and long that he could barely keep on his feet. For a moment the room seemed to spin and when he opened his eyes he was panting on top of her, her warm skin like silk under his cheek.

What the bloody hell had happened? Even as he opened his eyes, spasms of pleasure still assaulted his body. It was the most intense sexual experience he'd ever had, and damn him if he didn't want to repeat it. He couldn't. Not right away, at least. Still, what was wrong with him? Shouldn't he have had his fill of her? Shouldn't he be sated?

He gently extricated himself from her and seeing her still bent over the table, pulled her up and into his arms. He turned her, taking her face in his hands and kissing her tenderly. He'd meant it to be one kiss, but he couldn't seem to drag his mouth away from hers. And his bloody cock was hardening again.

"I had no idea," she said against his lips. "That was amazing."

"Yes," he agreed. It had been, and he should leave it there because it could never possibly be that good again.

"Is it always like that?" she asked.

He blew out a breath. "No. It's never like that."

Her honey-brown eyes flicked up, searching his face. He knew what she wanted to see there, knew she hadn't exaggerated when she'd said she was in love with him. He could see it plainly on her face.

But he could not love her back.

He picked her up and carried her to the bed, then stood on the side and pulled off his shirt and trousers. Her gaze slid down his body and now his cock did harden. Her tongue darted out to touch the tip of her lip, and he could hardly restrain himself. Her legs parted slightly, her body unconsciously welcoming him.

"Again?" she asked, her voice low and sultry.

In answer, he threw his shirt aside and climbed in beside her.

Later, she rolled over and gave him a drowsy smile. "I've gone all liquid inside. I shall never be able to rise from this bed."

"Good. I want to keep you here."

Her fingers trailed over his chest, her touch light but no longer tentative. "We have to eat again. In fact, I do believe we forgot to eat supper."

"You're right."

"I'll make us something." She began to rise, but he caught her arm and kissed her.

"Stay. I'll fetch us something. We can eat in bed."

"How decadent."

He winked. Brook found bread she hadn't burned to cinders, a bit of cold meat, and the last of the cheese. He gave the mother cat a bit of the meat and brought the rest to the bed with a flagon of wine.

He hadn't bothered dressing, and when he returned, her appreciative gaze was on him. He did enjoy the way she looked at him—as though there was one sugared plum left and he was it.

"This is the last of the wine," he said, hefting the container to test its weight.

"I'll sip sparingly." She took it from his hands and, pulling the sheet around her breasts, tried to drink it delicately. It dribbled down her chin. She tried to catch it with her hand, but it was a feeble attempt.

Brook took the wine back. "This is no time for delicacy. Drink like you mean it." He gulped from the flagon, exaggerating the gesture by throwing his head back. She laughed, took the bottle, and attempted to mimic his gesture. She looked ridiculous, but he admired her willingness to try.

They shared the simple meal, Lila brushing crumbs from the sheets and Brook telling her they could just shake them out and not to bother.

"I can't help it. When I was young I'd sneak cake into bed, and I was always so afraid of being caught, I'd try to erase all evidence."

"You were a wicked child," he teased.

"Not as wicked as Ginny."

"Your young sister? I thought her rather adorable."

"Ginny? You met her?"

"We played a brief game of hide-and-seek."

"Her favorite. You're right. She's not a wicked child. She's actually very sweet and good-natured. At least, I think so. The Vile Valencia won't allow me be near her for more than a few moments for fear I might contaminate the child."

"Contaminate her?"

"I'm infected with a horrible disease—the inability to marry." She tucked a strand of dark hair behind her ear. She had lovely ears, small and shaped like shells.

And if he was admiring her ears, he was truly daft.

"Ah. That is a dreadful ailment," he said with mock seriousness, "but I hardly think of concern to a child of three or four."

"It's an excuse. My stepmother hates me, and she would keep me from my father and my sister as much as possible."

"What crime did you commit?"

"I'm the daughter of my father's first wife." She

looked down at the mention of her mother, but not before he saw the sadness.

"You still miss her."

"Every day. She was the most kindhearted woman. She might have been a busy duchess, but she always made time for Colin and me. I remember her sitting on the floor with us in her silks and satins, playing with a wooden ball. She doted on me, gave me anything I wanted."

That explained quite a bit, Brook thought, although as the daughter of a duke, Lila would likely have been spoiled regardless.

"But do you know what I remember most?"

"What is that?" he asked, admiring the way her wide eyes shined.

"She always listened to me. I must have been a silly child, always prattling on about imaginary balls and gowns and princes. I hear Ginny playacting, and it makes me smile. I'm sure I was the same. But unlike Valencia, my mother listened to me. When I'd concoct some story about a knight and a dragon, she would crouch down, look into my eyes, and focus all her attention on me." Lila's gaze had drifted to the fire, and he knew she was far away. She'd gone back to the time when her mother was alive, when her life was still simple.

"She made me feel important," Lila said. "She made me feel loved."

Brook kissed her then because he could imagine her as a pampered but lonely child. All she'd wanted was love. That was all she still wanted, and damn him if he was another person who could not give it to her.

&

The rain woke him. The steady patter of it made him want to roll over and settle himself next to the warmth of Lila in the bed with him. But when he tried, he realized she wasn't beside him.

He sat, finding her immediately. She stood near the door, fastening a cloak over her shoulders.

"Where are you going?" he demanded.

She started and cut a look at him, her expression one of surprise but not guilt. "I'm thirsty," she said. "I thought I'd go to the well and draw a bit of water. Since I was up, I built up the fire and put more wood on it."

Brook stared at her. She'd stoked the fire and would go out into the night in the rain to fetch water? They should have had water inside the cottage, but he'd dumped it over her head. If anything, he should be the one to fetch water.

"I'll get it," he said, swinging his legs over the side of the bed.

"No." Lila held up a hand. "I'm already dressed and ready. Besides, the rain has slackened for the moment. By the time you dress, it's likely to start pouring again."

"Do you know the way?"

"Of course." She reached for the handle on the door, unchaining the lock. Then she peered back at him over her shoulder. "And when I return, you can warm me up again."

Brook watched her go, trying not to give in to the deluge of erotic thoughts that suggestion elicited. Instead, he lay back and closed his eyes. For the first time, he didn't look forward to the annulment of their marriage. He didn't want her to go, didn't want her to leave his bed. But he could hardly keep her as his wife until he tired of tumbling her and then seek an annulment. Even though the king had promised him an easy annulment, Brook could hardly justify treating the daughter of the Duke of Lennox—or any woman for that matter—in such a manner.

They could always stay married. They had passion, and in time he might grow to feel more for her. He might one day forgive her. She had a title and wealth and a long line of prestigious ancestors. That would please his mother. She'd give him children one day, which would also please his mother.

If he remained married to Lila, he'd have fulfilled his obligations as the second son of an earl quite sufficiently. He didn't care much about such matters, but he knew how Society worked and knew what was expected. Brook had never been against marriage. Even after the debacle with Lila when he'd been four and twenty, he knew some day he would propose again.

He just hadn't thought it would be to the same woman.

Now that he had her, why not keep her?

His chest tightened at the thought.

Why not? Because she hadn't wanted him. Because she'd laughed at him. Because she'd made him hate himself.

And yet, she was outside now—in the cold and the rain—fetching water. She'd tried to warm bread for him. She'd tended him when he'd been injured. She wasn't the same woman who'd refused his proposal.

And if he was honest with himself, he was beginning to like her, despite himself. He'd never spent much time talking to the women he bedded. For the most part, they were vapid actresses or widows. They wanted a bit of fun and not much more. Brook had thought he wanted the same, but was that all he wanted? He hadn't realized what it would be like to whisper secrets and confide intimacies with a woman. He hadn't known he wanted anything more than a tumble.

And perhaps he hadn't.

Until Lila.

He wanted to know everything about her, from the time she'd fallen off her pony jumping a fence to the first time she'd been kissed. And he'd found himself telling her about his life too, about his favorite dog when he'd been a boy and how he and Dane had played at Colonists and Red Coats. Brook, being the younger, had always had to be George Washington.

Even worse, in Dane's version, Washington surrendered to Cornwallis.

Brook hadn't known he wanted someone to share his life with, not simply his bed. Lila had shown him that. But why the devil did it have to be her to show him what he was missing? The one woman he could never forgive, could never love.

The mother cat padded over to the door and made a soft meow. Brook sat. He supposed that meant the cat wanted out, but why would she want out in the rain and cold of the middle of the night? The cat lowered her head, sniffing at the base of the door, and Brook realized something had attracted her attention. Had she heard a mouse or did she anticipate Lila's return?

Thunder rumbled in the distance. Shouldn't Lila have returned by now?

Heart beginning to thud, Brook pulled on his trousers, boots, and coat, not bothering with a shirt. She'd gotten turned around on her way to the well or back. He'd find her and bring her back before the rain started in earnest. Pushing his feet into his boots, he opened the door.

"Lila?" he called.

No answer.

The wind blew rain into his face, and he wiped it out of his eyes and squinted at the darkness. "Lila!"

The tree branches swayed, and in the distance, thunder boomed. The storm was coming closer. He needed to bring her inside before it worsened. He kept his gaze on the yard, fixed in the direction of the well, and when a burst of lightning lit up the sky, he was ready. But the lightning revealed nothing more than what he'd seen in the gloomy darkness.

The yard was empty.

Lila was gone.

trees and bushes. Beezle could slit her throat and leave
her for dead, and she'd be cold and stiff by the time
Brook stumbled on her body.

If some wild animal didn't eat her first.

She shivered from cold and fear, dragging her feet
in an effort to slow Beezle. She squirmed and fought
and slowed their progress as much as she could. His
arms were thin but wiry, and his grip almost painful. She could feel the indents of his fingernails in
her cheek, where his hand still covered her mouth,
and he'd pressed her injured wrist hard against her
body. The ache from her smashed wrist threatened to
overwhelm her. But she'd feel much more pain if she
didn't keep fighting.

The rain came down harder, the water running
over her face and obscuring her vision. She blinked it
out of her eyes, seeing the tracks her boots had made
in the soft dirt behind the kitchen. All Brook need
do is walk that way, and he would know where she'd
been taken. But of course, he'd look for her at the
well. By the time he thought to circle around to the
kitchen, it might be too late.

Fighting the feeling of helplessness, she dug her
elbow back and into Beezle's stomach. It wasn't a very
good blow, but it was enough to dislodge his grip
slightly. His rain-slicked hands slipped when he grasped
her again, and for a moment, she broke free. Lila
stumbled forward, lurching back toward the kitchens
and Brook. But her feet caught on the hem of her
dress, the slight delay giving Beezle enough time to
catch her again.

Her grasped her injured wrist, twisting it behind

her back. Lila screamed in pain. Beezle's hand clamped down on her mouth, but she shook her head until his hand slipped away.

"Brook! Here! Broo—"

Beezle covered her mouth again. For a moment the agony of her bent wrist subsided, and then pain exploded in her head. The blackness of the night widened and darkened, and when she saw the next flicker of lightning in the night sky, it was from beneath a canopy of branches.

He had her in the woods. She was as good as dead.

❧

Brook headed toward the well, wishing for more light so he might track her footprints. He could see the evidence of tracks back and forth, but they'd both been over that way many times the last few days, and he wasn't certain which were hers and which were fresh. He was almost to the well when he spotted the indistinct shape on the ground. As he neared it, he made it out to be the bucket.

Brook's throat closed, his lungs constricting painfully. He bent and righted the bucket, his fingers brushing the pool of water near the overturned opening.

Pieces clicked into place like the parts of an unfinished portrait. Investigations were always thus for him. He would see part of a nose or a mouth and when he had the whole image, that was when he knew what had happened or who was to blame.

The overturned bucket was one piece. She'd made it to the well. She'd filled the bucket. She'd been on her way back.

Why had she dropped the bucket? Where was she now?

The portrait might have lacked detail, but he could make out the face well enough.

Somehow Beezle had found them, and now he had Lila.

He thought he heard something—a voice—over the wind and rain, but when he stood and cocked his head, he couldn't make out anything but the crack of lightning and the whistle of wind through the tree branches. Brook stood, hands on hips, and stared at the yard. Beezle couldn't have gone far. Where would he have taken her?

The woods or the road. One would provide more cover; the other would provide a quick escape. They were in opposite directions, so Brook knew he had to choose well and choose quickly.

Beezle would want the woods if he intended to hide or if he intended to kill her. The fear punched him in the gut at the thought of Lila lying dead among the wet leaves and low-hanging branches. He pushed the fear back, unwilling to acknowledge it. Fear clouded his senses, and he needed all his wits about him.

He looked toward the road. Beezle hadn't walked from London. He had a horse or cart waiting for him somewhere, most likely somewhere off the road that ran in front of the cottage. He'd take her toward the road if he wanted to bring her back to London.

The road was three-quarters of a mile in front of the cottage, and the woods ran several miles behind it. If he made the wrong choice, it would cost him his life.

No—it would cost Lila her life. But with a dawning

horror, he realized losing her would mean the end of his life too.

Brook stood in the cold rain and turned toward the road. Then with a roar of frustration, he headed toward the woods.

He found the trail immediately. If it was Beezle, he'd been alone. She'd fought him. He could see Beezle had struggled to drag her away. The tracks hadn't been filled with water yet, so the trail was still relatively new. He was right behind them.

And then reached the spot where the hard impressions of her smaller boots faded. For whatever reason, she'd stopped fighting, and Beezle had pulled her into the woods with much less effort. In the darkness, Brook had to stop and examine the ground, the rain washing away the trail in places and clouding his vision. He might have been close behind, but Beezle had been wise to take her at night and during a storm. Brook could find anyone and anything in the labyrinth of Seven Dials or Spitalfields, but in the open country, he was not quite as skilled. He'd never felt the lack of his experience so keenly as when he reached the edge of the forest and the first covering of leaves.

Brook swore under his breath. Now the trail was even harder to make out. He'd start down one way, realize he must have missed a sign, and have to double back again. The only thing that kept him going was sheer determination and the fact that he hadn't found her body yet.

Finding her dead seemed all but inevitable at this point. The search was taking him too long. Beezle had had more than enough opportunity. Brook regretted not donning a shirt. He was stiff and cold, his clothing soaked through to the skin. The discomfort was nothing. Brook wouldn't give up until he had her in his arms again. A couple hours ago, she'd been warm and alive, curled beside him, safe. In a moment, his world had spun around, and everything he'd cared about, held on to—his pride, the past, her spoiled behavior—no longer mattered.

He just wanted her safe. Alive. Back in his arms.

Realizing he'd lost the trail again, he backtracked, forcing himself to concentrate. He couldn't think of her dead. Couldn't allow himself to imagine the bleakness of his life without her.

He let the numbness seep into his bones, his mind, his heart. With renewed purpose, he once again picked up the trail.

❧

"He's like a buff in search of a bone." Beezle swore. For the first time since he'd dragged her into the woods, Lila felt a sense of hope. Brook was following them. Brook would find her. Save her.

Beezle had dragged her for miles, through the pouring rain, across freezing creeks, over fallen logs. When she'd fallen, he'd kicked her until she rose again. When she asked a question, he cuffed her. Her breath came in short gasps, puffing into the cold, gray dawn like smoke. He hadn't killed her yet. She still had a chance to get away.

Beezle dragged her along behind him, his hand clamped around her upper arm. He'd quickly learned pressure on her injured wrist incited her to obey. If she slowed, he jerked her arm, and she'd cry out and try to increase her stride.

He'd pushed her behind a fallen log and knelt there with her, peering over the edge. Was Brook on the other side? She might have called out, but the rain poured so hard and so loudly on the fallen leaves that Brook would not have been able to hear her. Beezle, on the other hand, would punish her severely.

She might not have another opportunity to cry out once Beezle was through with her.

A moment later, Beezle yanked her up and pushed her forward again. She tried to slow his pace, dragging her heels, looking for any sign Brook was nearby. Beezle must have seen or heard him. Brook must have been close. Beezle yanked her arm, but when she didn't increase her pace, he twisted it. The sharp stab of pain made her gasp and double over.

"Get up or you'll think that twist o' yer wrist was a night at the theater."

Lila pushed forward, struggling to keep up with Beezle across the soggy ground and with her skirts weighed down by water and mud. For a time, she forgot all about escape. Beezle's pace was unrelenting. It seemed he yanked her along for miles and hours. Indeed, dawn had broken, though the storm meant the sky was still cloudy and dark. Finally, the trees thinned and Lila realized they were leaving the wooded area.

She whipped her head around, looking for a landmark, a tree, anything in her surroundings she might recognize. Had they traveled all the way back to the cottage? Perhaps they'd made it to the Longmires' property or the Spencer farm. But nothing looked familiar. No buildings stood in the clearing, no signs of life, only dead grass and a barren field. Beezle pulled her across it, Lila peering back at the woods, hoping Brook had followed them. He'd see them easily in this landscape. There was nowhere to hide. Gradually, she realized a road lay in the distance, and Beezle was headed straight for it. Lila's heart jumped with hope. Perhaps someone would come by and she would be saved.

She looked hopefully up and down the road, but it was deserted. Curse this storm! No one would risk the bad weather to venture out.

Lila narrowed her eyes at a dark shape about a quarter mile away. The road was not deserted after all. A carriage sat in a tree-shrouded nook. The horses had been unharnessed and stood under a scrubby tree. A man stood with them.

She was saved!

"Help!" she cried out. "Help me!"

Beezle gave her arm a brutal twist. "Shut yer potato hole, or I'll shut it fer you."

Lila obliged. He was leading her toward the carriage at any rate. If he wanted to take her there, the man with the horses was probably in league with Beezle. She couldn't allow Beezle to put her in that carriage. Once inside, he could take her anywhere. Brook would never find her. He had no horse and couldn't follow. This was it. She had to escape now.

Lila took a deep breath and waited for her chance. Beezle pulled her closer and closer to the carriage. It was rather a fine carriage to be out in the middle of the countryside. It couldn't have been Beezle's, and she did not want to know to whom it belonged.

As they neared, the coachman turned to look at them, and Lila stumbled. Something about him looked familiar. The horses too looked familiar. She stared at the trio, unable to place them in the gloomy light.

In the distance, lightning lit up the sky, and one of the horses reared up with fear. The coachman turned to calm the animal. At the same time, Beezle jumped with fright at the hack's sudden movement. Lila took the opening.

She tore her arm from Beezle's grasp and turned on her heel, running as fast as she could back toward the woods. The cover of trees was her only hope of escape. She could find somewhere to hide until Brook found her.

She heard cursing behind her, but she didn't stop running. Her lungs burned and the rain pelted her face, but she knew she could make it. She could hear the thump of his footsteps behind her. He was close, but she had the lead. She could make it to the woods. She could beat him.

Lila saw the rock jutting out of the ground cover too late. She swerved to avoid it, but it caught the edge of her boot. She lost her balance, stumbled, tripped over her skirts, and fell to her knees. Pain lanced up her legs where her knees hit the ground, the delicate skin gouged by the rocks and twigs. She tried to rise, but she knew it was too late.

Beezle grabbed her by the hair and closed his hand on her throat. She couldn't breathe. She struggled, but his grip tightened. Blackness hovered at the edge of her vision. Her lungs burned. Beezle's hands were like iron clamps, digging into the tender flesh of her neck. The world seemed to go dark then come back into focus again.

"I will enjoy killing you." Beezle's voice seemed to come from far away as the darkness closed in.

❧

He'd lost them. At one point, Brook had known he was close. The hairs on the back of his neck stood up as they often did when he had sighted his quarry and went in for the kill. He'd almost been able to feel Lila's presence, catch the scent of her perfume.

And then she was gone.

He'd backtracked. He'd retraced his steps. He'd started out in a dozen different directions, but he'd lost her. He'd gone over the same patch of ground twenty times or more, found the spot where she and Beezle had crouched behind a log. He saw the indent her shoe had made, and the impression of Beezle's bony legs. He followed the footprints to where they ended. A large tree limb had fallen, and it obscured the trail. Brook went around it, but he couldn't find it again. He set out from the tree limb in every direction, searching for some small clue—a broken twig, a bent leaf, a soft mark in the ground.

Nothing.

Brook stood in the center of the woods, the rain pouring down on him, and wanted to shout. This couldn't be the end. This couldn't be how he lost her. He needed to kiss her one last time. He needed to tell her he forgave her for the stupid way she'd behaved when they'd been little more than children.

He needed to ask her forgiveness for the pettiness of holding it against her all these years.

He needed to tell her he loved her.

Brook was the hero, not Beezle. Beezle wasn't supposed to win.

Only, this story hadn't been written by the London scandal rags. This story didn't have a happy ending. She was gone, and Brook knew he'd never find her in time to save her.

❧

She came to in darkness, the rain pattering on the roof outside.

Outside?

She lay on her face, the hard floor beneath her cheek. Lila sat quickly, regretting the action immediately. Sharp pain cut through her temple. Her throat was swollen, her neck sore.

"Good, you are awake."

Lila opened her eyes and turned in the direction of the voice. A female voice.

The curtains had been closed and the carriage lamps extinguished, but she knew that voice. She knew the form seated on the squabs beside her.

"Valencia?" she croaked, unwilling to believe what her eyes told her. And yet it made sense. She'd known the coachman—a second coachman—and the horses. They were her father's coachman and horses.

"Where is my father?" she asked. Lila's voice was stronger now, but she had to strain to force it past the swelling in her neck.

"London." Her stepmother's mouth turned upward

into something resembling a smile. "His Grace will not be joining us."

"I don't understand."

Valencia shouldn't be here. Had Beezle been taking her to her stepmother all along? Why, when he wanted to kill her? Why had he saved her?

Had he saved her?

Lila was aware of the sounds surrounding her now. The clink of metal and the stamp of hooves. Outside, John Coachman harnessed the horses.

"No, I'm sure you don't understand. You do not need to understand. All you need know is that your father will not be joining us. I've planned a short journey, just the two of us."

"Sir Brook is looking for me. I have to find him. Take me back to the cottage."

"Oh, I don't think so, Lillian-Anne. I didn't come all this way to have my plans thwarted by Sir Brook. He's already caused me enough problems."

Lila pushed up and onto the squabs across from Valencia. Before she could sit, her stepmother swung her umbrella, the ebony handle cracking hard across Lila's knee. Lila screamed at the insult to her already-injured knees and buckled.

"Don't you dare soil my velvet with your dirt and muck," she hissed. "Sit on the floor like the rubbish you are."

Lila stared at her. She'd always known Valencia didn't like her, but the woman had never dared speak to her this way. "I want my father," Lila said. "If you won't take me to Sir Brook, then I demand to be taken to Lennox House."

Valencia shook her head her vivid blue eyes glittering in the darkness and her blond hair shining like starlight. "You still do not understand, do you, simpleton? Allow me to make it perfectly clear. I am here to see you killed. That idiot loggerhead I hired couldn't accomplish the job on his own, so I have come this time to make certain he does it right. You, dear daughter, will never see your father or your husband again."

Nineteen

LILA STARED IN HORROR AT VILE VALENCIA. SHE caught the movement of the umbrella right before Valencia struck and ducked in time to avoid the worst of the blow to her head. The ebony and silver handle still cracked her across the side of her temple and ear. A warm trickle of blood slid over her cheek and down her neck.

She huddled on the floor, her arms over her head to ward off more blows. Instead of continued abuse, Valencia called out, and Lila realized John Coachman had tapped on the door.

"Drive on," Valencia ordered. "And you," she said, prodding Lila with her slipper, "had better stay down, or I'll kill you myself."

Lila supposed that meant Beezle was still nearby. Valencia was paying Beezle. Valencia had arranged to have Lila abducted.

The coach lurched forward then jerked back again. Lila heard the coachman yell and the creak and strain of the coach's frame as the horses pulled with all their strength.

"What is the matter?" Valencia lowered the window and yelled into the cold morning. Lila realized the brick at Valencia's feet, though not hot anymore, had retained enough heat to warm the interior of the coach. She almost had sensation back in her fingers.

"The wheels are mired in mud, Your Grace!"

"Well, get down and push!" Valencia raised the window, muttering under her breath about incompetent servants.

Lila prayed the coachman couldn't free the wheels for hours. The delay might give Brook enough time to find her.

If he was still looking for her.

He was. Of course he was. He might not have loved her, but he would not allow her to die. He would not allow Beezle to win. But would Brook even investigate the coach? Neither of them had ever considered that Valencia was involved in her abduction.

The carriage rocked back and forth as John Coachman tried to free it from the wet, muddy road. Valencia's mouth thinned into a line that made her look older than her thirty years.

"Why are you doing this?" Lila asked. She didn't expect her stepmother to answer. Valencia looked down at her.

"You gave me no other alternative."

"*I* gave you? This is my fault?" Lila had to tamp down the urge to sit and bellow indignantly. Such behavior would only earn her more thumps from the umbrella.

"Yes, it is your fault. I tried to send you away, but you would not *stay* away. You always came back." Valencia glared at her.

"Lennox House and Blakesford are my home. Where else am I to go?"

Valencia leaned down. "You may go to hell for all I care," she hissed.

Lila recoiled as though hit. "What have I done to make you hate me so much? To make you...how could you hire Beezle to abduct me?"

"I hired him to kill you, but he couldn't even manage that."

Lila gasped. "Why?"

"You're the last reminder of *her*. Your sainted mother. All I ever hear is 'When Isabella was alive.' He looks at you and thinks of her. You look just like her."

It was true. Colin looked more like their father, but many of her mother's relatives had remarked at the similarity between Lila and her mother. Lila had taken it as a compliment. Valencia had been jealous.

"The duke does not need you. He has another daughter now."

This was madness. Lila could not fathom the depths of Valencia's hatred if she had gone to these lengths to rid herself of her stepdaughter.

"You do not need to do this, Valencia. My father loves you." If he hadn't, he wouldn't have sent Lila away so many times to please his new wife. "And he loves Ginny. I'm married now. I am already out of your way."

Valencia sneered at her. "You still do not understand, stupid chit. If you hadn't seen Beezle murder that MP, I could have allowed you to live. But you saw too much."

"You had something to do with that murder?" Lila could barely force the startled words from her injured throat.

"Of course not."

The carriage rocked violently, and Lila feared the wheels had been freed from the mire. But the conveyance settled back again. It might have been easier to move the vehicle if Lila and Valencia exited, but Valencia would never agree to stand outside on the roadway in the rain. Lila would have jumped at the chance.

"But the murder tied that thug to Fitzsimmons. Bow Street will stop at nothing to catch Beezle. They searched his residence—if you can call it that—and do you know what they found?"

Lila nodded. Everything made sense to her now. Beezle had kept a bank draft or a letter or something that tied him to Valencia. Her stepmother had nothing to do with the murder of the MP, but the murder had shed light on her underground activities.

"Then the government already knows about you. It's too late," Lila said.

"Bow Street and the magistrates move slowly. I have time to see you dead before I go abroad."

Valencia was fleeing for the Continent. It was the only way to avoid imprisonment and the humiliation of a trial. But she'd wasted precious hours of her escape to go after Lila.

Valencia opened the window again. "What is taking so long? What do I pay you for?"

"We almost have it, Your Grace!"

We. Was Beezle behind the conveyance trying to free it? If she escaped and ran toward the horses, she might have a chance to get back to the woods and hide until Brook could find her. She needn't hide for days or even hours. Valencia could not wait that long to leave England.

Lila cut her gaze to the carriage doors. They were locked, but that would only take her a moment to undo.

"Idiots, all of them," Valencia hissed. Her flat eyes settled on Lila with a look Lila knew boded ill. "I suppose there is no reason to wait."

Lila couldn't agree more. She jumped for the door she faced, that farthest from Valencia, and turned the lock. Fingers fumbling, she pushed the latch. Valencia screamed, bringing her umbrella down on the back of Lila's neck. Pain exploded like a bright light blinding her. But it also propelled her forward. She pitched from the carriage, falling to her already bruised and battered knees.

More pain. More tears stinging her eyes. The only thing that drove her to her feet was the knowledge that Beezle was coming for her. She stumbled upright, found her bearings, and ran for the horses' heads. She could hear the commotion behind her, but she didn't dare look around. She ran as fast as her aching legs would take her.

Past the horses. Toward the woods. A few more feet. The tree line was coming closer.

Footsteps, hard and swift, sounded behind her. Lila pushed herself faster and harder. If she could just escape into the trees, she could lose him. She would be saved.

And then something moved in her peripheral vision. A man. Not Beezle. His hair wasn't dark. The coachman?

She stumbled and ran on, but the coachman was almost upon her.

"No!" she screamed just as his hand clamped around her arm.

❧

She fought like a wild creature, ripping and tearing at him with hands like claws, fingernails sharp as razors.

"Lila!" He shook her. "Lila, it's me!"

She stilled, the wildness fading from her eyes. Before he could say more, Brook pushed her behind him, shielding her from Beezle who had been right on her heels.

Beezle grinned, a skeletal stretching of skin on his thin face. "Now ain't this convenient."

"It is, rather, isn't it?" Brook lunged, not waiting for Beezle's attack. Beezle had a knife, but it wasn't in his hand, and Brook had no intention of allowing him time to grasp it.

With the rain still falling at a steady pace, the muddy ground slid under his feet. He knocked Beezle aside rather than tackling him, as he'd hoped. Brook went down to one knee, and Beezle kicked out, landing his boot hard on Brook's shoulder. He ignored the pain, throwing himself on top of Beezle and punching him hard across the face. Beezle's cheek opened, blood flowing pink as it mixed with the rainwater.

The blow would have felled other men, but Beezle was used to life in Seven Dials. He had fought his way to the top of his gang, and he did not observe the pugilist codes of Gentleman Jackson's. Brook could fight dirty as well. Beezle shoved a fist under

Brook's chin, pushing his head up. Brook fought to stay upright, attempting to dig his boots into the slick ground. One boot slid, and Beezle lost his grip on Brook's chin. Instead of pulling back, as Beezle expected, Brook moved forward, slamming his fore-head into Beezle's nose.

He heard the crunch and Beezle's grunt of pain before rolling away to lick his own wounds. His head hurt like the devil, but he'd broken Beezle's nose. That would buy him a few minutes.

"Brook!"

He searched the ground, spotting Lila's mud-caked boots. He held up a hand to stall her progress. He didn't want her coming to his aid, didn't want her anywhere near Beezle.

"Stay back. Get in the coach."

"I can't! I—" She looked back at the carriage as though a band of thieves was housed inside it. For all he knew, there was. He'd spotted the conveyance from the shelter of the woods and had approached cautiously. A few minutes of observation told him Beezle and a coachman were trying to free the coach from the wheel ruts where it had become lodged. He hadn't expected Lila to burst from the vehicle and appear on the far side.

He'd thought the coach empty, but now he wondered who might have been inside with her.

"Brook! Behind you!"

Heeding her warning, he sprang to his feet, ready to fight. Beezle was on his feet, too, dagger in his hand. He looked like Satan come from Hell. His face was a mask of red, blood dripping down his cheeks and pouring over his lips from his shattered nose. The twisted object that had been his nose gave him a strange, ghoulish appearance.

Brook didn't have a weapon, but he didn't need one. He hadn't survived in the rookeries without learning how to defend himself. He let Beezle come for him, sidestepping at the last minute when Beezle struck with the knife.

"Fast feet," Beezle said, his voice a gurgle.

"Faster than yours, I'll warrant."

"Don't need fast feet when you have a porker."

"Unless you can throw with some accuracy, you'll need fast feet to strike me."

Beezle's gaze traveled to Lila. "Maybe I'll strike her first."

Just then the coachman freed the carriage. He was covered in grime, but he'd dug the wheels out and now ran for the driver's box. The horses pitched forward, the carriage wobbling along.

"Lila, watch out!" Brook yelled. The horses would trample her if she didn't move quickly.

"No!" Lila screamed, turning to see the carriage stagger forward. To his shock, she raced toward it.

The lapse in attention cost him. He feinted to the side but not in time to avoid the slice of Beezle's blade.

❧

Lila raced toward the carriage as it gained speed. She couldn't allow Vile Valencia to escape. Brook would take care of Beezle—please, God, let Brook defeat Beezle—but Valencia would be halfway to the Continent if someone did not act to stop her. John

Coachman saw her, but he either did not recognize her or did not care if he trampled her. She skidded around the horses and reached for the carriage door.

Her hand slipped, groping air, before she back-pedaled and reached again. This time she caught the latch, forcing the door open. Lila hadn't expected the door to be unlocked. She was not certain what she expected, but it was not to see Valencia gaping, mouth wide, as Lila ran alongside the coach.

"Get away!" she screeched.

The horses had picked up speed, and Lila had to act. She dove into the carriage, her knees banging on the frame, her legs hanging out. She groped at the squabs, trying to catch hold so she could pull her legs in. Valencia let out a scream and slammed her feet down hard on Lila's forearm. With a curse, Lila dragged her body inside, covering her face from the worst of Valencia's assaults. Valencia was kicking like an irate toddler, and by the time Lila managed to curl her knees under her, her ears rang and her face was numb.

The carriage door swung wildly as the carriage churned along the muddy road. Rain blew in, leaving dark droplets on Valencia's crimson cape. Valencia gave one last kick then hurled herself across the coach at Lila.

"I'll kill you myself." Her gloved hands closed on Lila's throat. Lila twisted out of her grip, elbowing Valencia in the chin. She screamed and attacked again, swiping at Lila with hands bent into claws.

The gloves protected Lila from the worst of the attack, and since her own hands were free of gloves, she raked her nails down Valencia's cheek.

"Little bitch!" Valencia screamed.

"Just wait!"

Lila ducked, and Valencia landed a glancing blow across the top of her head. But Lila came up ready, slashing and slapping at Valencia. The other woman raised her arms to protect herself, and Lila grabbed her wrists and forced them down. Using the weight of her body, she trapped Valencia on the floor of the carriage.

"Get off me!" Valencia's words came between short gasps for breath.

Lila leaned down until her face was inches from her stepmother's. "This is your fault. All your petty jealousy has brought us here."

"Get off!"

"No!" She shook Valencia's arms.

"Why can't you die like your mother?" Valencia spat.

Lila felt bile rose in her throat, and though she would not have minded casting up her accounts all over Valencia, she swallowed the nausea.

"Isabella this," Valencia whined, "and Isabella that. I couldn't stand it."

Lila closed her eyes. She'd always thought if she tried harder to be agreeable, tried to include Valencia, tried to be friendlier, then her stepmother would like her. But Lila had never had a chance.

She realized the coach had stopped moving.

Lila opened her eyes. "There is one difference between my mother and you that would have ensured my father's love."

Valencia's brow creased. "What is it?"

"My mother *is* dead."

She climbed off Valencia and peered out the open

door. The carriage wheels had become mired in muck again. The conveyance was too heavy for the muddy roads. One glance at the box told her the coachman had fled. She looked about but saw no sign of him. She saw no sign of Brook either. They must have left Brook fighting Beezle at least a mile back. Lila supposed she'd have to deal with Valencia on her own.

At least there was one bright spot in her day—the rain had stopped.

"Hallo, there!"

Lila started as a man rounded the front of the coach, eyeing the horses with what looked like appreciation. He wore a wide hat, a thick coat, and boots up to his knees.

"Bad day for a drive. Did you lose your coachman?"

"Yes," Lila answered. "But it's no loss."

"Help!" Valencia screamed, kicking at Lila from inside the coach.

The man raised a brow and tried to peer past Lila. "You look like you've had quite a day, miss."

Lila could only imagine how she looked after a night in the rain and woods. "I'm not a *miss*. I'm Lady Lillian-Ann, daughter of the Duke of Lennox."

"I see." He took off his hat. "Mr. George Longmire."

"Longmire!" Finally, the fabled Longmires. "Brook Derring told me you would help."

"You know Sir Brook?"

"Help!" Valencia yelled. "Help! She's abducted me."

"Ignore her," Lila said. "Sir Brook is my husband." For the moment, at any rate.

She explained the situation as best she could, and though Longmire looked less than pleased at the prospect of holding a duchess prisoner, he agreed. He locked Valencia in the cellar and left Lila with Mrs. Longmire while he rode back to search for Brook.

Valencia screamed and cursed below them, and Mrs. Longmire attempted to make tea and hold a conversation above the noise. Lila judged Mrs. Longmire to be in her early forties. She was a small woman and a little jumpy, but she kept a clean, cheery home. She settled Lila near the fire, wrapping a blanket around her shoulders, ignoring Lila's protests that she would ruin the blanket with all the dirt on her.

Finally, warm teacup in her hand, Lila said, "Mrs. Longmire, you needn't pretend this is not strange on my account."

"Oh, we all need a touch of excitement now and then." She sat across from Lila and sipped her tea. Below them, Valencia railed at the injustice and threatened all manner of retribution. "Perhaps we can save our conversation for another time," Mrs. Longmire suggested in a shout.

"Very sensible of you, Mrs. Longmire," Lila shouted back.

She sipped her tea, allowing the warmth to infuse her. In a few moments, Brook would come and this would all be over. She could go back to her life—her life before Vile Valencia—and he could go back to his. The scandal of her stepmother's treachery would far outweigh the humiliation of her annulment.

Brook would be out of her life. All she would have were memories.

She felt as though they were Athens and Sparta at the end of the Peloponnesian War from the dry book she'd finally finished. Her time with Brook had been like the Golden Age, and now it was ending. All their battles and no real winner.

She closed her eyes against the sting of tears. She'd been a fool to fall in love with him. She'd been a fool *not* to fall in love with him, but she couldn't go back. She could only go forward.

Alone.

❧

Brook looked up, squinting at the sound of hoofbeats. He'd managed to evade Beezle's dagger thus far, but his strength was flagging. If Beezle's clumsy thrusts were any indication, he was at the end of his reserves as well.

Beezle turned toward the sound of the approaching horse as well. It wasn't the coach. Even if he hadn't seen the rider approaching, Brook would have known it wasn't Lila and the coach. His sense of panic at having lost her again didn't diminish. For all he knew, she could have been lying dead on the side of the road.

Beezle slashed at him again, and Brook jumped aside. The dagger caught his coat and ripped the wool before it came loose and Beezle spun around with the force of his jab. Brook was through playing. He had to find Lila. He needed the approaching horse.

Before Beezle could spin back to swipe at Brook again, Brook slammed into him, knocking him forward. Beezle jumped around, seeming to sense Brook's growing determination. He crouched and jabbed. Brook braved the tip of the knife to close in on Beezle, close enough to stick one foot out and hook it around Beezle's ankle.

Too late, the arch rogue realized his mistake. He'd left his legs unprotected. He went down, and Brook went after him. The two men fell to the muddy ground, Brook reaching for Beezle's waving hands to control the knife. Beezle tried to scurry away, and Brook caught his knee, pulling him down. He rose up, ready for Beezle's next attack, but the man didn't move.

Brook rose slowly, staring down at Beezle, whose chest rose and fell in jagged bursts. With one booted foot, he turned the man over. The dagger hilt protruded from Beezle's chest, just below the heart. He'd be dead in a matter of minutes.

Brook tried to summon regret, but none came. Beezle had died in the dirt, exactly where he belonged.

The horse and rider approached cautiously, and Brook glanced up. He knew the man, but he couldn't place him for a moment.

"Are you, Sir Brook?"

Brook nodded, wiping some of the mud from his face. "Longmire?"

"That's right. He dead?" He nodded at Beezle.

"Close enough. I need your horse. My wife—"

Longmire held up a hand. "She's at my house, safe with Mrs. Longmire. We locked up the duchess in the cellar. I hope we did right."

They'd locked a duchess in their cellar? The Duchess of Lennox? That had been the Lennox coach he'd seen.

"I just need to see my wife," he said, aware it wasn't the answer Longmire wanted. It was the only answer Brook could give. He needed Lila. He had to see her, touch her, hold her, know she was unharmed.

Nothing else mattered.

"What about him?" Longmire said with a nod at Beezle's body.

"He'll wait."

Longmire nodded. "Climb on. We'll go directly."

It was less than a mile, but it seemed an eternity before the small house on the hill came into view. Brook dismounted before the horse had come to a stop. He could hear a woman's screaming from the yard, and he didn't wait to be invited inside. He ran for the door and burst inside.

Now that the rain had stopped, the cottage was darker than the yard, and it took Brook a moment to make sense of what he saw. Finally, he realized he was in a small hallway with stairs before him. A door on his right was open, and through it he saw a woman rising from a worn but comfortable chair. He went toward her, toward the heat of the fire and the scent of chamomile from recently steeped tea.

"Sir Brook." The woman curtsied. "I covered her with the blanket. She was exhausted."

Brook turned and then fell to his knees. Lila lay curled under a thin blanket, head on the arm of the chair, mouth slightly open. Her cheeks were rosy from the warmth of the fire. She was beautiful, even with the smudges of dirt and the matted lock of hair falling over her neck.

He had to tell her he loved her. He had to tell her he didn't want an annulment.

The woman screamed again, and Brook realized it must have been the duchess in the cellar.

Lila would have to wait.

Longmire entered and Brook steered him back out again. "I need to borrow your horse as far as the posting house. I need to go to London. I need Bow Street or a magistrate. Hell, if that's who I think it is in your cellar, I may need the king himself. Will you take care of her for me?" He nodded toward the parlor and his sleeping wife.

"Of course, Sir Brook. And we keep the other locked in the cellar?"

"Until I return, yes." He glanced at the parlor again, at the faded yellow chair where his wife slept. "I'll be back for her."

At least that was what he intended before he returned to London and everything went wrong.

Twenty

Six weeks later

THE MEETING WAS AN INCONVENIENCE. LILA HADN'T wanted to attend, but she hadn't attended the last one, and Brook had refused to grant the annulment. He'd rescheduled and insisted she be present.

Lila couldn't think why. This separation was what Brook wanted. He didn't need her in his solicitor's office on Bond Street. Her father could sign for her. Her father was all too happy to sign for her.

The duke, Lila, and her brother were eager to put the events of the last several months behind them. Valencia was in gaol, awaiting trial for attempted murder. The duke was in shock, Colin was drinking too much, Ginny asked for her mother daily, and Lila seemed to be holding the entire family together.

Thankfully, Beezle was dead, and she did not have to fear him any longer. Lord Liversey, a member of the House of Lords, had been accused of ordering the death of Mr. Fitzsimmons, the MP from Lincolnshire she saw murdered. Apparently, Fitzsimmons and

Liversey worked together, and when Fitzsimmons found information damaging to Liversey, the other man paid Beezle to kill the MP.

The Duke of Lennox hated scandal, and she had inadvertently put them in the middle of it.

She looked at her father, sitting straight and rigid in the red leather chair opposite the tidy desk in the well-appointed room. He held his walking stick with both hands, his knuckles white on the silver handle. He did not need to be kept waiting for Sir Brook. He needed—they all needed—to leave London for a few months and travel to Blakesford, where they could lick their wounds and start over.

Lila stood, pacing the room, her slippers shushing on the Turkey rug as she pretended to peruse the law volumes on the lengthy bookshelf. How she craved the peace and solitude of Blakesford. There, she could cry without interruption. She could weep over Brook like a foolish schoolgirl until she had no more tears, until every thought of him didn't stab her heart like a thousand tiny needles in a pincushion. Why did he want to see her? He was the one who'd left her. He'd returned to London and hadn't even said good-bye. A magistrate had taken her statement and then a hired coach had returned her to Lennox House. Before she'd left, she'd insisted on checking on the mother cat and kittens one last time. They had been gone from the cottage, as had Brook.

She shouldn't have been surprised he'd abandoned her. Despite their lovemaking, despite their whispered confidences in the dark, Brook had given her no illusions. He'd been clear that he didn't hate her, but he didn't want her either. Not permanently.

"You should have spoken to him when he came to call at the town house," her father said, breaking the oppressive silence in the room.

Lila glanced over her shoulder. Her father was angry. A duke should not be made to wait.

"I should have," she said. But she'd been too much the coward when he'd finally called on her, several days after she'd arrived home. She'd feared he'd take one look at her swollen and bruised face and turn away. She feared he'd say exactly what he would say today—*I want an annulment*.

She expected it, but she wanted it done and over. She could not see him because worse than the look of disgust when he saw her bruised face, worse than hearing the demand for an annulment from his lips, was her own weakness. She did not trust herself to hold on to her dignity. She'd still wanted him too much, and the danger that she'd break down, declare her love, and beg him not to leave her had been very real indeed.

She'd tamped the urge down now, and it had faded like the bruises. But she was still tender, in flesh and spirit. She could face Brook Derring without dissolving into hysterics, but watching him sign the papers to be permanently rid of her would scar her heart forever.

She would never love again, and perhaps that was just what she deserved.

A floorboard creaked and the low rumble of men's voices floated into the room. Lila spun around, uncertain what to do with herself. Stand? Sit? On the chair? The couch?

And then the door opened, and the Earl of Dane entered. Lila dropped a curtsy, nodding as he said something she could not hear. The blood whirred too loudly in her ears because just behind Dane was Brook. He stepped in after his brother, his dark eyes going directly to her and holding.

His mahogany-colored eyes were as unreadable as ever. They seemed impenetrable pools of hardness in a face already replete with sharp edges and flat planes. He'd shaved for the meeting. She'd grown used to the light brown stubble interspersed with blond, and the clean-shaven jaw made his face look almost soft. It wasn't only that he'd shaved. His hair was slightly longer than the severe style she'd seen him wear during their brief marriage. He hadn't cut it, and it had begun to curl in a way that made her want to tangle her fingers in it.

Best not to think along those lines though.

She dropped her gaze from his, but that was a mistake. It allowed her to observe his clothing. He'd dressed for the meeting as well. He wore a dark blue wool coat, a stiff, white cravat, a cream waistcoat, buff breeches, and highly polished riding boots. She couldn't fail to notice how lean and muscular his body looked in the tight breeches. Considering she knew just how wide his chest was and how broad his shoulders, the snug fit of the coat did nothing to curb her imagination.

Her gaze flicked up to his again, and she saw what she'd been too overwhelmed by his initial presence to note before. He had shadows under his eyes. He might have shaved and dressed well, but he was not sleeping. Dare she believe it was because he missed her? More likely he was anxious to be rid of her and worried she would make the annulment process more difficult than necessary.

Brook's gaze drifted to his brother, and Lila realized the earl was speaking. "Mr. Scott will be here in a few moments. He regrets that he has been detained."

William Scott, brother of Lord Eldon, resided over the consistory court that issued annulments in London. Thankfully, Brook had arranged to have everything completed privately in the office of his solicitor, a Mr. McKinnon.

Dane had walked around the desk. "In the meantime, I suggest we all partake of McKinnon's fine whisky. I hear it's his own family recipe." He opened the solicitor's desk drawer with an air of one familiar with the furnishing's contents, and placed two glasses and a bottle on the desk. Lila knew she was not expected to partake, but she wondered who else was to be excluded.

The room was too silent, and when Dane poured the whisky, the clink of the bottle on the rim of the glasses made her jump. Lila tried to think of something to say, something to ease the tension. She should have been able to say something to her husband, the man she'd been in bed with just a few short weeks ago. But he seemed like a stranger to her now. And what use were pleasantries when what she really wanted to know was why he had left her without even saying good-bye. Did she not deserve that much at least?

Dane handed a glass to her father then cleared his

throat. "Brook, we'll have a drink while you and Lady Lila speak privately."

Lila started at the unexpected suggestion. Why had the earl told Brook to speak to her alone? She glanced at Brook, but the scowl he directed at his brother did not answer any questions or make her want to speak to him alone.

"What is this about?" her father demanded. "Lila has nothing to say to Sir Brook."

It still surprised Lila that her father had begun to take her side once again. It was as though now that Valencia was out of the way, he could see Lila again. She mattered again.

"I don't think that's quite true," Brook said, his voice low. He inclined his head toward her. "My lady, if you would give me a moment of your time, I would be obliged."

Lila narrowed her eyes at the man. This was not Brook. He sounded like Brook and looked like Brook, but Brook was not this polite to her.

"Whatever you have to say to her, you can say with me present," the duke said.

Brook glanced at Lennox then back to her again. "I can and I will, but I prefer to say it alone."

"I can vouch for my brother's good intentions, Duke," Dane said. "She will be perfectly safe and just on the other side of the door. McKinnon has a small parlor." He indicated a side door. "Step in there, my lady."

Brook walked to it and opened the door, gesturing her inside. Lila didn't quite know how to refuse. She gave her father a little shrug and walked across the room on wobbly legs. She hardly knew how she managed to stay upright, but she made it to the door. She kept her chin up as she passed Brook, buckling slightly when the scents of bergamot and brandy—smells she would now and forevermore associate with him—tickled her nose.

And then she was through the door and she heard it close behind them. She turned, almost falling backward when she all but collided with Brook, who was standing far too close behind her.

He caught her arm to steady her, then released it just as quickly, as though touching her might sully his kidskin gloves.

She stepped back, putting space between them, and waited for him to speak. He stared at her, his mouth in a flat line, his eyes hooded. A bracket clock sat on the table beside her, ticking and ticking in the strained silence. Brook opened his mouth, and she thought he might speak, but he only blew out a breath.

Someone had to say something, and she supposed she had better be the one to begin or they might stand there forever. "This is an awkward situation."

He drew in a quick breath when she spoke, his gaze flicking to her face.

"After all we have been through, it seems peculiar to stand here and converse"—not that they were conversing—"like strangers."

"Yes."

Lila waited, but he didn't say more.

"I am certain Mr. Scott will be here soon, and then this will all be over. You won't have to see me again."

"Right. About that…" But to her dismay, he trailed off and didn't continue.

"About what?" she prodded. "Is there a problem with the annulment?" It wouldn't have surprised her, as legally there was no valid reason for annulment. But Brook had the support of the king, and the king could do as he liked.

"I will sign the annulment. If that's what you want," he said.

She simply hoped he'd cited fraud as the reason for annulment and not declared her insane. Lila clasped her hands together too afraid to hope. "Isn't that what you want?"

He didn't speak. She could see his throat working, and the idea crossed her mind that he might actually be having trouble saying what he wanted. But how could that be? He was Sir Brook: the Inspector; Sir Brook: the Hero. Nothing stood in his way.

"If you've reconsidered the annulment because you don't want to hurt my reputation, I assure you, I will be fine," Lila said. "I'd much rather a sullied reputation than to stay in a marriage in name only. How awful to have to plan my entire life so I am never in the same place as my husband." She'd seen marriages like those before—husbands who stayed in the country while their wives were in Town. If the two happened to attend the same function, they pretended the other did not exist.

Lila couldn't live like that. If she hadn't loved Brook, it might have been an option. But how could she see him, know he was hers, and also know she could never have him?

"That's not what I want," he said finally. "A marriage in name only, I mean."

She furrowed her brow. "Then you *do* want the annulment?"

"Not if you don't."

Lila shook her head, began to speak, then paused, uncertain what to say.

Brook blew out a frustrated sigh. "I suppose I shall have to spell it out for you. You never did make anything easy."

"As though I'm the one who need apologize," she said, her temper rising. How dare he act impatient with her! "I am the one who was abandoned."

"Abandoned?" Brook's voice rose sharply. "What the devil does that mean?"

"You left me with the Longmires and never even said good-bye. I'd been out all night, fighting Beezle and then my stepmother, and you couldn't even speak a word to me."

"I'd been out all night tracking you! And if you recall, I fought Beezle and killed him for you!"

"For me?" She scoffed. "You made it quite clear protecting me and capturing Beezle was your responsibility. I suppose I should not have been surprised that when your task was complete you left me without so much as a by-your-leave."

"Is that what you think?"

She held her hands out in front of her. "Am I wrong?"

"Yes!" he shouted.

Lila had rarely heard him shout, and she drew back slightly, her gaze drifting to the door where she expected her father to burst in at any moment.

"I left you safe, sleeping under a warm blanket, in the Longmires' home. That is not abandoning you."

He advanced on her, and Lila held her own, refusing to back down or show her fear. "I fetched the proper officials so I might continue to keep you safe from your stepmother and any other schemes she might have concocted. Had we been in London, the matter would have been dealt with in hours. No one acts quickly in the country. It took almost a week to deal with all the details." He stood looking down at her, eyes blazing. "Everything I did, I did for you. And what thanks do I receive? You wouldn't even see me when I called on you."

"Because there was nothing for us to say to each other!" she shouted back at him. "You made your feelings toward me perfectly clear. You said, 'There is no hope for you and me.' I didn't need to hear it one more time. Even now I can see it pains you to have to be in the same room with me, to speak to me."

Tears stung her eyes, but she blinked them back, biting the inside of her lip to keep it from trembling. There would be a time and place for tears later. Not now. *Not now.*

"Is that what you think?" His hands closed like vises on her shoulders. "That it pains me to be here with you?"

He certainly looked pained—pained and angry.

"Yes."

"You're wrong." His hands slid down her arms and took one of her hands in both of his. To her shock and consternation, he slid down to one knee.

"What are you doing?" she breathed in little more than a whisper.

"Probably making a fool of myself. Again."

"I don't understand."

"Yes, you do. Do you remember our wager at the cottage?"

Their wager? Why did he mention that now? "Yes. I lost."

"Correct. I won, and now I want to claim my prize. One request. And you must do whatever I want."

"Are you suggesting—?"

He held up a hand before her voice could rise to a screech.

"Lila, I am asking you to marry me—or rather, stay married to me. That's what I want for my prize." He looked up at her, his dark eyes burning with anger, his face a scowl.

Lila shook her head. "No, Brook. I'm sorry. I cannot honor the wager."

❧

At her words, Brook died inside. She'd refused him again, and damn him if it didn't hurt as much this time as the first.

No. It hurt more this time because this time he knew what it was to have her lush body under his, to brush his mouth against hers, to taste her, feel her clench around him when she found release.

The damn woman refused to marry him even when she was *already* married to him!

He released her hand, but he didn't yet feel stable enough to rise to his feet. He might fall over...or throttle her.

"May I ask why you have refused me?" Not that her refusal meant anything. If he did not want the annulment, it would not go forward. Of course, he'd shove hot pokers under his fingernails before he stayed married to a woman who didn't want him. He'd sign the bloody annulment and then throw it in her face.

"Brook—"

"A simple answer will do." He stared at her waist, at the white, gauzy netting that overlaid her apple-green gown. Slowly his gaze traveled up and over her rounded breasts to land on her chin. The chin—a safe spot to pause. "A simple, 'I lied. I don't love you' will suffice."

She let out a short gasp. "But that's not true. I *do* love you."

Was it just his imagination or did her voice catch? She sounded close to tears.

"And now you lie again."

Too late, he saw her hand strike out. The blow landed on his shoulder and was probably intended to shove him back. He didn't even sway.

"I am not lying, you obstinate man. I do love you."

He grasped her wrist and rose to his feet. "Stop saying that."

"No."

He expected her to attempt to free herself, to pull her wrist free, but instead she all but fell into him, grasping his coat between both hands. "I love you. I love you. I love you."

He pulled her into his arms and took her mouth with his. He'd missed her lips, the scent of lily of the valley, the way she felt against him.

This was madness.

He tore himself away, his breath coming in harsh gasps.

"How can you expect me to marry you?" she asked, a tear rolling down a cheek as perfect as marble. "I don't want to be with a man who will never overlook the mistakes I made in the past. Each time I make another mistake—and I will certainly make mistakes—will you throw the past in my face? Will you dredge up my unforgiveable behavior? You cannot forgive me, and you do not love me. I want no part of that marriage."

She tried to pull out of his arms, but he didn't release her. He couldn't release her. Was she correct? Would he always hold on to the past?

"You're right," he said, holding fast when she tried to squirm away. "A marriage like that would be sheer hell. And if you were the woman now that you were seven years ago, I could not forgive you. But you've changed, and you're not that woman anymore." He stroked a finger down her silky cheek, wet from her tears. "The woman I married can admit when she's wrong. She's humble, kind, considerate of others. Granted, she can't cook or make a fire without endangering the lives of everyone around her—"

Her mouth dropped open in shocked outrage.

"But fortunately, I don't care about her domestic skills." He grinned. "Because, you see, I have fallen completely, utterly, irrevocably in love with you. And I have completely, utterly, and irrevocably forgiven you for the past. It's forgotten. It never happened."

She shook her head as if to deny what he said, but he only nodded more forcefully. "It's true. And if you marry me again, Lila Derring, I vow always to take the blame for every disagreement we have, always to let you have your way, happily to defer to you in every matter of refurbishment, and to love you with my whole heart from now until forever."

Lila wrapped her arms about his neck. "You cannot possibly keep all of those vows."

"I will keep the last. Is that enough?"

"Yes, my darling. My love." She kissed him lightly. "Yes."

He pulled her close, drinking her in like a parched man who stumbles upon a verdant oasis. The tender kiss was interrupted when the door to the office slammed open, and her father burst inside.

"What is the meaning of this? What the devil is happening? I heard screams. You, sir, unhand my daughter."

Dane stumbled in behind the duke. He gave an apologetic shrug. "I held him off as long as I could, Brother."

Brook hauled Lila against his side. "I'm afraid, Lennox, she is not only your daughter but also my wife."

"Not for long!" The duke waved the annulment papers in the air.

"Dane." Brook inclined his head toward the duke.

His brother snatched the papers from the duke, crossed the room, and handed them to Brook. Brook held them up and ripped them in half. "There won't be an annulment today. In fact, I believe what we need is another wedding."

"Well done." Dane clapped.

The duke staggered back. "I don't understand."

"I love him," Lila explained. "And he loves me too. We just needed a moment to settle that."

She looked at Brook as though to verify it really was true. He had forgiven her. He did love her. He looked at her with all the love swelling in his heart, letting her see it in his eyes.

"I don't need a second wedding," she said.

"Oh, yes you do. This time we'll invite everyone, and it will be the most lavish affair your father's money can buy."

The duke didn't appear to have heard them. He stared at the floor, muttering to himself. "What about the judge?" he asked. "All the arrangements made by the king?"

"Mr. Scott has no idea we expect him," Brook confessed. "I never intended to let Lila go."

"Then this was all a ruse?"

Brook shrugged. "I had to see her somehow." He looked down at Lila. "Do *you* forgive *me*?"

She cradled his face in her hands. "I do."

Epilogue

Dearest Madeleine,

I have returned from the wedding of my cousin Lady Lillian-Anne to that inspector, Sir Brook Derring. I must tell you that compared to my recent nuptials, this affair was quite vulgar. Our friends have always claimed Lila had good taste, but you and I doubted the veracity of that claim. I am not pleased (at least not very pleased) to be able to say that we were correct in our estimation.

The wedding was obscene—the profusion of flowers, the gluttony of food and wine, the lengths of silk and satin, the dancing—yes! Dancing after a wedding! Even my uncle the duke danced, and his poor wife not dead a month from hanging. The whole family is scandalized, and yet he danced with the child they call Ginny. Indeed, children were everywhere at the wedding. I would have left early, but I did not want to miss a moment lest I not be able to report the occasion to you in its entirety. Not to mention, the charlotte of apples and apricots was quite divine.

I must tell you that Sir Brook's family is every

bit as wicked as we had thought. The late Duchess of Lennox's treachery is nothing to the disgrace of the Derring family. I suppose the Earl of Dane and his sister Lady Susanna are charming enough, but the countess is outrageously uncouth. And Lady Susanna's husband, a Mr. Dorrington, who I suspect is no better than a common rogue and has fooled them all. Even the dowager countess has married a man who speaks of nothing but botany. I feared I should perish from the alternating shock and tedium. Fortunately, the plum pudding was rather delicious and fortifying.

Even stranger, the bride and groom insisted a kindle of kittens attend the ceremony along with the mother cat. The kittens were most adorable, if you like that sort of thing, but also quite naughty. One snagged the hem of my new dress. And perhaps most shocking of all was the behavior of the bride and groom. My dear Madeleine, they could hardly keep their hands off each other. I thought we might all witness the husband's claiming of his conjugal rights (as to that, I think they had already been claimed). I assure you I am quite overwrought from the event. If it had not been for the Banbury cakes, I do not know how I would have persevered.

Please do tell me all the news from Town. Have they concluded the trial of the lord suspected of the murder of the MP from Lincolnshire? Dear me, murders and plots and dancing at wedding breakfasts before noon. What is the world coming to?

Yours,
Lady Rose Pevensy-Lawson

Acknowledgments

Thank you to my fabulous agents, Joanna MacKenzie, Danielle Egan-Miller, and Abby Saul, for all their help and support. I'm so lucky to have you!

Thanks to my friend Gayle Cochrane, to whom this book is dedicated, for all your great ideas and cheerleading. Thanks also to the Shananigans: Sue, Lisa, Barbara, Susan, Ruth, Kristy, Patti, Connie, Nicole, Misty, Sarah, Flora, Monique, and Melanie!

Thanks go to Margo Maguire, who sparked the idea for this series, and Sophie Jordan and Lily Dalton, who brainstormed this book with me on those long drives to and from Buns and Roses in Dallas.

Thank you to my editor, Deb Werksman; editorial assistant, Eliza Smith; my production editor, Rachel Gilmer; and all the wonderful professionals I'm privileged to work with at Sourcebooks.

Most importantly, thank you to my friends, my family, and my readers for all you do to encourage and sustain me.

About the Author

Shana Galen is the bestselling author of passionate Regency romps, including the *RT* Reviewers' Choice *The Making of a Gentleman*. *Kirkus* says of her books, "The road to happily-ever-after is intense, conflicted, suspenseful, and fun," and *RT Book Reviews* calls her books "lighthearted yet poignant, humorous yet touching." She taught English at the middle- and high-school level off and on for eleven years. Most of those years were spent working in Houston's inner city. Now she writes full-time. She's happily married and has a daughter who is most definitely a romance heroine in the making. Shana loves to hear from readers, so send her an email or see what she's up to daily on Facebook and Twitter. Stop by her website at shanagalen.com.

Look for the dazzling new
series of breathtaking Regency
romance from Shana Galen

The Draven Club

At the height of the Napoleonic Wars, Lieutenant Colonel
Draven led a troop of younger sons of nobility—the best,
the brightest, but most importantly, the expendable—on a
suicide mission that changed the course of history. Now, the
surviving "Draven Dozen"—rakes and rogues before they
left for war, now a group of restless renegades—must settle
back into London Society and the world they left behind,
facing new threats to their lives…and their hearts.

Coming soon from Sourcebooks Casablanca